LOST LAKE

LOST LAKE LOCATORS BOOK FOUR

SUSAN SLEEMAN

EDGE OF YOUR SEAT BOOKS, INC.

Published by Edge of Your Seat Books, Inc.

Contact the publisher at contact@edgeofyourseatbooks.com

1

———

She was missing—maybe dead—and it was all Gabe's fault.

Kenna. His best friend for twenty-five years. Her four-year-old daughter, too. Gone.

Kenna. Lucy. Where are you?

He scanned the shoulder of the narrow winding road, headlights cutting through thick fog. One last attempt. His Lost Lake Locators team had already searched every route from Kenna's house to Lost Lake.

Nothing. Not a trace.

The others had returned to the office, urging him to come with them. He couldn't. Not after her voicemail around six p.m.—her voice shaking, whispering she was in danger. She'd said she was just leaving home, starting the one-hour drive.

That was nearly two and a half hours ago.

So where was she? Where was sweet little Lucy?

His fingers tightened on the steering wheel. Sweat slicked his palms despite the cold April air. "Get a grip, man. You're no good to her like this."

He reached the intersection for Lost Lake Road and forced his breathing to slow. She shouldn't have taken this turn. It didn't lead anywhere she needed to go. Unless Lucy had begged to see the lake.

No. The fear in Kenna's voice hadn't belonged to a woman stopping to sightsee.

Still, he and his team had no leads after searching for two hours. None. A quick loop around the lake would take fifteen minutes. That was all.

He crawled forward. Wind howled and buffeted the vehicle. He scanned both sides of the road through the thick mist.

Nothing.

Then—something.

A shadow in the ravine below. Large. Metallic.

His stomach sank. He coasted to a stop at the overlook and killed the engine.

Flashlight. He yanked it from the console and jumped out. Forty-degree air. Misty rain. He jogged to the edge. The beam sliced through fog, catching weeds and rock. The shape below was half-buried, indistinct in the shadows, impossible to make out.

He shifted the flashlight to his left hand and gripped a sapling, easing down the steep incline. Slow steps when every instinct screamed to run. His feet skittered down the slope. Brambles tore at his jeans. His heart pounded in his ears.

Closer. Closer he came.

The light caught a wave of turquoise.

Then cream trim.

No. Please no!

A vintage Volkswagen bus. License plate SUNSHN, the custom plate Kenna had added just last week.

Her bus.

"Oh, God. No. Please." He let go of the sapling and slid the rest of the way down, landing hard beside the vehicle.

He scrambled to his feet and yanked open the driver's door. Cream dashboard. A little flower charm hanging from the mirror. Every detail screamed *Kenna*. But maybe...

He lunged across the seat, ripped open the glove compartment, and jerked out the registration.

Confirmation. Kenna James.

"What were you doing on this road?"

Lucy's freckled face flashed in his mind. Fiery red pigtails. Wide grin.

Air locked in his lungs.

Stop thinking. Move.

He bolted outside and wrenched open the sliding door. The child's car seat was gone. Floofy Bear lay slumped on the bench seat, abandoned.

"No." A sickening weight settled low in his gut. "She would never leave her favorite bear."

He tore through the bus. Three suitcases. A box of toys. Too much for a short visit.

She'd been running.

From what?

Not Lucy's father. He wasn't in the picture. Never had been.

Sirens wailed in the distance. Too close.

Cold dread slid through him.

He pulled out his phone and called Nolan, their team leader, to ask if his fiancée, Mina Park, the local sheriff, found anything. "You hear anything from Mina?"

"No. You find them?"

"Not them, but Kenna's bus crashed in a ravine. Sirens are closing in on the lake."

"I'll call Mina. She might know what's going on. Hang tight."

Gabe shoved the phone into his pocket and clawed his way back up the ravine. He charged to the overlook.

Flashing lights painted the fog an eerie blue glow, and sirens wailed just down the road.

The sound of distress. Trouble needing intervention.

Patrol cars stopped near the beach. Deputies sprinted downhill, flashlights slashing across sand and water. Someone waved frantically then pointed at the water.

Gabe ran to the edge of the lot and zoomed in with his phone's camera. The image blurred with fog and motion.

His phone rang. "Nolan."

"Mina said they found a body floating in the lake. A man dragged it to shore. It's too late."

Something icy gripped Gabe from the inside. "Male or female?"

"She doesn't know yet."

He started toward the beach, every muscle shaking. "The child?"

A pause.

Nolan cleared his throat. "Empty car seat on the dock."

Gabe's legs gave out. He hit the ground, his palms striking dirt, lungs burning for air that wouldn't come.

Kenna. Lucy.

He'd promised to protect them.

Now what?

Either there was still a chance or this was a nightmare he'd never escape.

The callout proved accurate, and Detective Elaina Lyons swallowed hard, her pulse stuttering as she took in the scene on the beach below. A woman's drenched body lay face down on the sand and an empty child's car seat rested on the dock.

Her world narrowed to one desperate thought. A child

could've wandered off after her mother drowned, lost in the dark.

Then a darker possibility came to mind.

No one swam in Lost Lake in March.

The woman could've been murdered. And the child?

El tried to shut the thought down, but it was as if a neon sign flashed in front of her.

Another missing child.

Victoria's name echoed through her from the past.

No! Focus.

Hurry. Beat the threatening rain. Evidence would vanish if the weather turned.

She pulled on gloves and crossed the nearly empty parking lot. She joined Deputy Ewing at the taped-off stairway leading to the beach. "Did you call this in immediately?"

"Yes, ma'am." He straightened, his expression turning uncertain. "After interviewing the witness. Deputy Massey is with him now."

"Beach secure?"

"Yes. Trails on both sides are cordoned off."

"Keep it that way. Give the ME access. No one else without my say." She looked back at the scene below. "Any witnesses, besides the dog walker who found the woman?"

"No one else. Beach is officially closed this time of year. Sign on the chain strung at the opening warns people off."

A thick chain dangled between two substantial metal posts at the head of the stairway, the sign stating the beach closure from October through May. A deterrent for most people, but anyone determined to access the beach could easily circumvent it.

She faced Ewing again. "Remember, no one other than the ME and her team enters the scene unless authorized by me."

He cocked an eyebrow. "Not even Sheriff Parks?"

"That won't be a problem. She's standing by in her office for a report."

He nodded.

El slipped under the tape. Hand over her eyes to block the blowing sand, she quickly assessed the scene unfolding before her on a night when the moon had taken refuge behind thick clouds still threatening to drench the evidence. One weak light mounted on the changing room wall illuminated the immediate area but left the remaining space dark and quiet.

Deputy Massey stood near an older man wrapped in an emergency blanket and seated on a concrete bench, a dog straining at the leash.

The witness.

Moonlight broke through the clouds. She'd check the victim first, document the scene, then talk to him.

She couldn't miss a thing. Every detail mattered.

Footprints near the water. Drag marks. A phone. A half-empty water bottle. A child's toy rocking in the ripples.

She crossed the sand. The lake reflected the moon in glints, deceptively peaceful as the water lapped against the shore. The wind carried the faint smell of algae and something sharper, metallic. Blood or mud, she couldn't tell yet.

She knelt beside the woman and began snapping pictures. Her camera flash revealed the victim's pale skin, her forehead, an ugly purple bruise. Weeds tangled in her soaked red hair. Clothes clinging like rags. Wrists and ankles, raw and red, as if they'd been restrained. Dark staining on the woman's knit top, made lighter by her time in the water.

Blood. *Help me find who did such an awful thing to this defenseless woman.*

El narrowed her focus to the blood. No tear in the fabric

or obvious wound, so where had the blood come from? Her killer?

El turned to the drag marks. One line, coming from the lake. Probably from the witness who'd rescued her. Not the person who'd put her in the water. Did they drop her from the dock or were they strong enough to carry her?

"What happened to you?" El said under her breath.

"Obviously she drowned," Massey said behind her.

El turned slowly. "Did you look at her?"

He hesitated. "Our witness said he found her floating."

El bit back the sharp reply rising to her tongue. "Come here."

She angled her flashlight at the victim's throat. Raised, reddish welts bloomed under the light. "Tell me what you see."

Massey squatted beside her and went still. "Strangulation?"

"Likely." El stood. "Checking for petechiae in her eyes would help confirm it, but we're hands-off until the ME does her preliminary examination."

Massey nodded, his Adam's apple bobbing. "Right. Burst capillaries, red and purple dots in her eyes. Classic sign."

"ME's on her way. Hopefully she'll check that out and find some ID."

He scanned the shoreline. "Cell phone's over there but no purse. Might've gone under."

"As could the child. We need a dive team." El shot another look at the empty car seat and nausea rolled through her. "Sheriff Ryder's county is the closest one with divers. I'll get Mina on the line and get them over here."

"And what do you want me to do?"

"Bring some lights down here so you can photograph the entire scene then watch the trails. Make sure no one tries to access the scene and contaminate evidence."

He glanced at the water as if he wanted to say something else. She followed his gaze. This was a real circus. One where she was the ringmaster and everything depended on her direction.

She straightened and made eye contact with Massey. "We find that kid. No excuses. Let's move."

He bolted into action. but El allowed herself one more moment to take in the scene. The wind had died down, and Lost Lake was quiet now, too quiet, as if holding its breath. And in that stillness, the weight of the scene crushed El. The lifeless mother, the missing child, and the invisible clock ticking relentlessly against them all.

El shivered. She would never look at the lake the same way again.

Please God, the woman has died, but let me find the child. Watch over her. Care for her before...

No. She couldn't say it. Not even to God, who knew everything. She forced her attention away from the shadowy water. She had a job to do.

The witness was secure, the scene locked down. Now there was only one priority.

The child.

She pulled out her phone and dialed the office. "Mina. It's El. We're looking at a possible homicide. Possible missing child either in the water or the woods. Maybe abducted. I need search teams around the lake. Divers. ASAP. A K-9 unit, too."

Mina exhaled hard. "I'll handle it and keep you updated on their arrival times. Do we have an ID for the woman?"

"Not yet. ME's en route and hopefully she'll find something on the body. There's a cell phone near the water. Might get a quick ID there. I'll get it to our tech team as soon as possible."

A pause. Too long.

"You should know," Mina said. "Gabe Irving's friend, Kenna James, and her four-year-old daughter, Lucy, went missing tonight. They were on their way to see him and should've arrived at the inn more than four hours ago, but they never showed."

Gabe. How hard this must be for him.

They'd worked cases together before. Shared long hours, bad coffee, and an attraction between them they didn't dare to explore. And now this?

"Is this a coincidence or do you have reason to believe the woman might be Kenna and the car seat her daughter's?" El asked.

"It's probably them. Gabe found a VW bus registered to Kenna in a ravine near the lake."

"That's bad."

"Yeah. He's on his way. If he can ID the body, we need that." Mina's tone said this wasn't optional. "We're dealing with two potential investigations here. You'll need some help. I'll pull Ulrich off his current case and get him out there too."

A seasoned officer, Detective Burke Ulrich had joined their team when their department received a grant to work cold cases and he wanted to be close to Abby Day, a Lost Lake Locators team member. El would appreciate his help. Investigating a murder and missing child simultaneously required everyone to work this investigation, and he made things happen.

"How do you want to handle forensics?" El asked.

"With a scene exposed to the elements and a missing child, we can't wait for the state to send someone out. I'll try to get Sierra Rice from the Veritas Center out here."

The Veritas Center in Portland. Perfect. *If* they had the funds to pay for a nationally known private laboratory with experts in all areas of criminal forensics plus state-of-the-art equipment and techniques.

"We can afford that?" El asked.

"No way, but Nolan and his team have a connection to them, and he can hopefully get them to take this case pro bono."

"What are the odds of that?"

"Their forensic anthropologist has a son and is sympathetic to cases involving children. She can be persuasive, but all the partners have to sign off on pro bono work."

"Something to pray about then," El said, surprising herself. She and God had been on a break since Victoria died during El's rookie year. Not God's fault. Hers for not being able to let go of the guilt. But this child deserved her every effort, and that included prayer.

"I'll call as soon as I hear back," Mina said. "Anything else you need right now?"

"I'll let you know if something comes up." She ended their call and strode through the squishy sand to the phone lying too near the lake for comfort.

She photographed it then lifted it. The screen remained dark and water dripped from the case.

Even if the phone still worked, protocol prohibited her from checking for recent calls or texts. It was up to the tech staff to recover information. She bagged and pocketed it.

Nearby, a pink-and-blue squeezable unicorn toy rested close to the water. Even a minor wave could drag it into the water. She also shot pictures of it then slipped it into an evidence bag.

On the dock, her flashlight beam revealed muddy drag marks and boot prints in two sizes.

A car seat sat near the edge. Why was it there?

Had the woman and child been brought there by boat? But if this woman was Gabe's friend, the van was close enough to walk from. Why use a boat? Maybe they'd find answers when they examined the terrain around the ravine.

In any event, it could explain that the seat was used to keep the child strapped in for safety or to contain her movements. But where had the boat come from and who piloted it? Maybe the dog walker had seen something to clarify things.

She photographed the front of the seat, spotting a small pink sweatshirt tucked inside. Perfect for a K-9 to pick up on the child's scent and it would also contain DNA and fingerprints. She bagged it carefully and eased around to the seat's back. A large sticker of Bluey. The sight of the cartoon character punched her in the chest.

A young child, missing. Her job, to find her.

She clenched her hands to keep her emotions in check and crossed the beach to the witness and his black-and-white dog. The dog came to its feet and wiggled.

"Okay to pet him or her?" she asked the man in his late sixties, she guessed.

"Her. Jinx and sure," the man said, his voice deep and gravelly. "And I'm Curtis Williams."

"Detective Lyons, with the Lost Lake Sheriff's Department." Taking off her gloves, she squatted by Jinx and ruffled her wet fur. "I know my deputy already took your statement, but can you tell me what happened here tonight?"

He frowned, his whisker-covered chin dropping. "Jinx and I were on our normal nightly walk. As a border collie, she needs a lot of exercise."

Jinx lifted her head and looked at him as if he'd called her into duty. He gave her a hand signal, and she settled back down.

"We take this path every day at lunch and after dinner. Nothing out of the ordinary this afternoon, but tonight Jinx started barking the minute we hit the trail. I quickly saw something floating in the water. A woman. I charged in to drag her to shore. I can't even begin to tell you…"

His voice broke, and he clamped the back of his neck. "What it was like to discover she was dead. Took me a minute or two to get my bearings and call 911. Stayed by her side until the deputy arrived. Not like I could do anything for her anymore, but she seemed like she needed me."

"Did you see anyone else?"

"No, but I couldn't miss that car seat. Please don't tell me there's a child involved in this. That would be so much worse."

She couldn't discuss anything with him. "What about any vehicles in the parking lot? Did you hear anything from up top?"

"No. Nothing. Not unusual for this time of year and especially at this time of night."

"What about a boat or canoe?"

He shook his head. "Nothing there either."

"No sound of a motor or no lights out in the lake?" she pressed.

"No. No."

"And you didn't touch anything besides the woman?"

"Like I said, I could barely keep it together to call 911, much less think to do anything but wait."

She fished a business card out of her pocket and handed it to him. "If you think of anything else that might help, please call me immediately."

He studied her card and looked up. "Does this mean I'm free to go?"

"Yes, thank you for your cooperation. I'll escort you to the stairway."

"Let me in." From the parking lot above, a raw, desperate

voice broke through the fog. "I might be able to identify the body!"

Gabe!

El's chest tightened as he took on a linebacker stance, ready to bulldoze through Ewing, who stood his ground.

"El! Tell him to let me through. I know her! I might be able to identify the body." Gabe's tone had gone far beyond someone simply looking for a missing person to a personal loss deeper than she expected.

She had no doubt that if she didn't intervene, he would break through Ewing's defense.

"Hurry, El! I think I know who drowned."

El wouldn't correct him on the cause of death. No reason to traumatize him until she was certain. And she wouldn't let him get close enough to see the welts on the woman's neck for himself. Especially not if she wasn't his friend, Kenna.

El reached the top of the stairway and caught the anguish on Gabe's face. His strained expression changed things for her. This was no longer strictly professional. It was personal.

Having worked several investigations with the Lost Lake Locator team, she knew all six team members well. But Gabe? She'd had feelings for him for more than a year, and he felt the same. It didn't matter. They would never act on it, each for their own reasons.

She lifted the crime scene tape and let Williams and Jinx pass under. "Please call me if you think of anything else."

Williams gave a quick nod, glanced at Gabe with horror, and raced away, Jinx pulling at the leash to stay behind.

She turned to Gabe. "Mina told me about your potential connection. I'll walk you down."

He reached for the crime scene tape as if she'd given him clearance to barge through.

"Hold up." El raised a hand. "I'll let you take a look, but we need to do this by the book."

He paced, exhaling hard. "You think I care about the book when that could be Kenna down there?"

"I know how you're feeling. If it is her, we'll find out together, but you have to stay with me. Don't cross the line."

He nodded, jaw clenched. "Fine."

They descended toward the shore, grief radiating off him like heat.

And with every step, a single, icy thought tightened its grip.

If that woman was indeed Kenna, had Lucy followed her mother into the murky lake and lost her life too?

2
————

"It's her...it's Kenna."

The words scraped out of Gabe's throat as he stared at his friend twisted against the sand, as if the beach itself had rejected her. Drenched clothing plastered to her body. Hair straggly. Sand and weeds clinging everywhere.

They might call it an accident. Say she drowned.

But he knew better.

Kenna would never go into the water and leave Lucy behind.

Someone had killed her. There was no doubt in his mind. The only questions were who and why? Something he had no answer for.

Why, God? Why Kenna?

He didn't expect a reply. He sucked in air, bent forward, and planted his hands on his knees, concentrating on the simple act of staying upright.

"I'm so sorry, Gabe." El rested her hand on his shoulder.

The touch should have helped. Instead, it made everything real. Final. All he wanted was to shrug her off and sink into the sand until the crushing weight in his chest lifted.

But he didn't. That would be rude. Revealing. And he didn't allow himself that kind of weakness anymore.

He straightened, her hand sliding free, and forced himself to look again. The sight of Kenna lying lifeless sent nausea rolling through his gut. He squeezed his eyes shut.

The loss could still take him down. He'd lost military friends before, but no one as close as Kenna. Since she'd had Lucy...

"Lucy!" His eyes snapped open. "Where's Lucy? Tell me you found her."

"We don't know." El spoke softly, but frustration weighted her words.

"You don't know?" The words flew out before he could stop them. "I thought you were a good detective."

She flinched.

His fault, and he hated causing her pain, but finding Lucy came before anything else. Anyone else. Before manners. Before guilt. Even before finding Kenna's killer.

Don't take her from me too. Please keep her safe and bring her back to me.

El's jaw tightened. "There's a car seat on the dock. Odds say it belongs to Lucy."

"Her seat is missing from Kenna's van."

El nodded, but it was halfhearted. "I found a phone by the water, likely Kenna's. We'll get it to our tech team as quickly as we can. We should know more soon, but right now we don't have other leads. Mina's organizing a ground search with K-9s and a dive team for the water."

"Why aren't you searching?" His voice sharpened. "Doing something?"

"I *am* doing something." She crossed her arms, fire flashing in her eyes.

He'd gone too far.

Get a grip.

If he kept pushing, she'd freeze him and his team out of the investigation. Then where would he get answers? About Kenna. About Lucy.

"I've been securing the crime scene," she continued. "Procuring necessary resources. Making sure evidence is preserved so we can figure out what happened here."

"I'm sorry." He forced the words past his pride. "You didn't deserve that. I know you're doing your job." He paused, tamping down the rage clawing at his chest. "Have you found anything that might tell us where Lucy is or how Kenna drowned?"

Pain flickered across El's face before she masked it. "A few things bother me. First, the car seat. If it belongs to Lucy, why would Kenna remove it from the van and bring it down here?"

"No idea. But if it has a blue plaid cushion and big Bluey sticker on the back, it's hers."

El winced. "I saw the sticker earlier."

Gabe froze. He'd expected the confirmation, but hearing it left him hollow.

What had happened to the people he loved?

"Do you have a picture of Lucy?"

"Sure." He got out his phone, swiped a few times, and studied the sweet four-year-old's face. She had curly red hair and a ready smile that spoke to her outgoing personality. Her eyes were lit with joy, so full of life. Now, where was she? Had she died? Did someone have her?

He ignored the swell of emotions threatening to bring tears, swallowed, and looked at El.

"Can you text it to me?" she asked.

He tapped his phone screen to take care of it.

Her phone soon chimed. She checked her screen and smiled, but it was soon replaced with a frown. "Is it okay if we circulate this picture for law enforcement and an Amber

Alert? Maybe to the media if we don't make progress on finding her right away?"

He nodded. "You should know, when I found Kenna's van, I climbed down in the ravine to check on them, but the van was empty." He tried to think like she would. "Lucy's favorite stuffed animal was on the backseat. She never went anywhere without it."

El cocked her head. "Okay, say Kenna had nothing to do with bringing the seat here and someone else brought it. But who and why?"

"If the stuffed animal was left behind, it had to be someone who didn't know them well. Maybe someone planned to pick them up by boat." He shook his head. "But that makes no sense. None at all. Kenna was coming to see me. No need for a boat."

"Was this a normal trip or did she have a special reason for visiting today?"

"We don't have a normal routine, and it's easier for me to go there than for her to bring Lucy here. Oddly enough, she was just here last weekend. Spent the night on Friday and went back on Saturday afternoon. It was a spur-of-the-moment visit. but not like this one." He told El about the voicemail. "She called me around six. Do you want to hear it?"

El nodded and stepped closer to him. He played the message. Kenna's anguished voice squeezed his chest until even the smallest of breaths hurt.

El's expression darkened. "After hearing her panic, there's no way she would've made a side trip to the lake. Do you know anything about the danger she mentioned?"

"Not a clue. I want to see the car seat up close."

"I can't allow that." Her tone softened. "I shouldn't have even let you identify her at the scene. It's time for you to step outside the perimeter."

He glanced at Kenna again, searching for answers that weren't there.

El stepped in front of him to block his view. "There's nothing you can do here. Looking at her won't help. It'll only make things worse."

She was right, but how could he leave his best friend lying there all alone? Soaking wet. Cold. Tangled in seaweed and covered in sand. She needed him. Needed him to find who did this. Needed him to find Lucy.

"I can't leave her," he said hoarsely. "Can I stay until they take her away?"

El bit her lip. "There's nothing you can do for her, Gabe."

"I know. But I can't go." His voice broke. "If you want me out of here, you'll have to arrest me and haul me away."

Her expression softened, and she looked up the hill. He followed her gaze to see the ME arriving with her assistant carrying a backboard. Visions of the morgue flashed through his mind. Cold, dark, wrong. No place for Kenna. For his best friend.

El turned back to him and pointed across the beach. "I understand. Take a seat on that rock. But don't move until I tell you. Understood?"

He nodded and scanned the beach, desperate to do something—anything. He pulled out his phone. "I'm calling my team to start searching for Lucy."

She scrubbed a hand over her face. "I can't give any of you access to the scene."

"Trust me, I know that, but there's plenty of wooded areas you haven't secured. We'll search for Lucy there."

She hesitated, then nodded. "Go ahead, but promise you won't interfere once we begin our search."

"I promise." He meant it.

For now.

In a few minutes? Maybe not so much. If interfering was what it took to find Lucy, he'd do it. No matter the cost.

~

El kept Gabe in her peripheral vision as she stood beside Dr. Faye Briggs. The county's new medical examiner pulled on gloves, pink nails disappearing beneath latex. El had met the ME only once in her six months on the job, but she'd heard good things about the doctor's skills.

Her assistant, Theo, walked toward them from the lake, thermometer in hand. In his early twenties, he had a stocky build and was new to the job and the town.

El moved closer to the doctor, aware of Gabe's gaze tracking her every move.

She shrugged it off and watched Dr. Briggs squat by the body, insert a thermometer probe into the liver, then stand and look at her assistant. "What did you get?"

He held out his thermometer. "Air temp's fifty degrees. Water, forty-six."

Dr. Briggs nodded sharply, her focus lingering on the lake.

"Tell me you have the time of death," El said.

The ME turned to her. "I'd like to give you that, but the water's cold enough to stall everything. Plus, from what you said, our victim was exposed to the elements on the beach for an hour or so. That compounds things."

"So, no estimate then?" Disappointment crept into El's voice.

"I can give you my best estimate, but don't hold me to it." She looked at her thermometer. "Liver's at eighty-eight degrees and rigor hasn't set in. Plus, there's no lividity yet. I'd say she's been dead less than three hours, maybe two."

That made sense. Rigor mortis—the stiffening of

muscles after death—often helped determine the time of death. Lividity occurred when blood settled in the body after the heart stopped.

Plus... "We know she left a voicemail at six p.m., so that fits with this timeline."

Dr. Briggs nodded then glanced toward the lake. "If she drowned, it happened not long before she was discovered."

El checked her watch. 10:07. "So Kenna died between seven and nine p.m."

"Yes," Dr. Briggs said. "I'll have to confirm that in the autopsy, but it gives you something to go on now."

El jotted it down. "You said *if* she drowned. I've been questioning that. The welts." El pointed to Kenna's neck and waited for the ME to bristle at the observation.

The doctor studied her. "We'll be working together on this investigation and future ones. I'm always willing to hear a lead detective's theory. Also, call me Faye."

Pleased, El nodded. "And I'm El. It's short for Elaina."

She turned her attention back to the body. "Well, El, if you're thinking strangulation, I can agree with that. At least preliminarily. The blood has seeped into the surrounding tissue, so the bruises occurred perimortem."

"That's exactly what I was thinking."

"See these," she said, her voice low but precise as she angled her flashlight toward the victim's neck. "The bruising runs horizontally. The pattern's irregular. Fingertips, not a ligature. These smaller red and purple spots are petechiae or tiny ruptures from pressure cutting off blood flow. Classic signs of manual strangulation."

El imagined the scene. Big powerful hands around Kenna's throat. She clenched her jaw.

Faye paused, tracing just above the collarbone where the skin had darkened. "Her attacker used significant force, likely both hands. Likely a male. She fought back, but..."

Her gaze flicked to the faint crescents near the jawline. "He was stronger. She never had a chance."

"This says she didn't drown, right?"

"Not necessarily. Her attacker could've inflicted the damage, stopped short of killing her, then thrown her in the water alive."

El's imagination ran wild with that.

Faye lifted Kenna's hand and pointed to the tips of her fingers. "Skin is smooth and normal. No washerwoman's affect or softer waterlogged fingers yet. A clear sign she wasn't in the water long. Probably less than thirty minutes. Maybe an hour. But the fact that we found her so soon could contradict death by drowning."

"I don't understand."

"Drowning victims often stay at the surface for a short time. Struggling, submerging, resurfacing. Once unconscious, they slip under. In freshwater, they typically sink after that, though it's not always immediate."

"And if she was put in the water postmortem?"

"That's a different story. She'd sink at first. Floating wouldn't happen until decomposition kicked in—bacteria producing gases that bloat the body and increase buoyancy. In warm water, that can be a day or two. At this temperature, you're usually looking at a few days, maybe longer. Depends on the water, her body composition, currents, even what she was wearing."

The scene played out in El's mind, Kenna struggling, grasping. She couldn't imagine how she'd tell Gabe. It would push him past the edge he was already teetering on.

"Of course," Faye said. "This is all speculation. Air could've simply been trapped in her clothing, keeping her on the surface. Especially since she was found so soon. Not something we'll ever know unless your witness noticed it."

"He didn't mention it, but he was in shock. I'll ask him, but I doubt he would've noticed."

"Then it'll be up to my examination to reveal if she has water in her lungs."

"What about the blood?"

Faye lifted Kenna's shirt. "Just like I suspected. No open wounds. It's probably not her blood unless there's a wound elsewhere and the blood transferred here. My examination will answer that too."

"She also crashed her van into the ravine tonight. I assume the large bruise on her forehead is from that."

She bent to look at Kenna. "It's clearly perimortem so you could be right. If so, there'll be contusions from a seatbelt as well."

"In past investigations, I learned water washes some DNA away—especially loose material like saliva or skin cells—but some can remain. So we should still test her shirt for DNA."

"Yes, it gets trapped in the fabric fibers, particularly in porous materials like her cotton shirt, and we could find it."

"So how soon can you do the autopsy and get me that shirt for DNA testing?"

"First thing in the morning. Around nine, unless something more pressing comes in. Not likely though. In our little county, a potential murder takes precedence over everything else."

El gritted her teeth. "I'll be there."

Faye stood and spun to face her assistant. "Bag her hands, Theo, and let's get her to the van."

Theo slipped paper bags over each hand and sealed them with rubber bands. Then he unfurled a black body bag with a flourish.

"I'll have her stuffed inside in no time," he said loudly.

Gabe growled and jumped up, glaring at Theo. Thankfully, he was on the other side of the crime scene. If not, he'd be giving the assistant a piece of his mind, and El wouldn't blame him.

She was tempted to go to him, but she couldn't manage Gabe's emotions through this entire investigation. Her job had to come first. Not only did she have a murder to solve. She had to find a missing four-year-old.

~

Two thirty a.m. Gabe paced the team's conference room. Everyone on the team except Reece had changed clothes and was seated at the table, warming up from hours of searching for Lucy in the cold and damp. They hadn't found her or any sign that anyone had recently entered the wooded area.

Hayden, their team internet expert, stared at his laptop screen, deep-diving into Kenna's background. Gabe hated violating his friend's privacy, but they needed to know everything to find who killed her and where Lucy had disappeared to. Maybe when El arrived to update them as she'd promised, she'd have a lead.

Until then, they waited. Not something Gabe was good at.

Reece tugged on her wet T-shirt and picked up a full pot of coffee from the table against the wall. Tall with thick blond hair, she walked with a model's confidence, a remnant from her college days. Before joining the team, she'd been an ATF agent, though nothing in her appearance suggested it.

She stopped next to Gabe and held up the pot and a mug. "Coffee?"

Gabe wouldn't be sleeping until they located Lucy. Every bit of caffeine would help. He grabbed the mug and held it out. "Thanks for looking out for us when you probably want to get out of those wet clothes."

She waved her hand. "No worries. I'll change once I make sure you all have coffee and a snack."

"I hate to see you shivering." Sitting at the main table, Jude French stroked his neatly trimmed beard. "But we appreciate our team mom looking out for us."

"Betty Crocker at your service." Reece wrinkled her nose at him and poured steaming coffee into his mug.

Former sheriff Abby Day stood and stepped beside Gabe. She was petite, curvy, and had short hair. "You doing okay?"

"If this is a stranger abduction, you guys all know the first three hours are everything," Gabe said, as they were in business to locate missing people and things. "After that, the odds start working against us, and it looks like we're already beyond that time."

Gabe got the words out, but barely. What could he say after his best friend had died and her daughter disappeared? If he put words to his feelings he might completely fall apart. Something he wouldn't do in front of his team. Shoot, something he wouldn't do in front of anyone if he could help it. He had to remain a professional and in control.

Abby rested her hand on his arm. He stiffened.

"We're praying for you," she said. "For them."

He nodded, but he didn't know how much help he would get from prayer. He believed in God. Sure, he did. Had all his life. But had he lived his life for God? Not most of it. How could he have, growing up in a dysfunctional family like his?

"Gabe?" Abby asked. "You thinking about Kenna?"

No way he'd answer that. Would be the catalyst to that

breakdown. To the real man beneath the baggage. Only one person had ever seen that guy. Kenna.

But just because he wouldn't let Abby in didn't mean he wanted to hurt her feelings. He took a gulp of coffee and squeezed her hand. "Don't worry about me. I'll be okay."

She frowned. "You might want to run away from how this is affecting you, but you can't. So, remember we're all praying for you, and we're here if you want to talk."

He nodded, but right now he wanted to take action. He strode to the whiteboard to grab a red marker. "No more waiting for El to get here. We can't afford to delay. We'll get started on a plan of action."

"You've got too much of a personal investment here to take lead." Team leader Nolan Orr stood and tried to take the marker from Gabe's hand.

Gabe jerked it behind his back. "No way I'm backing down. No matter what you or anyone says."

Nolan cocked his head. "Even if it stands in the way of finding Lucy or Kenna's killer?"

Gabe locked eyes with Nolan. "Trust me. I can do this. I won't stand in the way."

Nolan watched Gabe carefully, as if hoping to make him squirm. But Gabe rarely did, and he certainly wouldn't now.

"You know I mean it," Gabe said. "You won't sway my opinion, so why waste time trying?"

Nolan hissed out a long breath. "Because I know it's the right thing to do." He looked around the group as if asking for assistance.

"Why don't I be your copilot on this?" Jude said. "You can run things by me before acting."

Gabe had to admit Jude's idea was a good one, even if the two of them had little in common. Jude was raised in a wealthy family until they'd disowned him. He chose to be an FBI agent when they wanted him to follow in their footsteps into a lucrative career. The one thing they did share—both were rejected by family. At times that shared experience helped them understand each other.

Besides, it didn't mean Gabe had to follow Jude's suggestions, but at least he wouldn't let his emotions make him do something he'd regret. "Works for me."

Surprise crossed Jude's face, and he held out a fist to Gabe. "We'll be the dynamic duo. No one can stop us."

Gabe bumped Jude's fist.

Nolan's frown disappeared, but tension remained in his shoulders. "Let's also agree that if any of us see you hindering the investigation, we'll tell you about it, and you'll back down."

"I'd be glad to have you call me on things, but I won't back down unless you convince me it's better for Kenna or Lucy."

Nolan gave a solemn nod and took his seat.

Consensus reached, Gabe let his shoulders relax. "Let's start with making a list of registered sex offenders in the area and getting out to question them."

"I'll make the list," Hayden said. "Then depending on the number of suspects we find, we can split them up so we can question them as fast as possible."

Gabe appreciated their computer expert stepping forward without being asked. "That's a great start."

Nolan nodded. "We have to assume El is doing or has done the same thing, and we don't want to step on her department's toes."

"I'm done playing nice, but I won't back down if I think we have an issue with one of them," Jude said.

"I wouldn't expect you to, but we could dialogue with El or Mina before you go full pursuit of the guy."

"I can coordinate with them," Gabe said. "But if in doubt, we'll err on the side of taking action. This investigation is different for us. We've never searched for a young child and certainly not one whose mother had been murdered. So we don't wait. Not with a child. Every minute matters to find her alive. In only a few hours, we may be looking at something very different."

The room went quiet and somber. Too somber. The kind of emotions that stopped action.

Gabe was setting the tone. He pulled his shoulders back. "Just keep me updated. We also have to assume that El made an immediate call to the National Center for Missing and Exploited Children."

A car horn blared outside.

Gabe jumped and hated that something so simple had startled him. But how could it not? This was El's signal letting them know she'd arrived and needed someone to let her in.

Soon he'd have fresh information on two of the most important people in his life. One was already dead, and El could be coming to tell them the other one had died too.

3

———

In the Lost Lake Locators' parking lot, El killed her engine but left her hand resting on the keys. She checked her watch. Nearly two forty-five a.m.

Fatigue gnawed at her, urging rest, but exhaustion wasn't what kept her sitting there. She didn't want to go inside. Didn't want to see Gabe's grief again under harsh lights with nowhere to hide.

Lucy was counting on her, though. She couldn't waste time sitting in her car because she was afraid of Gabe's response. Of her old memories. Of losing control of emotions she'd kept sealed for years.

She forced herself out and crossed the cracked concrete to the rundown inn Nolan had purchased as company head-quarters and the team members' home. Perched on an ocean cliff, the building sagged with neglect, its faded sign bearing the team name and logo.

The door opened. Green paint flaked loose and drifted down like insects.

Still wearing damp clothes from the search for Lucy, Reece stood in the doorway. "Welcome. Everyone's in the conference room."

"You haven't changed clothes," El said.

Way to state the obvious.

El always felt self-conscious around Reece, who somehow managed to look runway-ready even now. El wore no makeup at work, her hair scraped into a bun, a few strands escaping. Add to that unremarkable suits and collared blouses. Nothing feminine enough to invite criticism or dismissal in a male-dominated profession. Especially not in a town this small.

"I wanted everyone to have something warm to drink first. Come in, and I'll be right back." She bolted down the hallway.

El inhaled, steadying herself, then stepped inside the foyer clinging stubbornly to its mid-century decor frozen in time. They'd begun renovations but stopped after finishing the bedrooms. With the business off and running, investigations always took priority, and updating the rest of the inn had stalled.

She passed the dim sitting area, shadows pooling over threadbare chairs upholstered in faded orange and mustard. Down the hall, voices drifted from the former dining room, now serving as their meeting room.

She stepped inside. Old Formica-and-chrome tables had been pushed together to form a long conference table. The members of the team chatted, mugs of coffee and cocoa in front of them.

Not Gabe.

He stood at the whiteboard, marker clenched in his hand, action items scrawled on the whiteboard behind him.

She avoided looking at him, but caught the gaze of others around the table. "Looks like you've started planning."

"We have," Nolan said.

"And don't bother trying to slow us down." Jude lifted his chin. "We're backing Gabe one hundred percent."

"Of course you are." She glanced at Gabe, but he still hadn't looked her way. "Mind if I photograph the board so we don't trip over each other later?"

"Knock yourself out," Jude said.

She flashed several shots in consecutive order then stowed her phone.

Gabe finally turned, pinning her with an intense stare. "Your turn. What did you find?"

She didn't like the edge in his voice, but she would cut him some slack due to his stress. "We have preliminary findings from the medical examiner. She…"

His expression hardened. The words she needed lodged in her throat.

"And?" His voice dropped, dangerous in its low tone.

"I'm sorry, Gabe." She met his gaze. "The ME believes Kenna could have been strangled."

The marker clattered to the floor. A raw, animal growl tore from his chest.

El cringed inside, his pain freezing her in place. She'd expected a reaction, but nothing so extreme. She wanted to do something for him, but what? Other than a touch or hug —way too personal—and she couldn't afford to make a single mistake on this investigation. Touching him now would be one. A big one.

Abby Day shot to her feet and hurried over to him. Barely over five-feet-tall, she confidently circled her arms around his waist. "I'm so sorry, Gabe."

His arms hung limp at his side, and he didn't respond. Didn't say anything. Do anything. Nothing at all.

"We'll find who did this," Abby said softly. "And we'll find Lucy."

The mention of Lucy seemed to pull him back. He gave

Abby a brief squeeze, then eased away, his attention snapping to El. "*Could* have been strangled?"

"Dr. Briggs says the attack might not have killed her. She could've been put in the water alive. Finding the body quickly makes drowning a possibility."

"Explain."

El relayed the ME's explanation.

His face drained of color, and he set his hands on his waist. "Did you locate anything to help us find Lucy?"

Oh, how she wished she had a positive answer for him. "A toy unicorn floating near the dock. Small footprints in the sand close by and only a few headed toward the water. Then they stop, as if someone picked her up. Larger footprints were found nearby. All look like forensics will be able to make a good cast of them."

Gabe shoved his hands into his pockets. "Picked her up, but why? To put her in the water next to her mother or carry her away?"

"The dive team was delayed, so at this point, either is possible," El replied. "The footprints had clear heel-to-toe impressions with even depth and shorter strides versus toe-heavy impressions with deeper toe digs and longer strides."

"Means she was walking and not running," Reece said as she stepped into the room wearing dry jeans and a sweatshirt.

El nodded.

Reece took a seat at the table. "Could indicate she was removed from her car seat and led away before the violence escalated."

"And she was alive and calm," Abby said. "Alive at the dock."

"Which could also mean Kenna was complying," Reece said. "Possibly with someone she recognized. Maybe Lucy recognized them, too."

"A boyfriend?" Jude asked.

Gabe shook his head. "If there was one, she didn't tell me about him. We need to search her house and talk to her neighbors."

El nodded. "I'm headed to the office from here, and I'll apply for a search warrant."

Gabe gave her a pointed look.

"You don't have to say it. I get it. You want to come with me for the search. That might be possible. I'll let you know."

He gritted his teeth. "When will divers get there?"

"They promised to arrive as close to sunrise as possible. K-9s are on their way and the ground search will resume then, too."

"We'll be there," Gabe stated, his tone nonnegotiable. "We'll revisit our search area in daylight."

Finally, something she could say yes to. He could do that, but there was actually nothing else she could let him do.

Jude cleared his throat, gaining everyone's attention. "One thing I haven't heard anybody say is that abducting Lucy is our most probable scenario, but wasn't likely the goal. She wasn't a target, but a complication."

"How could you know that?" El asked.

"This murder was planned. Controlled. A person who thinks ahead, not someone who snapped."

"Controlled!" Gabe looked at him as if doubting the former FBI agent's take on events. "How can you say that? He strangled her. That feels more like he lost it."

"I can see where you're coming from, but look at the scene. Remote, but not random. No signs of prolonged struggle. He got close. Close enough to strangle her. That takes time. Control. Commitment."

"Or rage," El said, though she knew full well that strangulation was often motivated by control too.

Jude shook his head. "Rage is most often messy. This isn't. He chooses a quiet method. No weapon to trace. Then he disposes of her in water knowing no one comes out here this time of year, and she'd eventually sink to the bottom. Degrade. Delay your timeline."

No one spoke, as if they didn't buy his theory. El didn't blame them, but they should trust Jude's profiling experience not to lead them wrong.

Jude rested his hands on the table and leaned forward. "The guy I described isn't someone who snapped. That's a man solving a problem, to which he thought Lucy was a witness he didn't count on. He couldn't panic and kill her, nor could he leave her behind. So he abducted her, and he's holding her somewhere while he decides what to do with her."

"If you're right," El said, "then the smarter he is and more capable, the quicker he'll figure it out, and our clock is ticking even faster."

Gabe sucked in a sharp breath. "Let's hope Jude is wrong and the endgame isn't to kill Lucy too."

Jude challenged Gabe with a sharp look. "What other explanation can you come up with besides she wandered off or drowned with her mother, neither of which we have evidence to back up at this point?"

"None," Gabe said, the word barely escaping his lips.

"You'll also be looking for someone who's fit," Jude continued. "Someone who had the strength to move Kenna's body from the ravine to the lake."

"Could suggest a boyfriend," Nolan said.

"I don't think so," Jude replied. "This really isn't how the average boyfriend would behave. If they were upset with their girlfriend, the strangulation might occur after an argument. In the heat of the moment, but not planned. I'm not saying don't look for boyfriends, because you could always find one who fits this profile. I'm just saying it's not as likely as someone else."

"What motive would someone else have?" Gabe asked.

"To eliminate a threat. Perhaps she discovered something she shouldn't have and this is the only way they could silence her."

Gabe's shocked look said he was struggling to find a response. "I know you could be right, but I just can't see where she would learn something so serious that someone needed to murder her."

"You'd be surprised."

"He's right," El said from experience as a homicide detective. "People see things they shouldn't all the time, and it has nothing to do with their lives. Wrong-place-wrong-time kind of thing."

"Then how do you ever find out why they were killed?" Abby asked.

"Oftentimes you don't," El said, but at Gabe's tortured look, she thought it best to move on before he completely lost it. Like most men, he was a fixer, and he needed to act before exploding and taking matters into his own hands.

"I've secured the ravine for tonight," she said. "But will search the area in daylight too. Not only to look for evidence, but get the lay of the land."

"You think something else occurred there?" Nolan asked.

She shrugged. "We could find signs of a struggle by Kenna's van. Maybe that's where she was killed, and we'll find evidence of that. I'm also interested in seeing if it connects to the lake. Kenna and Lucy could've been taken away in a boat from there and brought to the beach."

Gabe's eyes narrowed as if he was imagining the scene.

Jude frowned at her. "Did the ME share any other information?"

"Nothing except that the autopsy is at nine. I'll attend, of course."

Gabe widened his stance. "I'm coming with you."

"Sorry, but no. You're not officially connected to this investigation. Besides, you don't want to see your friend undergo such an invasive examination."

His face paled, and he clapped a hand over his mouth. "I need some air."

He bolted around the table and brushed past her with such haste she had to work to stay upright. Wanting to reach out to him, she stood firm and tracked his progress out the door.

"I'll go after him," Abby said.

Nolan held up a hand. "Give him a few minutes alone to process."

Alone? He needed help. His pain was El's pain. His anguish, her anguish. His loss, her loss.

Never had an investigation brought up such intense emotions. Not even Victoria's. Perhaps the right thing to do was to recuse herself from the case. She could hand everything off to Ulrich.

Could, but she wouldn't let Gabe down. She would not only find Kenna's killer, but also locate her daughter, and along the way, she would support him through his turmoil.

El glanced around the group. "I have a few additional questions for Gabe, but other than that, I'm finished. Any questions?"

His solemn team members shook their heads.

Nolan focused on her as if training a sniper rifle. "In the event we don't find her right away, let's plan regular update meetings to pool resources. Maybe start at the end of the day today. We should have results by then, and it would be a good time to coordinate."

Many detectives would be put off by a private investigation agency like this one, but she knew their qualifications and skills, plus their success rate in finding missing people, so she nodded.

Nolan stood and gave a tight smile. "I know this isn't easy, and Gabe's personal connection compounds that. But he'll come around, so hang in there."

She started for the door, and Abby rushed to join her. "I'm praying for you and for a positive outcome to Lucy's disappearance."

"Thanks." El smiled at the petite woman. "That will make all the difference."

Abby squeezed her arm, and El stepped out the door. A brisk wind whipped from the ocean, and shivers ran over her body. Gabe was out there somewhere, grieving alone. Not surprising that he wanted to be on his own. He kept his private life private. He'd let her in a few times, telling her he came from a family with connections to illegal activities, but not what specifically had caused him to lock down his emotions.

She walked to her car, but was drawn to the ocean lookout. Maybe viewing God's majesty in His creation could lift her mood and help her trust Him to take care of Lucy.

She started down the cracked sidewalk and around the end of the long building. The lookout area spread out before her, lit by a single antique lamp on a post, the sound of ocean waves rushing to shore from the bottom of the cliff.

Near the security wall, Gabe sat on a dilapidated bench, shoulders hunched, elbows on his knees, staring straight ahead.

He wanted to be alone, but did he really mean it? He wasn't the sort of guy who didn't speak his mind. Meaning he wouldn't want her here. She turned to leave, her boot disturbing nearby gravel, the rasping movement of rock sounding like a clap of thunder in her brain.

He swiveled on the bench.

"Sorry," she said, and truly meant it. "I didn't know you were here. I came out to stare at the ocean and clear my brain before heading back to the office. I'll go now."

"The view's not working for me, but don't let me get in your way."

She hesitated, then moved directly to the wall, bypassing him to avoid seeing his anguish again.

She heard him get up and cross the gravel to stand beside her. "Did I miss anything at the meeting?"

She shook her head.

He took her arm and turned her to face him. "I won't let you freeze me out of this investigation."

"I know, but we'll have to work together. You can't go off on your own. Let me know in advance what you're doing so we don't have issues with contaminating evidence or jeopardizing the investigation. We both want to find Lucy, and Kenna's killer."

The fresh flash of grief in his eyes had her looking away at the ocean before she offered him some sort of physical comfort. Frothy waves rolled in, reminding her of the other body of water she'd left behind in the wee hours.

The lake had taken lives before. Would take them again. Might've taken one more last night. Even two. The second to be determined in the light of day.

What would Gabe do if divers found little Lucy's body in the murky depths of the lake?

4

———

Gabe appreciated El's concern, but if he let her in now, he might lose what little control he had left. His chest was already too tight, his thoughts too close to spiraling. On some level, he knew he needed her and he didn't have the heart to send her away, but he couldn't look at her.

Instead, he stared over the ocean raging below the bluff. The waves crashed against the rocks with relentless force, the roar swallowing everything else. When the water surged back toward shore, white froth glistened beneath a thin sliver of moon still fighting its way through the clouds.

It should have been beautiful.

He couldn't appreciate it. Not when his mind was locked on a single thought, one twisted thing to be thankful for.

That Kenna and Lucy hadn't gone to the ocean instead of the lake.

If they had, their bodies would never be recovered. No answers. No closure. Just endless water and unanswered questions. The relief curdled instantly into guilt, and a sudden chill worked its way through him. He shivered, though the night wasn't that cold.

El noticed. Of course she did.

"Is there anything I can do?" she asked.

Her voice cut through the roar of the surf, steady and professional. Too steady.

"The best thing you can do," he said, his throat tightening, "is work this investigation and work it fast. Find Lucy, and Kenna's killer." The words scraped his throat raw, and he gagged slightly as they left his mouth.

She pushed away from the low wall and turned to face him fully. "Then there's something I need to get out of the way. I don't want to upset you more, but I have questions. We can do this later at the office, but right now would be better."

"Go ahead," he said, even though the last thing he wanted was to talk.

She slipped a small notepad and pen from her pocket. In an instant, the concern vanished from her face, replaced by sharp focus. Her eyes narrowed slightly, unblinking, assessing, cataloging. It was the version of El everyone talked about. Methodical. By the book. Emotionally distant. He didn't know why she kept herself so locked down, only that she'd hinted at guilt from her past. Whatever it was, it had taught her how to shut feelings off like a switch.

She poised her pen over the pad. "Is there anyone we should notify of Kenna's death?"

Gabe swallowed. He'd been so consumed by his own grief he hadn't even thought that far ahead. "She's estranged from her parents, but they still need to know. *If* you can locate them. She grew up near Portland, but she never mentioned where they're living now."

"I can look for an address when I search her home. What about Lucy's father?"

"He's not in the picture. Never has been." He clenched his jaw. "Kenna said he was a one-night stand. She never even brought up his name."

"You have any theories on who it might be?"

He shook his head. "If I did, you better believe I would've tracked him down and pushed him to help support them. She struggled as a single mother, but she was proud. Too proud. She refused any financial help I offered."

El's pen scratched across the paper. Then she lifted her gaze. "Speaking of you. Where were you between seven and nine tonight?"

"What?" He stared at her, disbelief flashing hot and sharp. He dragged a hand over the back of his neck. "You think I did this? That I hurt Kenna? That's ridiculous. I was with the team at the inn until eight, then spent every second after I left until I arrived on the scene looking for her."

Her expression didn't change. Not a flicker of reassurance. Not a hint that she believed him. "Other than the team confirming your presence at the inn, anyone who can corroborate the rest of the time?"

The question landed like a slap. How could she even ask it?

"Not physically in my truck with me," he snapped. "But I was in constant contact with my team by phone."

"You know that doesn't physically place you anywhere," she said calmly. "So it doesn't confirm an alibi."

"You can track my cell phone."

"Can do. And we might be able to pull GPS from your truck. But that still doesn't prove you were with your phone or in your vehicle."

"Kenna texted from a gas station about a half hour after she left home." He pulled out his phone and displayed the text showing she needed air in a tire. "I went back to that gas station to confirm she'd been there and nothing had happened to her. Watched the video feed. The attendant can confirm I was there and I'd be on their video feed too.

Was right around eight. It would've taken me at least half an hour to get to the lake."

"We'll check on that, but it still doesn't tell us where you were for the last half hour."

She had a point. One he refused to respond to or argue with. Either she believed him or she didn't.

"This isn't personal, Gabe," she said quietly. "You know I'm just doing my job, right?"

He didn't know that. To him, it felt painfully personal. He bit his tongue, unwilling to say something he couldn't take back.

She exhaled. "Can you think of anyone who might've wanted to hurt Kenna?"

"I don't know the people in her day-to-day life," he said. "Only the ones she mentioned."

"Like who?"

"Mostly her coworkers at Little Pines Daycare. Especially the director who didn't get along well with the classroom staff. Kenna had a bunch of stories about how she always put profit before the children."

"Doesn't sound like the kind of person who should be working with children."

"I've picked Lucy up from daycare several times, and the woman has always been quite charming to me. Kenna told me that was a front."

"Why did she continue to work there, then?"

"It wasn't for the pay, that was for sure. She believed she needed to be there to try to protect these children and families. To help them whenever possible. She also believed in Safe Harbor. They're an emergency home for kids ages eight to seventeen. They're mostly funded by the New Tide Foundation, but I know the daycare center supported them too."

"I've read about group homes like that but never had cause to visit one."

"They help neglect or abuse cases, behavioral issues, and also serve as temporary placements. She said they successfully found permanent homes for most of the kids, and she loved volunteering there."

"You think this could be about the daycare or Safe Harbor?"

"I honestly don't think so. I mean, the director wasn't very nice to her staff, but I can't see any reason she would be involved in killing Kenna."

"I'll still need to interview the director, but we should move on until we have any indication that Safe Harbor or the daycare center have a connection to her murder." El made a note. "You're sure there weren't any boyfriends? Current or past. Someone she broke up with and it ended badly?"

"She said she didn't date. Claimed as a working single mom, and with her volunteer work, that was the last thing she had time for."

"Did you believe her?" El asked. "Or did you think she just didn't want to talk about it?"

He thought back over their conversations. "I believed her. She was pretty candid. Even more than I am. So, I think she would've said something."

"What about you? The two of you ever date?"

"What?" His denial came too fast. Too sharp. She probably wouldn't believe him. "Date? Us? Never."

"Why not?"

He hesitated this time. They were drifting dangerously close to territory he never shared. Even his teammates only knew the surface-level version of his past. And yet, something about El made it hard to hold the line.

"Gabe?" she asked. "Why not date?"

"Because we'd known each other since I was six and she was eight," he said, finally able to share a little of his past.

"We grew up together. Became friends. Dating wasn't even on the radar, and it never occurred to me."

"What about her? Did it occur to her?"

"If it did, she never said anything, which like I said, isn't—wasn't—in her character."

"How did you meet?"

Despite the ache in his chest, a smile tugged at his mouth. "I wanted to walk to school alone. My mom wouldn't let me. I'd seen Kenna heading out every morning by herself. She was older and cool when I was kind of a nerdy little boy, but one day I worked up the nerve to ask if I could walk with her every day. Oh, man, she teased me for being a big baby." The memory made him chuckle, and he paused to enjoy it. "But surprise, surprise, she actually agreed. And then my mom did too. Honestly, I think my mom was relieved. I was the youngest child, and Kenna was her ticket to a little freedom."

"Kenna must've moved on to middle school before you, but you stayed friends?"

He nodded, offering nothing more than he was ready to tell her.

"Was the rest of your family close to Kenna?"

Of course she had to mention his family. Stopped him from being able to look at her. He slid his gaze over her shoulder. "My mom genuinely liked Kenna, but our family wasn't well thought of in the neighborhood. Didn't mingle much with anyone. I'm still surprised Kenna's mom let her walk with me."

"Why wasn't your family well thought of?"

He should've known she wouldn't miss his comment and should've kept his mouth shut. He'd once given her that basic detail about his family, but she hadn't pressed him to find out why. Now she had a right to know, but he still didn't want to see her reaction when he told her.

"I doubt that's relevant to the investigation," he said, sounding more irritated than she deserved.

"The more I understand Kenna," El said without even a hint of emotion, "the better chance I have of finding who killed her. Faster too."

He didn't want to reveal anything else, but she might be right. After all, his family's history was a shadow that seemed to touch everything in his life. Who knows, maybe he even mentioned them because he really did want to talk about them.

He planted his feet on the ground, bracing himself. He'd only ever told this once before. To Kenna. "Crime was a way of life for my family. Tradition. My father and uncles were career con men. My oldest brother fit right in." He shook his head, still unable to meet her gaze. "By fifteen, I'd seen more deals go down than most detectives see in their whole careers. I wanted out. On my eighteenth birthday, I ran."

He glanced at her, expecting to see disgust.

There was none. Only surprise.

"I cut contact," he continued. "Learned how to survive on the edges of the system. Eventually earned my degree."

She nodded, thoughtful. "That explains why you tend to go rogue. Follow your gut instead of orders."

"Sharp eye. Nose for lies. Mistrust," he said. "Skills you don't lose once you learn them."

He was certain he should have changed by now, but how could he? No matter how far he got, the past always had a way of following him.

"Believe it or not," she said softly, "I understand more than you think."

He managed a wry smile. "You have a family full of felons, too?"

"No. Just a father who bailed when I was one. And a mother who supported herself as an exotic dancer." She grimaced. "When I was three, I was taken into foster care. Eventually my mom relinquished her rights to me, and I was adopted. I have great parents now."

So that was it. An explanation for the walls she'd built around her emotions. "Anything I haven't asked that I should know?"

Was there? He thought for a moment. "Yeah, I should tell you about Jude. You know he's a former FBI agent, but you might not know he was a profiler. He doesn't talk about it with anyone, but any theory he offers on an investigation comes from that profiler background, and we should pay attention to it."

"I'll keep that in mind."

"Sounds like you're skeptical of profiling."

"Not skeptical. I've never worked with a profiler, so *wary*."

"Jude was one of the best."

She tilted her head. "Why did he leave then?"

"That's his story to tell, but it has nothing to do with not doing the job right, so his skills can help with this investigation."

"Then I'm glad to have him on board."

As much as Gabe wanted to disagree with Jude about his first profile of their killer, Gabe was glad to have him, too. "That's all I have for now, but I doubt I'll get any sleep and my mind will keep looking for a possible motive. If something comes to me, I'll tell you when we meet at the beach."

Her mouth tightened, as if she dreaded the thought. Or maybe she dreaded watching divers search a lake for a missing child.

Heaven knows, he was dreading it far more than anything he'd ever faced.

～

From the hilltop above Lost Lake, El stared at the water, silent at dawn, the kind of silence that swallowed sound and secrets. Maybe not for long. Divers would arrive soon, and they might reveal the most horrific secret of all.

She shuddered, but not from the cold. Lucy had been missing for twelve hours now, and they hadn't made any real progress. Sure, they knew approximately when Kenna was murdered, giving them a timeframe, but they had no idea if Lucy actually was with her mother. But she had to be the reason for the car seat, so where was she?

You must answer that soon.

Statistics told her so. Seventy-five percent of all abducted and then murdered children were killed within the first three hours. They'd passed that milestone before they even knew she was gone. At the three to twenty-four hour mark—where they fell right now—a solid chance of finding them alive still existed, but they needed to ramp up their urgency, because hitting twenty-four hours?

No. No. No way she would go there before it was a problem. She'd just focus and do everything within her power to bring sweet Lucy home alive.

Starting with upping searchers, bringing in the dogs, additional door-to-door canvassing, along with evidence retrieval and processing. All scheduled by eight o'clock this morning. Not to mention, hunting for a boat potentially used to transport Kenna and Lucy from their van to the beach.

Vehicle tires crunched over gravel behind her. Had to be the dive team. Searchers from other jurisdictions and the K-9 team weren't due for thirty minutes. Plus, Sierra Rice from the Veritas Center forensic unit wouldn't arrive until eight.

Dread settled in El's gut as she turned.

Oh. Oh!

Not who she expected this early. Not at all.

All six members of the Lost Lake Locators team climbed from black SUVs. Led by Gabe, they approached with grim purpose as if they were in slow motion in a movie. If only that were true, she'd have time to prepare herself for their arrival, but all too soon they were standing in front of her.

All her fault for being caught off guard. They'd said they were coming at daylight, which it almost was, and they weren't the kind of people to stand around and wait for the day to get away from them.

"We're here to help with the search," Gabe said.

"You should've called first." She held his firm gaze and tried not to sound irritated when they knew better than to be there. "I could've saved you the trip. Nothing has changed. If you came to join in on the immediate area search and not the same place you searched last night, I can't let you do that. Not with your personal connection to the investigation."

"So what if we know Kenna and Lucy? Doesn't compromise our search abilities."

"Agreed, but until we have official details about Kenna's death, I can't rule any of you out as suspects."

Hayden settled his hands on his waist. "You're not seriously suggesting we had anything to do with Kenna's murder and Lucy's disappearance."

"It's exactly what I'm suggesting." El pulled her shoulders back. "I'm not saying I believe it, but until I prove otherwise, I have to follow protocol. Besides, if you find evidence, defense attorneys will question whether you planted it."

"What?" Gabe's voice shot up. "You know we'd never—"

"I know that, but juries wouldn't. They don't know your ethics would stop you from tampering with evidence."

Gabe broke eye contact and paced like a caged tiger. He stopped in front of her again and plunged a hand into his hair. "I'm the one with the real connection to Kenna. What if I stay here and the others search?"

"What do you think?" she asked.

Jude moved forward, resting a hand on Gabe's shoulder. "We could be accused of having our teammate's back and planting evidence for him."

"Fine," Nolan said. "We might not be able to access the cordoned off area, but you can't stop us from taking a better look where we searched last night. We can also use a drone to expand our search area."

She nodded, but before she could say anything, Gabe flashed his focus back to her. "That's not enough. I want to do more."

"Again, I'm sorry." She felt like a broken record.

"Come on, Gabe," Abby said. "It's better than walking away to do nothing while we wait for others to complete their work."

"I can't tell you what to do outside our perimeter, but I caution you. The same issue about planted evidence could arise. If you all do decide to search again," she paused to lock her gaze on Gabe, "it might be better if you don't join the team."

The storm brewing in his body erupted. His breath came in quick bursts, eyes shifting from dark and stormy to helplessly lost. He opened his mouth, then closed it.

"I'm sorry, Gabe," she said. "I wish things were different, but we have to solidify your alibi first."

"I told you where I was."

"And I believe you, but you were alone in your vehicle and no one can corroborate your alibi."

"I was on the phone with my team."

Hayden moved closer to her. "You need to get the GPS data for his phone for Kenna's time of death. That'll prove his phone wasn't here. Since he was talking to us most of the time, we can confirm he was with it."

She was way ahead of them. "I've already requested phone records, but providers are notoriously slow responding."

"Then I'll get Mina to expedite it," Nolan said. "Or are you threatened by me going to your supervisor?"

"Not as long as I know about it."

"Fair enough." Nolan pulled out his phone. "I'll call her right now."

He stepped away just as a dive team vehicle pulled into the lot.

"It's about to get busy," El said, letting her gaze drift over the team members. "I suggest you leave before that happens."

Gabe looked at his teammates. "You all go ahead. I'll wait here until you're done."

Drat! Not what she wanted him to do. At least he wasn't compromising her crime scene, but he'd be front and center if divers found something. If they pulled Lucy's tiny body from the lake, she'd be at the beach and not by his side. She didn't want that for him. Didn't want it at all.

"I wouldn't recommend staying. The search could take hours." She was thinking of him, though guilt lingered for trying to get him to leave.

"I'll stay with Gabe," Jude said.

Better than Gabe being alone, though she would've chosen Abby or Reece for the job. They both had stronger interpersonal skills. Jude could border on being a smart aleck, but from what his teammates said, he had a deeper, more sensitive side she'd never seen.

"Thanks, man," Gabe said. "But your time would be better spent searching."

Jude planted his feet. "Feels like I should stay."

"I think he should stay, too," Abby said. "He's your backup. You might need his help."

Gabe watched her carefully, perhaps deciding if Jude was staying because of his role or because he thought something terrible was about to happen and Gabe would need him.

Gabe's focus drifted to the van where the diver had flung open the back door and was unloading equipment.

He took a sharp breath. "Fine. Hang back with me."

The diver hefted up his oxygen tank and fins and started across the lot. He gave Gabe's departing team a curious look, but continued ahead until he stopped in front of El. "Lead diver, Vance Porter."

"Detective Elaina Lyons." She shook hands with him. "Thanks for coming."

He released her hand and peered over the lake. "We put our boat in at the nearby access ramp. My partner will be here soon, and we'll get started."

She nodded, trying to control emotions sitting right on the surface like a cyst waiting to erupt.

Please, please. Please don't let them find little Lucy in the water.

Gabe's mind swirled with the activity buzzing around the crime scene. The dive boat motored up to the dock, and divers were shimmying into their wetsuits. Multiple vehicles, carrying search personnel from nearby jurisdictions, rolled into the lot behind him.

A sturdy-looking handler with two dogs, a German shepherd named Scout and a Labrador retriever called Diesel, met El and Ulrich near the water. Scout was on a leash, patiently waiting for his assignment but Diesel was hooked to a metal stake as if he was a backup dog.

Everyone shared somber expressions. Somber like a funeral, and Gabe didn't like it. Sure, they shouldn't be joking and laughing, but their attitudes said they'd already reached a conclusion.

They didn't expect to find Lucy alive.

Jude dropped his hand from shading his eyes as he stared at the water. "Looks like El's doing a great job organizing everything."

Gabe nodded. "I'm impressed. Even keeping me from participating is the right thing to do." She might not have let him help, but he had to give her credit for successfully coordinating a major investigation.

"You think anything more of my theory I tossed out?"

"Unfortunately, yes. Finding indications of a boat at the ravine suggests premeditation, and Lucy didn't just wander off, but the killer took her."

"Kenna's voicemail said she was scared. Say this was the guy she was afraid of. Why would she meet him when she had Lucy with her?"

Gabe couldn't imagine the pressure she must've been under to bring Lucy to such a meeting. "She must not have thought he would harm her, but obviously, she was wrong. It cost her life and maybe Lucy's too."

"So that clock's ticking down even more on you, then."

"Yeah, standing here while everything's going on around me is infuriating. If El doesn't give me an opportunity to get involved soon, I'll find a way." Gabe's focus zoned in on Ulrich.

He spoke to the canine handler, who turned his attention to the large German shepherd. The guy gave a sharp nod and opened the evidence bag containing Lucy's sweatshirt to hold it to Scout's nose.

"Let's hope we get results soon," Gabe said.

Scout perked up, his whole body vibrating as he danced in place.

"Search!" The handler freed the dog from his leash.

Scout transformed from obedient partner to driven hunter, every sense locked onto his task. Nose to the ground, he moved with purpose and each step was silent but charged with energy. His ears swiveled to catch the faintest sound, nose working in quick, sharp sniffs. When he picked up a trace, his body changed. Muscles tightened, tail stiffened into a steady line.

He surged ahead, weaving in a focused pattern as he followed an invisible trail to the woods on the beach's south side. At the dirt path entrance, he barked.

Once. Twice. Sharp and urgent.

He glanced back at his handler, who'd followed him.

"Looks like he found something," Jude said.

Not taking his eyes off the dog, Gabe nodded. Scout's tail wagged in severe alert movements as his body quivered with restrained excitement.

The handler squatted down, and Ulrich crouched beside him. Together they pawed through fallen pine needles with gloved hands.

Ulrich came up holding something sparkly. El carefully made her way across the sand, looking as if she was avoiding stepping in other footprints that would be cast by Sierra.

Ulrich said something to her and then held out the object. She took it in her gloved hand and stared.

Gabe held his breath.

She stilled, then slowly looked up at him, eyes narrow and tortured.

His heart stuttered.

"That could only mean one thing," he said. "They found

something belonging to Lucy. You could be right and someone took her. Maybe she struggled and it fell off as they walked away. This could either confirm that or confirm she wandered away, but at least we won't find her in the water."

"Could be," Jude said, sounding like he didn't believe the last two options were probable.

Gabe still wasn't ready to admit that someone had taken Lucy, because if they had, she could be in terrible danger right now, and he had no way of finding her.

His sweet little princess in the hands of some crazed abductor.

Frightened. Terrified. Alone.

And not only couldn't he find her, here he stood, doing nothing to save her.

5

———

Daylight barely skimmed the smooth, glassy lake that was still now as if it had never taken any lives at all. But El knew better as she stood at the water's edge, watching faint ripples spread from Vance Porter's headlamp as he made his way to the surface.

Somewhere beneath that calm skin of water, answers waited.

Porter surfaced, eyes narrowed beneath his mask, clutching something in his hand.

El's stomach dropped. What now?

First, the dog had found a child-sized bracelet, which she'd bagged and stored in her cargo pocket. It gnawed at her like a cancerous growth to her body, and every moment since then, she'd been aware of what it could mean.

Now this?

She'd opted not to show Gabe the bracelet until Scout and his handler completed the trail search, but if, in fact, Porter had found something to indicate Lucy had drowned, she couldn't hold back from getting Gabe's positive identification that the item belonged to Lucy.

Porter pushed through the water toward the dock and

waved for her to join him. Before she even reached the worn wooden planks, he'd hoisted himself onto the edge, water sluicing off his wetsuit. He removed his fins and stood, the item in his hand.

She tried to hurry, but the slippery dock dipped and bobbed under her feet. To keep from face planting, she slowed her steps and was also careful to skirt around drag marks on the wood that the light of day made more obvious.

Porter held out the item dripping in his hand.

She steeled herself with a deep breath and looked at a pink Converse sneaker with random black and red stars dotting the canvas. Small. Barely the length of his open palm.

A child's shoe.

She gently took it in her gloved hands, legs going weak.

"I've seen girls wearing these in my daughter's daycare class," Porter said, voice choked.

"How old is she?" El asked and clutched onto the shoe.

"Four going on five."

"The right age," she mumbled because there was no point in saying aloud the size could very well fit Lucy.

Porter nodded, expression tight as he looked at the dawning sky. "I heard the mom died here. I can't comprehend what the child's dad must be going through. I would totally lose it."

She didn't mention Lucy's father wasn't in the picture and didn't even know this child existed, much less that she'd potentially drowned or gone missing. "Is this all you found?"

"For now."

El's shock receded, allowing logic to take over. "If she drowned, wouldn't she be found close to the shoe?"

"Most likely, if she was wearing it. Bodies don't drift far in lakes like this, no currents or inflow. Assuming she drowned, when her lungs filled, the water weight pulled down, and she would've sunk almost straight down from where she disappeared. Of course, there are a lot of factors that could influence her location. This should be treated as a starting point for a search grid rather than a guarantee."

The thought pressed heavy on El's chest. If Lucy was in the water, she probably hadn't floated away. Hadn't escaped the darkness below.

El tried to control her thoughts, but images flashed in her brain. The slow descent through murky water. Silence enveloping the sweet little girl and swallowing every sound. Reaching the bottom, and the faint sway of weeds brushing against her motionless limbs. Lying there, waiting for the moment the lake would decide to give up what it had taken.

Somewhere below, answers could still be waiting. And maybe something worse. A shiver cut through her, colder than the wind skimming the surface.

Stop. Move on.

She held up the sneaker. "I'll take this into evidence and let you get back to it."

Porter nodded grimly, dropped to the dock, and put his fins back on.

She bagged and pocketed the sneaker before turning toward Gabe. Whether she liked it or not, and no matter the pain it might cause him, she needed to ask if this shoe and the bracelet belonged to Lucy.

She crossed the sand and climbed the steps. Several onlookers lingered in the parking lot within hearing distance. Not surprising, but a nuisance. As long as they stayed outside the crime scene, there was nothing she could do about them.

Keeping the evidence in her pockets, she approached Gabe. "Too many people around to talk. Let's go to my cruiser."

She didn't wait for him to ask if Jude could come along, but stepped off, ignoring questions from spectators. Normally, she was careful to project a good image to the public, but if someone came to gawk at a crime scene hoping to see gore, she didn't have time for them.

In her vehicle, she waited for Gabe to settle in the passenger seat, then turned to face him.

"What's going on?" The question shot out like a fired bullet. "What did you find?"

She reached into her pocket for the bracelet and handed the bag to him. "Scout found this near the head of the trail to the woods. Does it belong to Lucy?"

Frowning, he turned the bag in his hands, studying the bracelet carefully. "I've never seen her wearing any jewelry. Kenna didn't have money for such things, but that doesn't mean it couldn't be hers."

"Maybe when we search their house, we'll find a picture of her wearing it. And of course, we'll give it to Sierra. It could contain DNA that would link it to Lucy."

He nodded, but it was reserved. "What did the diver bring up?"

She withdrew the shoe from her pocket.

He gasped.

"Lucy's?" she asked.

"Yes." The solemnly spoken word lingered in the car like a bad smell.

He turned the bag in his hand, then held it out to El and pointed at a single star filled with purple. "Lucy always begged me to move to their town because she missed me. So she colored this star. Said it was special and when she looked at it, she'd think about me and not miss me so much."

"Then you can definitely confirm this belongs to her?" El asked, hating every second of it.

"Unfortunately, yes." He looked up, moisture wetting his eyes. "Did the diver find any other trace of her?"

"None yet."

He swiped angrily at the tears. "Could be a good sign."

"It could," El said, making sure he knew she believed it. "The diver said if she drowned while wearing the shoe and it came off, she likely would've sunk straight down. He would've found her close to it, which he didn't. But there are situations where that could vary."

Gabe released a long breath. "But it's possible she wasn't wearing the shoe. Maybe it came off when she was taken out of her car seat and it fell into the water."

"At some point, the small footprints we found on the beach indicate she could've walked there with both shoes, so that might not make sense."

"Fine, then it came off another way and was tossed in the water." His desperation was nearly palpable.

"You could be right. We won't know anything until the divers finish."

He looked away. "When do you plan to search her place?"

"After the divers are done." She didn't explain her reasoning, but he had to know she wanted to be on scene if Lucy's body was discovered. "Plus, Mina arranged for Sierra Rice to handle forensics, and she'll arrive around eight. I want to get her started on both scenes before I go to Kenna's house. Then there's the autopsy."

"Whatever time you go to her place, I'm coming with you."

"Just like I couldn't let you search today, I can't let you do this either."

"But I know Kenna and could potentially see something important you'd overlook." He locked eyes with her. "If we stay together every minute, you'll see that I don't plant evidence or take anything."

"I don't know... I..." She shrugged. She wanted him there but really shouldn't allow it.

"Hayden called in a favor with a buddy at my phone company. They're emailing my phone records, including any coordinates, to you ASAP. You should get those before you leave for Kenna's apartment. If you cross-reference the calls with coordinates, it'll prove my alibi, and then you'd be free to let me help."

He was right. That could solve their problem. "That would work."

His shoulders relaxed, fists unclenching, but his forehead remained furrowed.

She wanted to press her fingers against those ridges and help him relax more, but there was no point. She might ease his tension momentarily, but this man she'd come to care for so much wouldn't be able to relax until they found Kenna's killer and precious little Lucy.

With every passing moment, frustration mounted and Gabe couldn't wait any longer. He had to do something to help. But what? El had instructed deputies to keep him outside the perimeter, and they carried out her orders to the letter.

She'd been involved with the searchers and was talking to one of them now.

The more he considered how she treated him, the more he thought he'd be foolish to trust whatever was building between them. If she cared for him, he would've expected her to make an exception for him. To let him help with the investigation. Man, he was wrong. Way wrong.

Even worse, he understood her reasoning, but only in

his brain. Otherwise, her actions felt like a knife to the back. Especially from a woman he'd developed feelings for.

He'd probably been a fool to feel anything for any woman. Especially one like El, who represented the life he'd always tried to prove he was worthy of. He wasn't. Not with his family. And he never would be.

So let it go.

One of the divers surfaced and tossed his fins into the boat. His gaze zoned in on the beach, and he strode through the lake toward El, each step sending ripples over the water. His hands were empty. Good. Very good. Unless he was bringing bad news. Maybe they'd found a body. Found Lucy, and he'd surfaced to make recovery preparations.

He marched up to El. Talking. Hands waving.

What was he saying? Gabe had to know. He focused on El, waiting for her reaction. For her body to stiffen or shoulders to collapse. A firm nod was her only response.

The diver stepped away, heading for the dock.

She reached into her pocket, drew out her phone, and tapped the screen. Gabe watched. Time dragged. She suddenly stopped. Turned. Stared at him. Tension sizzled in the air. She gave a slight shake of her head and crossed the beach to the stairway.

She had news for him.

Dear God, what is she going to say?

Waiting to hear the worst possible news, he shoved his hands into his pockets and fought the urge to flee from having to hear it.

She slipped under the fluttering yellow tape and stopped close to him. "I got the email from your phone company. Your alibi holds."

Good news, but... "What about the diver? What did he say?"

"They finished searching the immediate area and didn't

find anything else. He asked if I wanted him to expand the search."

Gabe let out a slow breath like air leaking from a forgotten balloon. "Did you tell him to do it?"

"Yes. Our suspect could've used a boat. Other factors could've caused her to sink away from the shoe, so I had him extend it another five thousand square feet. He said it'll take about five hours. I have too many other priorities to deal with to wait for them to finish."

"Makes sense," he said, though he wasn't sure if he could leave while they were still searching the water for his sweet Lucy.

El glanced at her watch. "I've got about forty minutes until Sierra arrives. Enough time to search Kenna's vehicle and the ravine."

"Can I come with you?" He expected a no, but still foolishly hoped she wouldn't say it.

"With your alibi checking out, for once, I can say yes." She gave him a clipped smile. "Give me a minute to tell my deputy where we're going. Then we can head out."

He nodded, and she whirled around to march over to Deputy Ewing. His eyelids were drooping and his shoulders sagging. In a forceful, almost stern tone, she directed him to call if Sierra arrived while she was away or if anyone else discovered new information. Lastly, she reminded him no one was allowed on the crime scene without her permission.

She strode back to Gabe, her posture stiff, and her gaze intense. She might've shut him down, but she would do everything possible to find Lucy, not quitting until they had results. She had the same intensity that drove him. She would burn the world to save a kid. He suspected something in her past fueled that driving force. He badly wanted her to share the reason with him.

"I'll drive," was all she said, whipping past him toward her vehicle.

At about five ten, she was a good four inches shorter than him, but he nearly had to jog to keep up. He'd barely settled in the passenger seat when she made a quick U-turn and whipped onto the highway.

He clicked his seatbelt. "Seems like you know where you're going."

"I mapped it out and reviewed satellite photographs after I left the inn."

"Did you get any sleep at all?"

She shook her head.

"Me neither."

"Then let's hope we're both alert enough to do our best work today."

"A good reason to have two sets of eyes on things." He glanced at her. "Have you ever worked a missing person case before?"

Pain slashed across her face, and she gripped the wheel tightly. "Once."

"Was it a child?"

She nodded but didn't continue.

"Seems like it didn't turn out well."

She ran a hand over her hair, smoothing the bun she wore daily, already cinched back like she was heading into battle. She claimed it, along with her serviceable suits with white button-downs, helped other guys forget she was a woman and treat her as an equal. Something that shouldn't occur in law enforcement today, but still did.

"I was just a rookie." Her flat, emotionless tone and rigid posture said something different. "I responded to a missing child report. A five-year-old taken from a public park. I was first on scene and followed department protocol. But..."

Her words drifted off, and she cleared her throat. "I

made a critical misjudgment. I believed Victoria had simply wandered off, so I didn't immediately escalate it to a potential abduction. By the time the truth became clear, it was too late. Victoria was never found."

"Oh, man. That must've been rough."

"Especially when her parents blamed me and demanded a case review. I was cleared of misconduct, but I..." Her voice choked, and she shook her head.

"You never forgave yourself."

"Exactly." She glanced at him. "We're almost to the ravine."

Okay, point taken. She didn't want to talk about the guilt. For some reason, that hurt. Maybe he'd come to care for her enough that he expected she would share her past struggles with him. But why? He hadn't done so. Sure, he'd told her about his family but just the facts, like a book report. He hadn't shared how they still impacted his everyday life.

"Less than a quarter mile now," he said, though her study of the ravine would have already told her that. "The overlook area comes up first. Pull in there."

She fixed her attention forward, mouth snapped closed. Just as he suspected. She didn't intend to discuss her guilt and how it drove her life.

She eased into the small parking area, reached behind her seat, and retrieved a camera. Hanging the strap around her neck, she slipped outside before he could say anything else. Not that he really had anything to say. He wouldn't press her because he wouldn't want her to push him.

He led the way to the ravine. Yellow crime scene tape had been strung at the road, and a deputy stood near his patrol car.

El approached him and gave him a quick nod. "Anything happen overnight?"

The deputy hooked his thumbs in his duty belt. "All quiet."

At least from the road. No way this guy could have any idea what occurred on the lake or wilderness sides below.

He lifted the yellow tape for them, and they stepped to the edge of the ravine. Daylight allowed Gabe to clearly see Kenna's van wrapped around a large tree at the bottom, undercarriage tangled with tall plants and grass. A powerful ache filled his gut, and all thoughts of El's guilt evaporated.

He had to look away before he lost it. Long skid marks on the road surface peppered with taillight fragments he hadn't seen in the dark, caught his attention. "Looks like a broken taillight. Like she was forced off the road."

El frowned. "We need to wait for an expert to make that determination."

"It's obvious to me. The scuff marks are lateral with sudden direction changes. Plus, the J-shaped or curved skid doesn't fit normal driving behavior."

She raised an eyebrow. "Something you learned when you were a state trooper?"

He nodded. "I investigated my share of accidents. Not many showed signs of force like this, but I saw a few."

El faced the ravine. "Finding paint transfer and a broken taillight on Kenna's van will help confirm your theory."

"Then let's move." He started forward, but El raised her hand. "I need to photograph the scene before we disturb everything."

"I did tell you I searched the van last night, right? I didn't know it was a crime scene, and I didn't think about disturbing the area. My only concern was getting to Kenna and Lucy to make sure they were okay."

"Of course. What's done is done. We'll deal with the scene as it is now and protect it going forward." She removed the lens cap and began taking pictures.

Gabe concentrated on remaining calm. No way he wanted her to decide he was a problem and make him wait at the road.

She snapped the lens cap back on. "I'll lead. You follow."

He'd never been a follower, but he was thankful to be there and would do his best to comply with her every instruction.

She grabbed tree branches and grass to ease her way down, much like he'd done the night before. The vegetation held her smaller body more securely than his. He gave her a solid headstart then followed, moving slowly and carefully to avoid plummeting down the hill and taking her with him.

At the bottom, she glanced back. "Stay here until I tell you it's okay to move."

Planting her feet on the thick bed of pine needles, she lifted her camera. She circled the vehicle, the camera's sharp clicks disturbing the quiet.

It gave him something to focus on other than the van and what had happened to Kenna.

"Black paint transferred on the back, along with vehicle damage." El dropped down behind the vehicle and clicked away.

"I know the van didn't have any damage before. She was seriously into everything retro, and the VW was her baby. She kept it in mint condition. She named it Sunshine and splurged on custom plates."

"Can you have your team contact repair shops in the area for any black vehicles brought in with front-end damage?"

"Sure." Gabe got on his phone and texted Nolan. "Could take some time with such broad criteria."

El continued around the vehicle but halted next to the driver's door. She grimaced, then looked at him. "Join me over here."

Professional El had taken over—sharp, to the point, demanding.

With anyone else, he might be irritated, but he loved seeing the confidence in her law enforcement abilities.

He headed her way, pausing to study the van's tailgate. The shattered taillight matched the pieces on the road.

She pointed at the ground. "Blood. Looks like a struggle."

He'd walked over this area last night to open the door, but hadn't noticed blood in the dark. "I would've contaminated this area when I raced to the driver's door."

"Couldn't be helped, but now that we know it's here, we can avoid further contamination."

He studied the blood, his brain flooding with terrible possibilities. "Do you think this is where her killer gained control of her?"

"Seems probable, but Kenna didn't have obvious wounds that would cause this blood." El pointed at the ground where a one-foot circle of blood saturated fallen leaves. "Maybe she injured her assailant. Maybe with a knife."

"She doesn't carry one, but she could've used something else." Gabe dropped to the ground and shone his phone's flashlight under the van. Something silver sparkled back. He took a quick picture.

He hopped up and swiped to the photo to show El. "A blood-tipped screwdriver."

"Say that was Kenna's weapon. What was she doing with a screwdriver?"

Yeah, what? He stared at the picture. An idea came to mind. "Her license plates. She just got those custom ones and needed a screwdriver to change them. She could've left it in the van."

"She'd need to be a strong woman to keep her wits about her and remember that while a man was attacking her."

"She would've done everything within her power to protect Lucy."

She wouldn't be protecting her sweet baby girl anymore.

Who would, if Lucy was alive? Not her father or her family. Kenna had asked Gabe to take care of Lucy if anything happened to her, but she'd never made it official.

A new shockwave traveled through him. Could the responsibility for the little princess actually fall on him? He loved the tiny tyke beyond anything he'd ever known, but he was the last person who should be raising a child. He didn't even have his own life together. How could he parent a child?

One thing was clear. He could never let her go into foster care.

El lowered her camera to rest on her chest. "Leave the screwdriver for Sierra to collect. Let's follow the blood trail."

He followed her over pine needles and leaf debris. She paused several times, squatted, and shone her flashlight on still damp smaller splotches of blood. Wet, the mist to blame, but they'd still turned brownish red.

She stood and looked him in the eye. "Someone continued to bleed. Maybe reached the point of needing immediate medical intervention."

Thankfully, she stopped before saying who might've needed that intervention.

No way he could handle her saying the pool and trail of blood could belong to Lucy.

6

———

El stood at the water's edge in the ravine with Gabe near what remained of a crumbling dock disappearing into the murk a few feet away. If the killer had used a boat to move Kenna and Lucy, this could've been his launch point.

She looked at Gabe. "I assume you noticed that there weren't any drag marks."

He nodded. "Which means if he moved her in a boat from here, he had to have carried her. He also would've had to carry the car seat. Kenna must have been restrained enough for him to not worry about her escape while he carried Lucy in her car seat over here."

She scanned the shoreline again. A deep V-shaped gouge marked the bank, the kind a metal hull left when someone beached in a hurry. Freshly trampled grass fanned out from the spot, helping confirm her theory.

"He might've already killed her by then," El said, wanting to say anything but that.

He cringed, but his only response was a sharp nod.

"Something I haven't resolved," she said. "How would the killer know Kenna was coming to see you? Or that he would succeed in running them off the road where he had a boat waiting?"

"My phone isn't tapped, if that's where you're headed. Hayden audits all our phones weekly. Mine was cleared two days ago."

"Doesn't mean hers wasn't compromised."

"If it was, she knew him. Or at least trusted him enough to let him get close to her phone to tamper with it."

"She also could've told him herself—shared her plans before she left—and he trailed her from there. Could've convinced her to meet him at the overlook."

"That might explain why she came here." Gabe's breathing had grown labored. The weight of what could've happened in this ravine had to be catching up with him.

"But who?" she asked. "And why? If he docked his boat here to move them to the beach, he would've had to know in advance to have the boat ready."

Gabe pursed his lips, but stood motionless. "I don't get it, though. Not after her frantic phone call. I just can't imagine her stopping anywhere for any reason."

"She wasn't just sightseeing, that's for sure, and the transfer of her body and Lucy in the boat confirms premeditation and not some random road rage." El's phone announced a text, interrupting her unpleasant vision of Kenna's and Lucy's terror as they were run off the road. "Hopefully her phone will survive being soaked, and the electronics expert will be able to tell us if she was meeting someone. I'll also request her phone records, but you know how slow phone providers are getting back to you. That can take some time."

She quickly read the message from Deputy Massey.

Forensics is here and asking for you.

She typed back. *On my way.*

"Forensics just arrived." She slid the phone into her

pocket. "I'll send them down here to process the van and the surrounding area in addition to the beach."

Gabe opened his mouth, seemed to reconsider, and turned toward the hill. He was a man of few words, and when he did speak, he took on a devil's advocate kind of role, and what he had to say was important. But whatever he'd been about to say just now, he kept it to himself.

El filed the moment away and followed him to the steep incline, quickly skirting the blood near the van.

At the base of the hill, he paused and waited for her to go first. She understood. He was positioning himself to catch her if she lost her footing on the loose vegetation. The gesture was so quiet and natural that it caught her off guard.

Tears pressed at the back of her eyes. Odd timing. She was working a murder and an abduction, not on a social outing, but the small kindness told her exactly how he must've treated Kenna and Lucy. No making a production of it and without expecting anything in return.

She swiped her eyes then climbed without incident. So did he.

They drove back to the beach in silence. El parked several rows behind a white panel van with the Veritas Center logo on the side, the rear doors thrown open. Two women in white Tyvek suits were rummaging through equipment bins stacked three high in the cargo area while Jude stood nearby, talking.

El recognized both women. Chelsea Vale, one of the center's forensic photographers, had glossy black hair and was still in the cargo bay. Sierra Rice, forensic expert, dropped out of the van, her blond ponytail bouncing, as El and Gabe approached.

El reached for the door handle. "Have you met the Veritas team?"

"Yes."

"Then let's go."

They made their way through a cluster of onlookers who called out questions. El kept her eyes forward and her answers consistent. *No comment. No comment. No comment.*

"Glad you're back," Jude said. "I was hoping you'd arrive in time to give Chelsea and Sierra instructions."

"Thank you both for coming on short notice." El offered the women a genuine smile. "I mean that."

"Of course." Sierra's smile was brief and professional. "We'd never turn our backs on a missing child. Has she been found?"

The warmth in El's chest cooled. "No. Let me walk you through everything, and then we can set your priorities."

Sierra settled on the van's rear bumper, and El gave her a thorough account. The body, the beach, the ravine, the boat, the blood near the van, the screwdriver.

"I recovered a few items from the scene that were at risk of contamination or exposure," El added. "They're in my car. Bagged."

"I'll check the packaging before we process anything else." Sierra stood and glanced toward the beach, her expression sharpening. "Looks like the beach has been significantly compromised."

"The outer perimeter, yes." El kept her voice even and tried not to take offense at her comments. "We cordoned off the area around the body and some of the waterline. But finding Lucy is our top priority, and I had to give divers, search teams, and my people access."

"Understandable," Sierra said.

El appreciated that Sierra didn't push it. "The victim's van is in the ravine, our secondary scene about a mile up the road. We believe she and her daughter were transported from there to the beach by boat."

"You have a positive ID on the victim." Sierra's eyes

moved to Gabe, then back. "But do you have anything placing the child at the beach?"

"Nothing direct," El said. "DNA could tie the toys and car seat to Lucy, but that only confirms ownership."

Sierra tilted her head. "Best option would be prints or DNA recovered from the boat or dock, assuming we locate any. Do you have her prints on file?"

El turned to Gabe. "Do you know if Kenna kept an identity kit for Lucy?"

"I gave her one from our department when I was a state trooper." His jaw tightened. "We can look when we search her place to see if she finished it. Her prints are probably on the car seat too."

"We should recover small latent prints from the seat," Sierra said. "They won't be definitive on their own, but they'd give you something to work with temporarily."

Gabe's expression shifted. "Same for DNA?"

"Identical limitation. Without a confirmed sample to compare against, nothing is ironclad." She paused. "This one will be difficult."

"One more thing." El met Sierra's eyes. "You'll find blood near the van, a significant amount. Kenna didn't have any obvious wounds to account for it. It could belong to her attacker. Or to Lucy."

She let that possibility hang in the air just long enough to land.

"We also found a bloody screwdriver under the van," El said.

"Knowing Kenna, she didn't go quietly," Gabe said. "She found it and used it on her attacker, leaving what we believe is his blood on her shirt."

"I'll pick up the shirt from the ME as soon as possible and give it to you for DNA testing."

Sierra straightened. "Blood on the beach or dock?"

"Nothing visible."

"Then the blood at the ravine is our first priority. Being outdoors, the rain would compromise the spatter patterns and dilute the samples." She looked at El. "Unless you need us somewhere else first."

"You know better than I do. I'll defer to you."

"We'll have one of our techs drive all recovered evidence to our lab early this afternoon. That way we can begin processing it. If you locate anything else, make sure you get it to us to include in the delivery."

"Thank you, I really appreciate your sense of urgency," El said sincerely. "Is there anything else we can do for you?"

"I think we have everything we need to get started."

"I could stay with them," Jude said. He'd been quiet so far, which for Jude was an achievement. "In case they need anything."

"It would help to have someone on-site," El said carefully, then looked at Sierra and Chelsea. "Only if that works for you."

They both nodded.

"Then I'll brief him on the secondary scene before you head out." El caught Jude's eye and held it for a moment, a warning that said be professional, before turning back to Sierra. "The minute you find anything new, call me. Anything. After all, even the smallest of details could be the lead that brings Lucy home."

In the dressing area outside the autopsy suite, El zipped the white protective suit to her chin and pulled on her gloves. She'd attended more postmortems than she cared to count, none of them easy, but this one sat heavier than most. Could be because she didn't want anything else revealed that would cause Gabe additional pain.

In fact, El would've liked time to digest anything she learned before telling him. That wasn't possible. He'd insisted on accompanying her and was waiting in the lobby, likely driving the receptionist crazy by pacing.

She could picture it clearly.

She'd tried to talk him out of accompanying her. He wouldn't hear of it. If someone murdered one of his best friends, he'd said, he wanted to understand every detail, not to satisfy curiosity, but to find the killer faster. She understood that, but she didn't have to like it.

Please help me share whatever I'm about to learn in the best way possible.

Dressed, she pushed through the swinging door with her elbows, to keep her gloved hands free of contamination, to the small, ancient room. The layered smell of chemicals and biological decomposition left a queasy feeling in her stomach.

Dr. Faye Briggs and her assistant, Theo, stood at the single autopsy table beneath a circular overhead light. El had expected to arrive in time for the initial Y-cut. She hadn't. Faye had already worked well past it and several organs rested in a bowl or on the nearby scale.

Faye looked up, scalpel in hand, her N95 masking most of her face. "Detective. Good. I started earlier than scheduled. Figured by the time you arrived, I'd have more to tell you."

"I don't mind missing the first cut." El moved closer. "Time and cause of death?"

"Little has changed from my initial assessment. Death occurred between seven and nine p.m. The cold continues to complicate determining a narrower window."

El had expected this answer, but was glad to have it officially confirmed. "And cause of death?"

Faye set her scalpel on the tray, her eyes steady on El. "The body tells a different story than drowning. The lungs are dry. No frothy edema fluid in the airways, no water aspiration into the alveoli. Also, microscopic algae from the lake aren't embedded in her lung tissue like they would be if she'd inhaled water while alive. I'm certain she was dead before she hit the lake. Someone staged it to look like a drowning, probably to buy time or mislead us. Or even hoped to hide the body in the lake."

El stepped closer to the table, peering at the neck under the harsh lights. "Strangulation, then?"

"Yes, manual strangulation." Faye pointed to the Y-incision she'd made across the neck. "Bruising shows thumb and finger marks around the throat with deep muscle hemorrhaging and petechiae confirming it. No hyoid or thyroid cartilage fractures. She was killed on land, then dumped. Cause of death is asphyxia from vascular compression, and manner is most definitely homicide."

Thank goodness the doctor had determined the cause of death, but El didn't much like thinking about the terrible way Kenna had lost her life. "Does this mean the blood on her shirt is a separate matter?"

"I found no wounds on her body to account for that quantity of blood on the shirt."

"The blood's likely from her attacker, then."

"It could belong to the child." Faye drew her eyebrows together. "Sorry. I hate to go there, but it could be a reality in this investigation."

El's stomach dropped. "Would that volume of blood loss on the shirt be dangerous for a child her age?"

"I can't determine an exact volume from the shirt. It's

just a visual estimate, and stains absorb unpredictably. I've bagged it for the lab if you want serologists to quantify the blood. Even fifty to a hundred milliliters could be life-threatening for a child that small, but that's speculative until results confirm the source."

"We're working with the Veritas Center expert."

"They can handle the shirt and estimate the quantity of blood at the abduction site. At her age, losing just fifteen to twenty percent—about two to four hundred milliliters—is dangerous. At twenty-five to thirty percent, it's life-threatening without immediate treatment, and over thirty to forty percent is often fatal, since kids decompensate much faster than adults."

The image of the dark, wet ground near the van moved through El's mind. She had confidence in Sierra's skills, but oh, how she desperately wanted answers now. "Our forensic expert is working that scene right now."

Please. Let the blood belong to the attacker.

"The blood on the shirt looks like less than half a liter, but if there's more at the abduction site—"

"There is." El forced herself to say it plainly when if it fit the quantity for a male attacker, it was more than enough for Lucy to be in great danger. "We'll know more once Sierra finishes the scene."

"It's all speculative until then." Faye looked down at the body, her gloved hand hovering near the neck. "I also ran a high-resolution CT scan before I started. It shows internal hemorrhaging in the throat muscles. Deep intramuscular bleeds that don't fully align with the external bruising pattern."

"Meaning what?"

"The injuries suggest prolonged or multistage compression."

"I'm not familiar with that," El said.

"There could've been an initial phase of restraint to seduce her. That would be broader, superficial force, leaving those external marks to subdue her. Then more targeted pressure causing the isolated internal hemorrhages without adding new surface trauma. It indicates a sustained assault with some control over the application of force, but exactly how many methods or the intent behind it? That's for you and the behavioral analysts to interpret. The pathology just points to escalation, not necessarily expertise."

"Law enforcement, military, martial arts?" El ventured, her mind racing through profiles.

"Could be." Faye held her gaze. "Or someone practicing for future kills."

El gaped at the doctor. "You're talking serial killer?"

"I'm presenting possibilities. What you investigate is your decision."

El moved a few steps away and mulled it over. She didn't like where this development pointed, but she couldn't ignore it. She'd need to run a ViCAP search. The FBI's Violent Criminal Apprehension Program was built to track and correlate information on violent crime, especially murder. If an investigating officer entered data on a similar unsolved murder, she should be able to find it.

Eager to move the process along so she could get out of this room, she stepped back to the table. "Any indication she was sexually assaulted?"

"None."

"That's a blessing for sure."

Faye nodded and pointed at the dissected shoulder region. "I found micro-tears in shoulder and neck muscles. These are consistent with a van accident, but could also be from abrupt traction or forcible manipulation."

"The kind that could occur if someone was grabbed from behind with sudden, violent force," El suggested.

"That's right," Faye said. "If that occurred, the pattern suggests the victim wasn't in a defensive posture or facing the assailant at the moment of impact, implying a rear approach without prior awareness or resistance."

"An ambush." El's mind started to piece together the fragments. "Kenna would've had to survive the crash. Climb out of the van. Then maybe lean into the backseat to get Lucy. He came up from behind. Surprised her, and she grabbed the screwdriver we found. She injured him, and his blood was transferred to her shirt."

Faye nodded slowly, setting aside her probe. "That scenario aligns well with the injury pattern. But it's still hypothetical until we cross-reference with the vehicle forensics, toxicology, and scene reconstruction. No scenario is locked in yet."

El could see it. Kenna bending into the van, reaching for her daughter, and then nothing. She could imagine Kenna's shock and fear. Imagine Lucy's terror. And of course, Kenna stabbing him.

El swallowed away the awful feeling in her gut. "Besides using the screwdriver, did Kenna fight back?"

"Could be," Faye said. "Several nails are broken. I collected biological material from under the others. I'll have the state lab analyze all of it."

A state lab would take forever. Not something El wanted to wait for. "I know you have guidelines to follow for submitting samples, but could you redirect those samples to the Veritas Center? Our agency is covering the cost."

Faye nodded vigorously. "They're on our approved list, and faster results would be great."

"Thank you." El let the words carry weight. Her eyes

moved along the body and stopped at the wrists. "You haven't mentioned the bruising."

"It was up next. It's accompanied by micro-punctures at both the wrists and ankles. The pattern is consistent with zip ties, specifically, a textured variety. Serrated or ribbed inner surface."

That was something. A specific tool, a specific pattern. Something to search in ViCAP. Something that might connect this to another scene.

"So, she was definitely restrained," El said.

"Yes, and one more finding." Faye pointed to the back of Kenna's right hand. "Trace blood, barely visible to the naked eye. No wound to explain it. Same situation as the shirt. Either her attacker's or Lucy's. I'll send it for analysis with the other samples."

El studied the hand for a moment. Of everything recovered so far, this might be the closest thing to a direct link. "I mean this genuinely. I'm glad you took this position. You bring skills this county hasn't had access to before."

Faye waved her off. "Just doing my job."

"You're doing it exceptionally well." El paused. "I hope small-town life holds its appeal for a while and you don't leave us for a big-city lab."

"It does." Faye's eyes above the mask crinkled, likely from a smile. "And whatever comes next in my life is in God's hands, not mine."

El nodded. She suspected the routine cases that filled most of a county examiner's calendar would eventually frustrate someone with Faye's training, but she kept the thought to herself. "Is that everything so far?"

"One more thing," Faye said, her voice quieter now. "Probably the most significant finding of all." She waited a beat. "Kenna was twelve weeks pregnant."

The words landed like a lightbulb dropped from a

height. El stood, unable to move past the initial impact, her mind already turning over everything they'd assumed about motive, about the killer, about why Kenna had died.

Things had just changed. Big time. This pregnancy could be the reason for Kenna's murder, and El had been looking at this wrong from the beginning.

7
____

Gabe didn't like the look on El's face.

Her expression was tight, controlled in the way people got when they were holding something back. Whatever she'd learned in the autopsy, she wasn't ready to tell him. Or maybe she just didn't want the receptionist to hear it. Either way, the finding bothered her.

He crossed to her. "What is it? What did you find out?"

"Not here." She tucked an evidence bag with clothing under her arm and took his elbow to steer him toward the door.

Not good.

He held the glass door open for her. She moved through without slowing, already heading for her vehicle in that focused, forward stride that meant her mind was occupied. He caught up to her as she clicked the key fob and the doors unlocked. They slid in together, and he turned to face her before she could reach for the ignition.

"Okay," he said. "Spill."

She took a moment to set her phone in the dashboard holder. Not stalling—organizing. There was a difference with El, and he'd learned to read it. "First off, Kenna didn't have air in her lungs. She definitely didn't drown."

"Not unexpected."

A sharp nod. "In addition to the external strangulation marks we saw, Faye found hemorrhaging inside the throat muscles. She believes someone used two methods of strangulation. Possibly the first to subdue her, the second to end her life."

"Man! Two methods. As a deputy, I saw that once before in a murder case of a former Marine and his wife. What do you make of it?"

El stared past his shoulder, not quite meeting his eyes. "We might be looking at someone with law enforcement or military experience."

His thoughts exactly. "Kenna never mentioned anyone like that in her life, but our search of her house might show us something." He filed it away and moved on. "What about the blood on her shirt?"

"She didn't have any injuries other than the strangulation, so not her blood."

His mind went somewhere dark before he could stop it, and he had to hold himself still for a moment before he could say it out loud. "Then it could be Lucy's."

El shifted to look at him directly. Her fingers curled around the wheel, released, curled again. "It could be from her or the attacker. We need Sierra to search the car seat. The fabric is dark, and I didn't see any blood, but that doesn't mean it isn't there."

"The amount on the shirt would be a significant loss for a child."

"Could be, but let's table this discussion until we know more from the scenes." Her voice was steady, but it had that cautious quality, the one she used when she was managing something she didn't want to spiral. "Speculating right now doesn't help anyone."

She was right, and he knew it. He pushed the image to that place in his mind where he kept the things he couldn't afford to feel yet. "Did Faye find anything else?"

"Micro-tears in the shoulder and neck muscles. That kind of injury happens with an accident like hers, but also when someone is violently startled. Most likely grabbed from behind."

"Like the killer coming up behind her to take control."

"Exactly. There were also traces of blood on Kenna's hand. Not hers either. We'll get the DNA to Sierra to run."

"Could be her attacker again."

"Possibly," she said quickly. "Faye also found evidence of binding at the wrists and ankles. The marks suggest a specific type of zip tie. The impressions are distinctive enough that we may be able to match or cross-reference them through ViCAP."

"Our team can look into the zip ties, if you'll let us."

She didn't hesitate. "We're stretched thin right now. I'll take the help."

He sat back. "I didn't expect to get so much to go on from a small-town ME."

El's eyes narrowed slightly. "She's overqualified for the job if you ask me, but she likes living here. We benefit from that." A long breath. "Before we talk about next steps, there's one more thing."

She turned away and looked out through the windshield, her leg beginning to bounce against the floorboard in a low, restless rhythm.

He'd been waiting for this. Whatever it was, it was what had caused her tight expression the moment she'd walked out. He pressed his palms flat against his knees, the pressure grounding him, giving him a place to put the tension building in his chest. "Go ahead. Say it."

She turned back slowly and held his gaze. "Kenna was twelve weeks pregnant."

She let her statement hang in the air. An enormous silence followed.

"She was…" He stopped. Started again. "But she never…" The words wouldn't organize into anything useful. A headache formed behind his eyes, and he pressed two fingers to his forehead.

How had Kenna not told him? They'd been close. Or at least he'd thought they were close. Something this significant. Something life-changing. And she hadn't said a word.

That stung in a place he hadn't expected.

"You didn't know she was seeing anyone?" El asked quietly.

"She never mentioned it." He lowered his hand. "Maybe she didn't know about the pregnancy yet. Or maybe she did, and that was what she was coming to tell me."

"Then we need to find out who the father was, and whether the pregnancy had anything to do with her death."

The contents of his stomach turned over. "What kind of person kills someone over that?"

"One who should be behind bars." El closed the folder. "Finding Lucy has to stay our priority, but while we work Kenna's house for anything that leads us to Lucy, we search for evidence of this relationship at the same time."

"I assume the ME is running DNA on the fetus."

"Yes. I arranged for a fetal tissue sample to go to the Veritas Center. Means we could have the father's profile in twenty-four hours or so. Doesn't mean he'll be in the database, but when we find our suspect, we'll be able to determine if he's the father."

El's phone rang. She grabbed it before the second tone. "Go ahead, Massey."

Gabe leaned slightly toward her side of the car. Tried to listen in, but he couldn't make out Massey's words. He only heard the efficient rhythm of someone relaying information. El's fingers drummed once on the steering wheel and went still.

"And what did he want?" she asked.

She bit on her lip while Massey answered.

"If he's right, it sounds like it sank," she said. "Get the dive team on it."

She listened again, and her shoulders went rigid. She kept her phone pressed to her ear, eyes sharp, body entirely still. Listening hard.

Then she slowly relaxed, and her fingers dropped back to the wheel. "Good work, Massey. Now we need to find this guy." She tilted her head as she let her free hand open and close against her thigh. "Fast-track the warrant. Text me the details the moment you have them. We'll head straight there."

She ended the call, slotted the phone back on the dashboard holder, and started the engine in one fluid sequence. "Our witness called back. Said he remembered seeing a floating seat cushion from a boat. Didn't know if it was connected to our scene, but it had 'Property of H. H. Mason' painted on it."

"There wasn't one in the water by the time I got there."

"Gone before I arrived, too. Witness said it was torn, looked old. Probably got waterlogged and sank." She checked her mirrors. "The dive team just found it."

"And since you said we're heading over there, I'm guessing you know who H. H. Mason is."

"The witness knows of him, but hasn't actually talked to him and doesn't know what the H. H. stands for. Says he keeps to himself, but there's a mailbox with those initials at a place about three miles south on Lake Road." Her phone buzzed against the holder. She glanced at the screen, then at Gabe, and something sharpened in her eyes. That barely contained urgency he'd come to recognize. "Mason's address."

Adrenaline sizzled through him like an electrical current switching on. "Then what are we waiting for? Let's book it!"

～

El pulled into the long driveway and parked in a wide clearing surrounded by soaring evergreens. She killed the engine and sat for a moment, studying the property.

Mason's house was barely more than an oversized shack. The siding had once been red, but time and weather had left it a dull, brownish rust. Peeling at the corners. A few boards visibly warped. A boathouse down at the water's edge was in markedly better condition, freshly painted in the same red the house used to be, its lines clean and deliberate.

"Truck could mean he's home." Gabe pointed at an old pickup sitting in the driveway. "Or it might not run."

She studied the vehicle. Rust crawled along the wheel wells. Electrical tape held a cracked side mirror on. "I've seen worse on the road. You probably have too. Either way, we approach like he's inside."

"Agreed." She turned to look at him directly. "And you're not carrying a badge right now, so stay behind me. Sidearm stays holstered unless a life-or-death situation calls for it."

He crossed his arms. "I'll let you go first, but I'm drawing my weapon now, and that's not negotiable."

She held his gaze.

"I won't let anything happen to you." His voice was even,

not aggressive. "You know I have plenty of experience, and I won't overreact."

She did know that. It was the only reason she didn't press it further. "Fine, but remaining behind me holds."

"You have my word."

She was out of the vehicle before he finished the sentence, moving quickly enough to get ahead of him. She pulled her sidearm and crept over beds of fallen pine needles and leaves, both softened by the morning mist. She went to the building and signaled for Gabe to remain at a distance.

At the front window, she held back for a moment, then took a quick look through the dirty glass.

No lights. No movement. No sign of Mason.

She took another quick peek, then glanced back at Gabe and shook her head.

His expression tightened with disappointment. She didn't waste time, but headed for the two front steps leading to a small platform while signaling for him to join her. The porch groaned under her boots, loud enough to announce her to anyone inside.

If Mason opened fire, they could die. Not on her watch.

She directed Gabe to move to the side of the small platform. She shifted as far as she could to the other side, then knocked hard on the splintered door. "Police, Mr. Mason, I need to speak with you."

Tapping her foot, she counted sixty seconds. Knocked again. Harder.

"Police. Come to the door, Mr. Mason."

Quiet surrounded them until a bird fluttered in the evergreens and went still. She glanced at her watch. Two full minutes had passed.

She looked at Gabe. "Doesn't appear to be home. I'll try

the knob, but we don't have a warrant so even if it's unlocked, we won't go in."

He frowned. "Then what's the point of checking?"

"If he didn't lock it, he thinks he's coming back soon."

Gabe's gaze moved toward the water. "Could be down in the boathouse."

Using her sleeve to protect any evidence, she tried the knob. It turned freely under her hand.

"You might be right." She stepped off the porch. "Let's check it."

He waited for her and fell in behind without being reminded, his footsteps entirely silent on the wet ground. Thankfully, his law enforcement experience had taught him how to move silently.

She knocked on the boathouse door and called out Mason's name.

Nothing.

She tried the knob. It turned. She released it and stepped back.

"What?" Gabe's voice was low, strained. "You're not going in here either? He could've killed Kenna. He could have Lucy."

"I know." She *did* know. That was the problem. Her every instinct pulled her toward that door. "If I let that lure me inside without the warrant, I hand his defense attorney the case on a platter. Everything we find in there becomes questionable. I'm not doing that to Kenna or Lucy." She stepped back. "We go back to the car. We wait for the warrant."

He stared at her with something between a grudging respect and disbelief that she was leaving.

Was he right? Was she deciding too quickly to go back to the car?

She turned toward the car. Then stopped.

A small window was set high on the boathouse wall.

She'd missed it on the approach. One corner of the glass was cracked, and a triangular piece was missing. An open gap no bigger than a fist she could look through.

She changed course, moved beneath it, and rose up on her toes to bring her face level with the opening.

It hit her then. She whipped back. Stepped down. Couldn't form a word to say. Just stood for a moment with her hand resting against the wall.

"What?" Gabe's voice was low. "What did you see?"

"It's not what I saw." She turned to face him.

His eyes were wide, his mouth pressed into a hard line, the muscles around it taut with something he was working to contain. "Tell me. Now!"

"It's the smell coming through that window. There's only one thing that produces that kind of odor." She held his gaze. "A decaying body."

8

───────

Gabe's mind went directly to Lucy. He couldn't stop it. Every dark thought his brain could manufacture landed in the same place. Her face, her size, how small she would look on a dirt floor. He opened his mouth to say it out loud, then couldn't.

El had already turned back to the window. She rose up on her toes and looked through the broken pane for a longer count this time, her hand braced against the weathered siding.

"There're metal tracks and a garage door that opens over the water," she said, her voice low and even. "Tracks run full length and down into the water. Boat cradle's empty."

"Could be the boat that put in at the ravine near Kenna's van."

"You could be right. Nothing to suggest that here, though. All I see are walls covered in fishing gear and an old tarp spread out on the floor. Looks like something under it."

A body?

She stepped down and turned to face him. He knew that expression. She'd already figured out what he was thinking as she'd done many times in the past. Helped fuel the connection between them.

Her gaze softened. "Before your mind goes where I think it's going, Lucy hasn't been missing long enough for her body to reach this level of decomp. Not even close."

He exhaled. She was right. He knew she was right. His training knew it too, even if the rest of him had temporarily stopped listening. "You'd need at least three days minimum to reach this odor level. Probably more, given the cold."

"Exactly." She held his gaze a moment longer, making sure it had landed. "And there's no guarantee it's even human. Could be an animal."

He wanted to hold onto that. He tried.

But until someone went inside and confirmed it, he wouldn't believe it. "One thing this does give us," he said. "Exigent circumstances. We don't have to wait on the warrant to make entry."

She nodded. The law was clear. If waiting for a warrant created a genuine risk of death, serious injury, or the destruction of critical evidence, officers could enter immediately. A potentially decaying body qualified without argument.

"We need N95 masks." She dug out her keys. "They're in my trunk."

Standing still wasn't helping anything, and moving helped. "I'll get them."

She didn't argue, probably thinking it was better for him to take action. She held out the key fob and clicked the trunk open.

When he came back, she'd successfully pulled on disposable gloves. He handed her a mask and unfolded the other one.

"Stay here." She released the elastic straps on hers.

"You're not carrying a badge anymore. Technically, you shouldn't even be on this property."

He knew she was right. He also knew he wouldn't stand back while she walked into an enclosed space alone with whatever was under that tarp.

She didn't wait for him to argue. She turned and pushed the boathouse door fully open.

"Police. I'm coming in," she announced.

The smell followed the door.

Even from where Gabe stood, it reached him. Thick, acrid. The nauseating smell bypassed rational thought entirely and went straight to something older and more instinctive. Despite the mask, it coated the back of his throat and made his eyes water. He controlled his gag reflex through sheer will.

He didn't want to think about what it was like inside. What it was like for her.

He gave her three seconds. Then he moved to the doorway and stopped in the opening, one hand on the frame, and looked in.

The space was dim, the only light coming from El's phone flashlight and the gray wash filtering through a high, cracked window. The metal railway ran down the center of the floor, old iron tracks, orange with rust, disappearing into the dark water at the far end. The cradle sat empty, its crossbars rusty with age. Fishing gear covered the walls in no particular order. Nets, rods, coiled rope, a pair of waders hanging from a nail.

And in shallow water between the tracks, a beige tarp unfolded, in the kind of deliberate spread someone had arranged rather than haphazardly left behind.

El stood over it, her back to him. She'd peeled back one corner and was looking down into the gap, her phone light aimed at whatever was beneath. Her free hand rested on her hip with the stillness of someone who had done this before and had learned to keep their body quiet even when nothing else was.

She heard him at the door. Turned and looked at him, and shook her head once. Not at him being there, just delivering the answer to the question they'd both been fighting off.

"Older male," she said. "Shirt saturated in blood. Looks like a stab wound to the chest."

He absorbed that.

"Another murder." He paused. "Could it be Mason?"

"I've never seen him. No photograph to compare." She shifted her gaze back to the tarp. "I can't confirm identity yet."

"How long has he been here?"

"Extensive insect activity, despite the cool temperature." She studied the body another moment. "It all suggests he's been here for some time, but I won't guess further than that. Dr. Briggs will have to give us the timeframe."

Gabe looked at the tarp, at the shape beneath the peeled-back corner. The smell pressed against the inside of his mask in steady rhythmic waves.

"We need a full search," he said. "Both structures."

"Yes." She straightened, dropped the tarp, and switched off her flashlight. "Which makes the warrant even more critical than it was twenty minutes ago." She was already thumbing her phone as she walked toward him. "Texting Massey for an update on that warrant. And I'll do a quick property search to see if I can confirm H. H. Mason as the owner. If so, I'll look him up on the DMV for a photo. If we can confirm his ID, it changes the shape of everything."

Gabe stepped back from the doorway to let her out, and they walked the worn path back to the patrol car together without speaking. The silence wasn't uncomfortable. It was the particular quiet of two people each processing and waiting until they had something worth saying.

He got there first.

"If someone was willing to stab Mason," he said, "then killing Kenna was nothing to them." He paused. "And Lucy—"

He didn't finish it. He didn't need to. El glanced at him sideways as they reached the vehicle, and the look on her face told him she'd already been chewing on the same thought.

She opened the driver's door and reached for the computer mounted to the dash. "Let's find out who he is first," she said. "Then we figure out what it means."

Another crime scene. Another murder. Another investigation. All under El's authority, and she was already running on fumes. She'd hand this off to another homicide detective if she could, but she was the only homicide detective in the department. Thankfully, Ulrich had arrived on-site to help, and the Lost Lake Locators were on the job behind the scenes, too.

If not for them...

She shook her head, shoving the worry aside to focus on the scene.

Ulrich had joined Faye and her assistant at the boathouse, offering support as needed. Gabe remained in El's vehicle, coordinating his team's efforts for a deep dive on H.H. Mason and a search for the specialized zip ties used on Kenna. He also hoped to get updates on their progress.

El could examine the boathouse and house, but would have to wait to run a ViCAP search. She would love to start now on her vehicle's computer, but like many small departments, without a robust electronic communications program, they had to restrict ViCAP access to an in-station computer only, for security reasons.

Faye nodded at Ulrich, then strode toward El with the determination El was coming to associate with her.

She rested her hands on her hips. "No wallet or any other form of identification. The missing wallet could mean we're looking at a simple robbery."

"Or the killer might be trying to hide his identification. Howard Mason owns this property. I ran him in DMV. No Howard Mason with this as his primary address, but I did find one where the photo is a match. At least, best I can tell with the decomp. His address is listed as Seaside Harbor."

Faye's brow furrowed. "Then we could be looking at Howard Mason. I'll run his prints and investigate further before you notify next of kin."

"What about cause of death?"

"Stabbing's obvious, but I can't confirm this caused his death until the autopsy. Also, I've preliminarily placed time of death between four to six days. I'll do my best to narrow it down."

"Stabbing to the chest looks clear-cut to me, but I know you uncover surprises all the time."

"We do. Of note. Insufficient blood near the body for the stabbing to have occurred there."

"So he was killed elsewhere and dumped in the boathouse." El let that sink in. "I didn't see any blood trails near the boathouse."

"The tarp is covered with grass stains. If the stains are fresh, the killer probably rolled him up in it and dragged him over."

"He was smart enough to avoid a trail outside, then dump Mason in the boathouse, probably hoping no one would check inside and discover his body."

Faye tilted her head. "Do we have a murder spree going on in the county or is this incident related to your other investigation?"

El explained Mason's boat and his potential involvement, either willingly or involuntarily. "Kenna's killer needed a boat. Mason's was convenient. The killer didn't want a witness to the theft, so he silenced him. Crime of opportunity."

Faye pursed her lips. "Or they were working together, and the killer turned on him."

"Possible. Mason doesn't have a criminal record, though. It does appear as if he was quite involved with the community in his younger days. Now we're checking for current friends or associates with records."

"You didn't say if Mason has family."

"A daughter—Talia Vogel—in Seaside Harbor. After you confirm his identity, I'll notify her."

Faye offered a tight smile. "We're moving the body now. I don't usually work Saturdays, but with the missing child, I'll do the autopsy at nine tomorrow. You or Ulrich attending?"

Good question. El hadn't considered it at this point, but this was one task Ulrich could take on. "I don't know yet. Depends on what we find, but Ulrich will be in charge of this scene so you can communicate with him."

Faye's head bobbed in a sharp nod, and she hurried back to the boathouse. El popped her trunk to grab her forensic kit and waved Gabe over.

He ended his call and joined her without hesitation. "My team's still working on the damaged vehicles in for repair, zip ties, and a deep dive on Mason. Other leads they've chased haven't panned out and aren't worth detailing now."

"We can talk about it later. Warrants are in. Let's search both places before the predicted rain hits. Follow me."

If he was surprised by her invitation, it didn't show as she headed for the boathouse, his steps falling in behind.

Faye and Theo wheeled the gurney toward their van, passing El. The body bag was strapped down against the bumpy ground. They nodded but didn't speak. Good. El wasn't in the mood for small talk.

At the boathouse, she distributed gloves from her kit to Gabe and Ulrich. "Do a cursory search only. No disturbing evidence. Leave that to forensics. Photograph anything that could potentially generate a lead. Any questions?"

Both men shook their heads. She turned and stepped in.

The air had cleared some since the body had been removed, but death's scent lingered. And if there was any doubt of what had occurred there, flies on the overturned canvas confirmed someone had lost their life.

El scanned the room, taking in the fishing gear on the walls. Most of the larger items were painted with *Property of H. H. Mason* in black. "If I were to willingly aid in an abduction and murder, I wouldn't use gear stamped with my name."

"Maybe he offered the boat, but didn't know what it would be used for," Ulrich said. "Then he learned the truth, confronted the killer, and paid for it."

"Sounds plausible." She crouched by the canvas, hunting for a manufacturer's tag. All she found was Mason's property mark. "Everything here seems to be his. Look for anything out of place or unusual."

Ulrich's phone chimed. He got it from his pocket. "Text is about you, Irving," Ulrich said. "Gas station attendant confirmed your visit and emailed a copy of the video feed proving you were there."

Gabe looked like he wanted to say "I told you so," but he didn't say a word.

"I'm glad that all checked out," El said, but it still left an uncomfortable feeling in the air, and they worked in silence, the only sound the water slapping the boathouse door in rhythmic waves.

Wasn't hard to imagine the killer stabbing Mason then slipping the boat out and escaping from the scene. "Anyone see blood spatter or pools?"

"Negative here," Ulrich said, edging along the wall toward the garage door.

"Same," Gabe replied from the other side of the boat cradle.

"Hold up." Ulrich squatted down. "Shiny object in the water. Looks like a Zippo lighter."

"Don't leave it submerged," El said, excited over a potential lead. "Take a picture first, then bag it."

"Roger, that," Ulrich said, digging out his phone.

Wishing she'd spotted it herself, El pushed through the water to him as he fished it out. "Engraving on the front."

She extended a gloved hand. "Let me see."

Ulrich studied it a moment longer, then reluctantly handed it over.

"One word. CHAMP in all caps." She flipped it over, opened the lid, and checked the bottom. "That's all. Chrome's worn like it was carried in a pocket for years."

"Assuming Mason is the deceased, he was in his late sixties. If he smoked, it could've been his for decades."

"Mind if I have a look at it?" Gabe asked.

El slashed through the frigid water and handed it to him. "You think it belonged to the deceased or our killer? Or even someone else?"

"Not sure. Too many possibilities." Gabe turned it over in his gloved hand. "Could be a nickname."

"CHAMP?" El continued to stare at the lighter. "Sounds like a boxer. Or a football player."

"Or a military call sign." He tapped the lighter. "Or

someone's reminder to keep winning or fighting. Like a personal motto."

El frowned. "All plausible."

Gabe handed it back to El. "That's what makes this tricky. It's a lead, but a very vague one."

She exhaled, tension coiling in her chest. "So many possibilities for one word."

Gabe nodded. "Exactly, and the right one will tell us everything we need to know."

She passed the lighter back to Ulrich and got out her phone. She brought up Faye's contact and typed, *Any sign Mason smoked?*

Her reply came fast. *No nicotine stains on his fingers or teeth. No smoker's wrinkles. No cigarettes or lighter in pockets. Lungs will tell for sure.*

Keep an eye out. El pocketed her phone and updated the men, then turned to Gabe. "Please have your team search 'CHAMP' linked to Mason or his associates."

"On it." His thumbs flew over his phone's screen.

This could be the break she needed. Sure, it might be a dead end. The lighter could belong to anyone, even drifted in with the water. But if it was tied to another suspect, that person might desperately come looking for it. Even the killer, desperate to avoid any trace leading back to them.

One thing her law enforcement career taught her for sure—desperate people did desperate things.

El shoved hard on Mason's front door, and the stench hit her full in the face. She stepped back, bumping into Gabe. He caught her by the shoulders before she could stumble.

"I smell it too," he said, his hands still warm on her shoulders.

She wanted to lean in to him. Instead, she eased free and tugged the mask back into place. "Question is, who is it?"

"One way to find out."

She pushed the door fully open. Floor to ceiling towers of boxes, plastic bins, loose furniture, stacked magazines, black garbage bags knotted tight and bunched together in no particular order, packed the entryway. The clutter ran all the way to the back of the house, leaving a narrow corridor.

Gabe didn't say anything. He didn't have to.

"It's too dangerous for both of us to go," she said. "I'll do it. You stay put."

He took a step forward. "You said it yourself. You knock into one of those stacks, the whole thing comes down on you."

"I'll be careful. Give me five minutes. If you don't hear from me, come in after me."

She stepped off before he could argue. She doubted he would give an inch, and this was her job.

She threaded through the narrow aisles, letting her nose pull her deeper into the house. Past the furniture, past the collapsed towers of magazines, past bags that rustled when she brushed them. In the kitchen, only the sink and the top of the stove were visible above the clutter. The smell thickened, and she pressed a hand over her mask.

A stack of old CRT televisions had toppled. A small dog lay crushed beneath them.

She let out a slow breath. Not a homicide. Not a person. But the sight still landed somewhere in her chest and stayed there. She loved animals. The dog hadn't deserved this.

Question was, was this an accident or had someone purposely knocked over the TVs to take out the dog?

They'd need a necropsy to evaluate his cause of death. After that, she'd see to it he received a proper burial.

She moved on. In what appeared to be the living room, a

recliner was positioned next to a small table and lamp, all sitting oddly clear of surrounding chaos. An empty coffee mug sat on the table. She bagged it for DNA and prints, then kept moving past a flatscreen balanced on stacks of bright fuchsia tote bins.

Two bedrooms were chock-full, allowing no entry. The third bedroom had a narrow path, then opened up to a bed and a brass lamp with a tattered shade on a small night-stand. No phone. No laptop. No tablet. She'd been hoping for one of them. They tended to provide a wealth of knowl-edge about a person more than they ever meant to give.

She and Ulrich had received calls in the boathouse, but maybe Mason had a different carrier and couldn't get a signal on his property. If that was the case, there was no point in having an electronic device here. Maybe he spent his weekends deliberately off-grid. If he needed a computer, there was always the library in town or even a friend's place. Worth checking for sure.

The bathroom was clean, uncluttered, and almost entirely bare. No medications, no personal items, nothing that said anyone actually lived here. Same as the kitchen. Both rooms had the flat, neutral quality of a space that was used occasionally at best.

A door at the back of the kitchen stood unlocked and slightly ajar, leading to the yard. Maybe Mason hadn't closed it, thinking he'd be back. She left it exactly as she'd found it and made her way out through the front entrance.

Outside, she lifted her mask and pulled in a long breath of fresh air. Gabe was waiting, his expression concerned.

"I don't think anyone was living here." She shared details of what she'd discovered, choking back her distress over finding the dog.

"Then where did the dog come from?"

"Back door was open. Could be a stray. I didn't stop to

look for a collar." The image of the dog surfaced again, small and still under the heavy TVs, and she pushed it away. "I'll order a necropsy right away. The vet can check for a tag or an implanted chip and the dog's cause of death."

"Let's assume Mason is the deceased. If the dog belongs to him, and whoever killed him also killed the dog…" Gabe shook his head slowly. "That's a particularly cruel person we're dealing with."

He was right. A brutality to the killing went beyond the practical. Killing a man who could fight back was one thing. Killing a dog that couldn't. That was something else entirely. She filed it away and moved on.

"We need to search the truck." She started plowing through tall grass toward it. On the way she used her radio to call in the license plate and wasn't surprised by their response.

"Dispatch confirmed the vehicle belongs to Howard Mason," she said, pulling open the unlocked driver's door.

Gabe circled around to the passenger side and leaned in. "I'm not really sure if that helps confirm our deceased's identity or not, since he didn't have keys in his pockets."

"Keys are in the ignition," she said, then took a good look at the cab and swallowed a groan. Fast food wrappers, empty cups, loose mail. Work clothes stained dark red, the same red as the boathouse paint. "He's been painting the boathouse."

"He must really love fishing," Gabe said. "Keeps the boathouse spotless, then lives like this. Makes no sense. It's like we're looking at two different people."

"Good point." She glanced at him, but he was too busy pawing through the trash to look at her. "And one we shouldn't rule out until we know more about who we're looking at here."

"Hopefully the ME will get a fingerprint match, and

then Hayden's deep dive will give us the other details we need."

"Right. Tell him to look at electronics, too. There's no phone, no electronic devices at all, in the house. No network connection either. If we don't find anything here, have him check library records or whether Mason used a computer at a friend's place nearby."

She started searching her side of the truck, bagging the mail for Gabe's team to sort through later. In the center console, a pair of binoculars peeked out from beneath empty candy bar wrappers.

"What was he watching?" she asked, more to herself than to Gabe.

"Or who?"

Gabe's ominous tone settled a cold feeling low in her stomach, but she kept going. She bagged the binoculars, set them on the torn seat, and continued digging. A half-eaten chocolate bar stuck to her fingers, and she shook it loose. "This guy has never met a trash can in his life."

"Got something." Gabe straightened from the passenger-side floor, holding up a brown leather gadget bag. He unzipped it and lifted out a camera. "Thirty-five millimeter. Top brand. This wasn't cheap."

Now they were getting somewhere. "Any film in it?"

He turned it over, studying it. "Yes, with sixteen frames shot."

"We need to get this to Sierra ASAP to have the images developed."

"Is she heading back to Portland today?"

"Doubt it. I can't see them finishing both the lake scene and this one today."

Gabe's expression sharpened. "I know your department is stretched thin with the murder, but we can't afford to sit on this. Not with a little girl still missing."

Victoria's face appeared in El's mind. The photo her parents had provided, that chubby-cheeked smile, her innocent blue eyes. Without warning, El's brain jumped the track to her parents, her gut twisting at the raw anger on their faces. The blame. The indignity of being told she had no right to be there.

"El." Gabe's voice was close, steady, and insistent. "You with me?"

She blinked back the familiar ache. "I'm fine. You're right."

Her phone rang, the call from Ulrich. It must be important if he was calling from the boathouse instead of waiting for her to join him again. She answered immediately. "You're on speaker with Gabe unless you have sensitive information."

"You decide if it's sensitive. It's about the boat we think the killer used."

"Go ahead."

"It's been found tied to the dock at one of those pricey vacation homes across the lake."

"Why leave a stolen boat at someone's house?" she asked.

"Place belongs to one of those summer-only families. He must've thought it wouldn't be found until the family showed up for the summer. What he didn't know was, they had a caretaker who checked on the property every two weeks. He found the boat and called it in."

"And you confirmed it belonged to Mason?"

"They found boat cushions labeled *Property of H. H. Mason*. Boat registration is current and in his name."

"It's urgent to get Sierra's team to process the boat for prints and DNA," she said."I want you to take charge of the boathouse scene."

"You got it!"

She ended the call and took one last look across the cab. "Bag the camera. We'll get it to Sierra to include in her afternoon lab shipment, and then we'll head straight to Kenna's place."

She didn't wait for his agreement but turned and stepped away from the truck, breathing deep and fighting off her memories. Her worry for Lucy.

Please. Please don't let this investigation end like Victoria's.

9

Gabe normally didn't like riding shotgun, and when El parked outside of Kenna's house, he jumped out before her patrol car came to a stop. He charged ahead to Kenna's one-bedroom bungalow. Painted a bright orange, the familiar building stood out in the complex of four bungalows. He stopped in the driveway that ran between the buildings.

"Not the best neighborhood, is it?" El asked as she stepped up beside him, a large toolbox-like evidence kit in her hand.

With El's fresh perspective in mind, he took a look around. He'd been there countless times over the years and had really stopped paying attention to the sketchy neighborhood. Each visit, he'd checked out Kenna's building to look for security and repair issues and ensure she and Lucy stayed safe.

Today, he could see the peeling paint on the houses around them, lawns needing mowing, weeds popping up in the grass, and long crumbling sidewalks.

"Neighborhood's sketchy, and I didn't really like her living here, but it was all she could afford on a daycare teacher's salary. I tried to help by supplementing her salary, but she refused to take any money from me."

"Sounds like she might've been too proud."

"I'm not sure if it was pride. Her parents kicked her out when she was sixteen and told her she wouldn't amount to anything. So paying for everything on her own was like proving she could succeed."

"I can see someone doing that."

Gabe nodded as memories returned. Nearly every one of his visits there had been a positive experience he'd looked forward to each time. Sure, Kenna had hard times, and he'd come here to help her through them, but in the end, they could always find something to laugh about.

He wouldn't be laughing today, and the only reason he would return again would be to go through her things and pack them up. After all, he was the only invested person in her life besides Mrs. Z., who lived next door, but Kenna had to be seeing someone to have gotten pregnant. Or it was another one-night mistake.

"What about security cameras?" El asked. "I don't see any."

"Another thing I wanted to do for her, but she wouldn't let me. Due to her limited finances, we didn't usually exchange Christmas gifts, but I tried giving her cameras one year. She said she couldn't afford to reciprocate and made me take them back. Wouldn't even let me do a doorbell camera, but she promised to save up for one."

"That's unfortunate, but understandable from her point of view." El set down her kit, got out disposable gloves, and handed a pair to Gabe. "Let's get to the search."

He slipped them on. El followed suit then retrieved his key from the bin. He'd surrendered it so she could come and go from here as needed.

On the small stoop, she made ready to insert the key, but stared at the door. "Four locks. Only one key."

"What in the world?" He joined her on the stoop and stared at them. "She's never had more than one lock. Let's check the back."

He jumped from the stoop and jogged around the side of the house to an equally worn door in the back. "Four locks here too. Not sure what to make of it."

"Seems like she was afraid."

"Yeah." Gabe's gut clenched. "Why didn't she tell me about this?"

"Maybe it's a new situation, and she planned to mention it when she got to the inn."

"Could be." He pointed at a long window. "I've always managed to get in here."

He didn't wait for her to stop him, but went to the window. He jiggled it, then jimmied the lock with a key from his pocket until it gave way.

"Seems a shame to install that many locks on the doors when there's easy access like this."

"Not so easy. You have to know the trick for it to work. I'll go unlock the door." He slipped through the opening and unlocked the back door so she could enter through the mudroom.

She glanced at him. "Are you sure you're okay to do this search?"

"I'll be fine," he replied with confidence he didn't feel.

She eyed him for a long moment, that intense law enforcement stare, and gave a sharp nod. "Follow me. Don't touch anything until I tell you it's okay."

"Got it." He filled his lungs with oxygen and followed her inside.

She led him down a short hallway to the main living space. The combination living area and neat and tidy kitchen smelled of Kenna's favorite green apple incense. He studied the kitchen then her living room, her personality in every object. He figured seeing her lifeless body had plummeted him to rock bottom, but being here cemented the raw emotion in his heart. She would never be coming back here. Maybe not Lucy either.

His knees turned to liquid. He grabbed the island countertop.

El rushed over to him. "You've lost all color. Sit down. Now."

He waved a hand. "Give me a minute, and I'll be fine."

She shook her head and took his arm to force him onto a turquoise counter stool. The cold metal chilled his body and helped cool him down, slowing the heat flushing across his face.

El eyed him with practiced discernment. "You stay here. I'll search."

"No. Wait. I might find something with meaning for me and not you." He pushed off the stool. "I'll start with the desk where I can sit down."

She watched him for a few moments, then let out a breath. "Don't move anything. If you find something of interest and you need to move it to get a better look, give me a shout."

He didn't wait for additional approval and stepped into the living room, decorated with furniture bought from thrift shops. Kenna had draped blankets and quilts in oranges and yellows over the cushions. The place looked lived-in but homey at the same time.

The small desk was barely wider than the chair he sat in. He opened the single drawer and found only typical desk items like pens, pencils, and a pack of crayons.

He moved to the stack of drawers on wheels sitting next

to the desk. The large bottom drawer held file folders, all neatly labeled with printed labels. He quickly ran his fingers over the titles.

"You should come over here," he called out. "I found bank statements, monthly bills, and her will. Also looks like a child ID packet for Lucy."

El left the kitchen drawer she was searching to make her way through the room, her phone in hand. "Pictures before we pull anything out."

He scooted his wheeled chair out of the way.

She squatted to take the pictures. "I'd like to look at the will first. See if anyone stands to gain from her death."

"It's not like she had much money."

"But her death might not be about money. It might be about custody of Lucy's parentage."

"I doubt Kenna would spell that out in her will. She didn't want the father to be part of her life while she was alive. Why would she want him to be involved after she died?"

"You never know." El drew the folder out and laid it open on the desk. "Not many pages."

She ran her finger down the document, and he eased as close as he could to read it too.

"She left most everything to you," El said, then continued her finger down the page. "She leaves several personal items to a Mrs. Irina Zaitsev."

"Mrs. Z. She's Kenna's neighbor across the driveway. They were good friends despite their age difference, and she's like a grandmother to Lucy."

"Sounds like you know her. That should help when we interview her."

Sure it would, but sadly, he had to tell the lovable older woman Kenna had died, and Lucy was missing.

"No mention of a significant other?" he asked, changing the subject.

"None." She flipped the page, revealing a guardianship clause for Lucy.

"Wow!" El whipped her head around to look at him. "Did you know Kenna wanted you to be Lucy's guardian if anything happened to her?"

"She talked to me about it. I agreed, too, but I figured it was one of those offhand comments, you know? Not something she would've put in an official document." He swallowed past the hard lump in his throat. "I shouldn't be surprised. Other than Mrs. Z., there really wasn't anyone else in Kenna's life."

El tapped the document. "She goes on to state that she doesn't ever want her parents to raise Lucy. You said they kicked her out when she was sixteen. Why?"

"Believe it or not it was because of her faith. She was the strongest woman of faith I've ever met. No, thanks to her parents. It started in childhood when a friend took her to church on Sundays. Then in high school, she got really involved. Her parents weren't believers, and they didn't want that stuff in their house. Said if she wanted to live under their roof she had to give up this God thing. She couldn't do that, and they stuck to their guns, telling her to pack her bags and leave."

"Talk about harsh," El said. "Is that the last time she saw them?"

He shook his head. "Hoping they'd want to be grandparents, she went back after Lucy was born. But since Kenna wasn't married and had a child, they shunned her again."

"Don't take offense to this, please, but if she was such a strong woman of faith, how did she get pregnant out of wedlock?"

"Even the strongest of Christians make mistakes. But she never considered Lucy a mistake. She always believed Lucy was a blessing from God, and she wanted her child raised in the faith. She knew her parents would never do that."

El gave him a quizzical look. "Do you plan to take custody of Lucy?"

Did he? Gabe sat back, trying to digest the fact that he had a major decision to make. Did he care for Lucy, or allow her to go to foster care? He couldn't imagine doing either one, but he would have to make a choice at some point. That was, if they found her alive. Something he believed would happen. And he would be so thankful that he would want her with him forever. At least he prayed he'd want that to happen.

El took photographs of each page of the will, then closed the folder and slid it into an evidence bag. "I'll try to get Sierra to process the scene, but I don't want to leave valuable evidence behind."

"You think someone could come looking for it?"

"I think it's possible." She retrieved the financial folder and withdrew recent bank statements.

Gabe leaned closer, not surprised to see a balance of only $26.11 in her account. "As you can see, she barely had enough money to live on."

"No big deposits for sure." El flipped to the next month, then month after month before she closed the folder. "This doesn't immediately look like our murder is financially driven. Unless, of course, she'd found an illegal way to make money and it went bad on her."

"You mean like selling drugs?"

"Or something like that." She lifted her chin and looked him square in the eye.

He eyed her. "You can't be thinking of prostitution. No

way. And if you are, let it go. I told you how strong of a Christian she was. No way she was prostituting herself."

"Desperate means often require desperate measures."

"I'd like to think if she was that desperate for money, she would've asked me for some." He took a long breath. "Who knows, maybe that's why she was coming to see me."

"Could be. Hopefully the forensics will provide us with a lead, and we can determine why she needed to see you." El arched a brow. "Was it common for her to visit you?"

"No. Lucy has a tendency to get carsick so I usually came here. I told you, she visited me last weekend. She claimed it was simply because I'd been so busy and we hadn't seen each other for a while. But I've been thinking about it. She was kind of uneasy. Not afraid. Restless."

"Maybe Mrs. Z. knows what had Kenna so worried."

"It's possible."

El bagged the file and flipped to the ID file. She withdrew an envelope holding necessary items to identify Lucy if needed. "We've got both DNA and fingerprints here."

"Finally, a break in our favor," he said.

El bagged the packet then checked the final files before closing the drawer. "You looked through those envelopes on the desk yet?"

He shook his head and picked up the stack. "Bills. None marked *past due* on the envelope, but a look at the actual statements will tell us if she was struggling to meet her monthly bills."

"Keep at it. Let me know what you find." El strode back to the kitchen, a purpose in her steps.

He opened each envelope and examined the statements. "All of these accounts are current. Doesn't include her rent, though, but it'll be easy enough for my team to confirm with her landlord. She didn't have a computer. Used a tablet, and

I don't see that here. Could be on her bedside table, or she could've taken it with her."

"When you're finished checking out the desk, we can search her room together."

"I have an envelope of photographs to look through before I'm done." He didn't expect to find anything unusual in the pictures. Kenna only printed photographs she wanted to display in the house. She surely wouldn't display some super-secret problem that had scared her into adding three locks on her doors and ended with her death.

He reached for the envelope, then paused. Viewing pictures of the two of them would be a tough task. He swallowed and withdrew a thick stack of pictures. The top photo was of Lucy's last birthday party. Her beaming smile tore at his heart.

Oh, baby girl. Where are you?

He breathed slowly until he could continue. Five more birthday party photos were next in the stack, each labeled on the back with dates. Kenna and Lucy in various positions, both widely smiling. Lucy wearing the bracelet found near the beach.

His heart sank. He was pleased to have the bracelet confirmed as belonging to her. It told them she might've wandered off in the woods, and they would find her. On the other hand, it cut him to the quick to know that she'd really been present and something forceful enough had happened to cause her bracelet to fall off.

Or maybe she took it off and left it as a clue for them. She was waiting somewhere for him to find her. Terrified. Counting on him.

He forced himself to continue and turned over the next photo.

"What?" He sat forward, searching every detail of the photo. "You have to see this picture of Kenna with a man in front of a glass-fronted building. I can't make out the guy's face, but he's wearing an old green army jacket and a black baseball cap."

El rushed in, and he held out the picture.

She squinted at it. "Can't see a logo on the cap."

"If it's a logo cap, several sports teams in the area have them. Like the Portland Winterhawks or the Hillsboro Hops."

She frowned. "Either way, the picture doesn't have enough to ID this man."

Gabe flipped it over. To check for a date. "She took it only three weeks ago, and wrote, *Our second chance*."

"Is it Kenna's handwriting?"

He nodded. "But what in the world did she mean by that?"

Gabe flipped the photograph back over.

"She's looking at him like he could be her boyfriend." El continued to stare at the picture. "Maybe she saw the boyfriend as a second chance at life with a dad for Lucy?"

"Yeah, maybe. She clearly feels something for him. My gut says I know him from somewhere. It's his stance that seems familiar to me."

She drew an evidence bag from a large cargo pocket. "I'll bag the photos to take as evidence."

"Maybe Hayden or a Veritas expert can somehow use that picture to identify the guy."

"We can hope." She gently placed the pictures in a bag and looked at him. "Hey, hey, don't look so discouraged. We'll find her. I promise."

He held up his little finger. "Pinky swear?"

She gave him a funny look.

"Oh, right, you don't know about that," he said, feeling embarrassed for revealing something so personal when this search should be all business. "It's my thing with Lucy."

She gave him a tender look and held out her little finger. "Pinky swear."

They twisted fingers, but only for the briefest of moments.

She immediately jerked free. "Finish up here, and we'll move to the bedroom."

Yeah, he should've kept things all business. Oh well. It was over, and despite her tender look, he shoved the interaction into the recesses of his mind and went back to reviewing items on the desk. Unfortunately, nothing else provided a lead.

"I'm done." He stood.

El met him in the hallway leading to the only bedroom.

"I always wished Kenna could afford a two-bedroom place," he said as he stepped into the room. "But that wasn't in her budget."

She'd placed a double bed in one corner and a small child's bed in the other. He'd never forget the Saturday morning when he took them to a thrift store and Lucy spotted the worn Bluey comforter now covering her mattress. The simple joy of a child. Something he hadn't experienced much in his life.

El went straight to the shabby nightstand holding only a single vintage lamp. She pulled out the drawer. "No tablet."

"Like I thought, she probably took it with her. I didn't see it in her van, though."

"If it's in there, Sierra will find it."

He opened slatted bifold doors to her closet. Hanging on a hook, he found a green US field jacket. "Found the army jacket in that picture."

She left the nightstand drawer open and joined him at the closet. She snapped several pictures, then took the jacket out. "Could be the connection to a military attacker we're looking for."

"Or if you believe what she wrote on the back of the picture, it belongs to the boyfriend." He pointed at the shoulder, his heart thumping with excitement. "A few short dark hairs. Color matches the guy's hair in the picture. Could give us DNA and most importantly, the name of Kenna's killer."

10

Gabe wanted to rush out of the room and get the jacket to the forensic lab for testing, but he forced himself to remain calm. Not only so El didn't pull him off this investigation because he couldn't control his emotions, but also to see what she had to say. To get that second opinion is so important in law enforcement. In life generally.

Her eyes lit up. "Definitely too strong of a lead to leave here."

"When word gets out about Kenna's death, the jacket owner could come back for it. Especially if he's the killer. Or even if he isn't, he probably doesn't want to get involved."

"I have large evidence bags in my kit in the family room. We can go bag it there."

He followed her, but hadn't missed her strong emphasis on *we*. She wanted him to accompany her. She didn't need his help, but she couldn't leave him without supervision.

They made quick work of bagging and labeling the jacket, then returned to the bedroom where El looked under the bed, while he completed his closet search.

She soon got to her feet. "Nothing here. Moving on to the bathroom."

He finished the last storage box and followed her to the only bathroom.

El went straight to the mirrored medicine cabinet, revealing toothbrushes and toothpaste, along with children's acetaminophen and ibuprofen, and a bottle of adult acetaminophen.

"No illegal drugs." She closed the door and squatted to look under the sink. "Nothing here either."

Gabe grabbed the trashcan and held it out to El. "A positive pregnancy test."

"She *did* know she was pregnant. I'll bag it for DNA and prints."

Another secret Kenna had kept from him. "With the test sitting on top of the trash, the father could know too. Or what if she was seeing two men and the second man found out it was the other guy's baby?"

El looked at him. "A definite motive for murder, but you didn't even know about one guy, do you really think she was hiding two men from you?"

"Doubtful, but we have to look at all possibilities. Maybe her neighbors have seen men coming and going and can help us figure that out." Gabe didn't wait for El, but hurried through the house and into the living room.

He fixed his hands on bended knees, and dragged in air, his lungs aching for it. His heart aching too. He didn't want to spend a moment of time thinking he didn't know Kenna as well as he thought. But he had to do his job and that meant considering things he didn't want to think about.

El entered the room, and he expected her to give him a lecture on going ahead of her.

When she didn't say anything, he rushed out the door. She had to secure the building and he went to the back of her vehicle, where she couldn't see his emotional meltdown, giving him time to clear his head.

El soon joined him and opened her trunk to secure the evidence and her kit. "The jacket is too good of a lead to wait on getting the DNA processed. I'll have a deputy pick it up and bring it to Sierra to include in the package she'll have delivered to the lab today."

She took out her phone and talked with Ulrich. And Gabe looked across the drive at Mrs. Z.'s bungalow, where she sat on her porch in an old cane rocker. The bright blue house color had faded, but lovingly tended garden beds surrounded the structure. Still, the building needed major repairs that her money didn't stretch to. Gabe had offered to help her, but like Kenna, she refused financial help. He'd settled for making minor repairs for her.

El pocketed her phone. "We'll meet up with a deputy and give them the jacket, pregnancy test, and photos of the suspected boyfriend."

"I appreciate your sense of urgency. This could be the guy who has Lucy." With that horrific thought in his brain, he headed across the drive.

Mrs. Z moved her rocker in a rhythmic dance. As he got closer, he could make out her pink-and-purple house dress with a flowered apron over the front.

She caught sight of them, came to her feet, and waved. "Gabe. Gabe. Yoohoo. Over here."

She met him at the top of the steps and swept him into a fiercely tight hug. Her body round and padded, she always smelled like vanilla and honey. "Land sakes. It's been way too long since I've seen you."

He pushed free of her arms. "Sorry. I'd like to have come by more often, but we've been swamped with setting up the new business."

"Kenna told me you all have made quite a success of it. She's not home, as I'm sure you know, since you were just there."

Of course she saw them arrive and him go around to crawl into the house. She didn't miss a thing, which would make her a valuable witness.

But before asking any questions, he had to tell her about Kenna and Lucy. "Why don't we sit down?"

She drew her eyebrows together and looked past him. "And who is this?"

"Oh, sorry. Meet El Lyons."

"El? Like the letter L? What kind of name is that?"

If El was offended by Mrs. Z.'s comment, she didn't show it. "It's E-l. Short for Elaina."

"Well now, that's a beautiful name, and I'll call you Elaina." She gestured at the rockers. "Have a seat. I'll run inside for some iced tea and the sugar cookies freshly baked for Lucy. They're her favorite but she won't miss a few of them."

Gabe reached for Mrs. Z.'s arm. "Let's sit. There's something I need to tell you."

Those eyebrows drew together again, and she frowned at him. "It's about Kenna and Lucy, right? Why they're not home, and why she didn't tell me where she was going? Probably didn't tell you either or you wouldn't have had to crawl through that wonky window."

Gabe didn't speak, but helped ease her into the chair. Considering she could already be unsteady on her feet at times, he didn't want her standing when the shock hit her.

He pulled the nearest rocker closer to her and took her hands. "This will be hard to hear, but you like straight talkers so I won't tiptoe around it. Kenna's body was found last night. She was murdered."

She gasped and jerked her hand free to clutch her chest. "No. No. I refuse to believe it."

"I thought the same way, too, but I've seen her. She didn't survive."

She started sobbing, tears flowing over her cheeks. She dug a tissue from her apron pocket and dabbed at her eyes. She suddenly sat forward. "Lucy! What about Lucy?"

Gabe wasn't sure he could get the words out to tell her, but he had to. "She's missing. We don't know if she wandered off or if someone took her."

"Someone?" She planted her hands on the rocker arms. "You mean like the killer?"

"That would be the most likely scenario."

El silently approached and knelt in front of Mrs. Z. "We're doing everything we can to find her and find out who killed Kenna."

"We? That doesn't sound like something a friend would say. Exactly who are you?"

"I'm the detective in charge of finding Lucy, and Kenna's killer."

"She's working with me and my team," Gabe said. "We hope to find leads in Kenna's bungalow. Also to ask if you know anyone who might want to harm her."

"Kenna?" She waved her hand. "You know she was the sweetest, most lovable person, and no one would want to do her harm."

He nodded, but obviously one person wanted to harm her. Someone not only had means, but motive and opportunity too. They just had to find that person. "Did she have a boyfriend?"

"You of all people should know that." She gave him an appraising look.

He took it to mean he would know that if he'd been around more often. "She never mentioned anyone to me."

"Me either, but she's had a male visitor for the last couple of months."

"Do you know his name?" El asked. "Or can you describe him?"

"I don't know his name. I do know he arrives late at night. Often leaves early in the morning." Her chin lifted a fraction, lips pressed into a thin line, as if she didn't approve of this behavior. "But before he leaves the house, he flips up his hood. Then keeps his head down, and I can never get a clear look at his face."

Probably what he and Kenna intended.

El held out her phone, the screen displaying the picture they'd found in the house of Kenna and the unidentified man. "Is this the guy, and did you ever see him wearing a jacket like this?"

She peered at the picture. "Yes. Yes. That's him, and I saw him wearing that jacket a couple of times. He had a sweatshirt on underneath with the hood pulled up."

"So he was a big guy?" Gabe asked.

"Yeah. Kind of like you except a little bulkier. But tall and he had kind of a swagger when he walked. You know, like some of those young guys you see on television."

Gabe didn't know exactly what she meant, but the man having kind of a swagger could help them.

"What about a vehicle?" El asked. "What does he drive?"

"That's the odd thing." Mrs. Z. leaned back in the rocker. "He parked down the street. Like he and Kenna didn't want anyone to know who he was or that they were in a relationship."

"Maybe she thought you would recognize him if you saw him," Gabe said.

"Me? Not hardly. I wouldn't recognize any younger man unless he was from church. That's the only place I really go besides doctors' appointments."

"Maybe she didn't want anyone to know a man spent the night at her place," El said.

"You don't think she was...that they were doing something they shouldn't do outside of marriage? No. I can't believe that about Kenna."

Gabe could tell her about the pregnancy, but he didn't think she needed to have another loss to grieve. He met El's gaze, encouraging her not to say anything. She opened her mouth. Gabe held his breath.

"Did Lucy ever mention him?" she asked, and Gabe started breathing again.

Mrs. Z. shook her head. "I also wondered if he came over when he did so Kenna didn't have to introduce him to Lucy."

"Which would suggest a more casual relationship," El said.

"I didn't get any sense that she'd fallen in love. At least not by her behavior. It didn't change. Wait, I take that back. She was suddenly worried about her and Lucy's safety. Made her put all those locks you had to have seen on her door."

"Did she ever discuss that with you?" Gabe asked.

"Sort of. But she never gave me a good answer about why she suddenly felt unsafe. Nothing around here scared the rest of us. I was worried that something had happened at her place, and she was hiding it from us."

"I'll check police reports to see if there've been any incidents in the area," El said.

Mrs. Z.'s face narrowed in a scowl. "You'll keep us updated if you find anything, right?"

"Of course."

"One thing you could check for at her place if you haven't already found it. The last month or so, she spent a lot of time scribbling in a journal. The book was green with a big black cross on the front. I asked about it. She side-stepped my questions and said it had to do with her faith."

"But you didn't believe her?" El asked.

Mrs. Z. shook her head. "And you know what? It wasn't like her to lie. I can't say she was downright lying to me, but she was avoiding telling me the truth."

Gabe made a mental note to tell Sierra to look for the journal and Kenna's missing tablet.

"Has anyone approached her house since she left?" El asked.

Mrs. Z. shook her head. "Unless of course they came when I was sleeping, which at my age is getting less and less."

"What about the other neighbors?" El stood. "Could one of them have gotten a good look at this guy or know why Kenna added the locks to her doors?"

"It's doubtful," Mrs. Z. said. "They're never home, and it's been hard to connect with them. Besides, I have the best view of Kenna's front door. If I didn't see this guy, they probably didn't either."

Gabe gave her hands a squeeze and stood. "We still need to talk to them."

"Of course you do. Stop back before you leave. I'll have the cookies packaged to take to Lucy for when you find her."

Gabe nodded and swiftly jogged down the steps before he let Mrs. Z. catch any doubt in his expression over finding his little princess.

"You didn't see a journal in the house, did you?" El asked when she caught up to him in the middle of the driveway.

He shook his head. "She could have brought it with her, and it's in the van."

"I'll text Sierra to be on the lookout for it and the missing tablet." She woke up her phone and thumbed the screen quickly before shoving it back in her pocket. "Do you think the guy in the picture is the father of Kenna's unborn child?"

"Seems possible." He scanned the other bungalows,

looking for security cameras but not seeing anything mounted on the exteriors.

Disappointment settled in. He couldn't lose hope. He had to stay positive, not only for himself, but for El. As much as she was acting like a tough detective, he knew her insides were tangled up with past guilt. Maybe she was even too stressed to see how much he cared about her and wanted to help her. Not only in her life, but in this investigation.

Gabe never expected to be back there. Never expected to lay eyes on this sprawling ranch painted a crisp white with black shutters and trim. Never expected to see the house he'd come home to every day for eighteen years. But there he was, standing out front of his parents' house.

El inched closer to him. "You don't have to do this. I can question them on my own."

"They won't talk to you or anyone in law enforcement." He took in a deep breath. "Might not even tell me anything since I was once a state trooper."

"But really, all we want to ask is if they know how to locate Kenna's parents."

"With their distrust of law enforcement, they'll think we want to arrest her parents. Not that they care about anyone but themselves, but they'd never want to be considered snitches."

El rested her hand on his arm. "Maybe they've changed."

He didn't have to think about that for even a second. "No way. They're career criminals all the way, getting deeper in as time goes by. And their choice of livelihood means we can't even meet each other halfway."

"Then maybe we should take a moment to pray that

they'll be forthcoming." She took his hand and began praying.

He listened and believed what she was asking for, but did he really believe prayer presented on his family's behalf made a difference? He'd offered prayer after prayer for years without any response from God, so he'd stopped praying.

Was he selling God short by doing that? Was God simply telling Gabe it wasn't the right time for his family to change now but they could in the future? Or had he read God's answer right and his family would never change?

El ended the prayer and squeezed his hand. "Ready?"

Ready? Was he ever. Maybe it was her comforting, encouraging, and loving gaze that left him thinking he could do anything.

"Let's do this." He led the way up the familiar walk and rang the doorbell.

Who would answer? His mother or his father?

His gut clenched. He couldn't do this. He took a step back. Then another.

El moved closer, letting the edge of her hand touch his. The warmth. The compassion. Caring. Support. He could do this. With her at his side. With God at his side.

He raised his shoulders.

The door slowly opened. An older version of his mother stood before him. Her hair had grayed, her skin wrinkled, and her shoulders were stooped.

Her eyes lit up. "Gabe! Oh, my goodness. My Gabey boy. I always prayed you'd come home."

She reached her arms out to him. The little boy in him wanted to be swallowed up in them. The adult remembered the many times she'd forced him to go along with his father on a criminal activity. The adult took center stage, and he couldn't accept a hug. "I'm not here on a personal call. Is Dad home?"

Her excitement faded. Slowly. As if she couldn't let go of hope for reconciliation. His heart ached for her. For himself, too. But he couldn't do anything about it unless they'd changed.

Her posture stiffened. "He won't be back until dinnertime. You could stay and have dinner with us."

"Thank you, but no," he said as politely as he could muster. "Actually, I don't want to talk to him and was hoping he wouldn't be here. Can we come in for a minute?"

For the first time, his mother shifted her gaze to El. "And who might you be, my dear?"

El held out her credentials. "Detective Elaina Lyons. Lost Lake Sheriff's Department."

His mother's gaze flashed to his face, her eyelashes batting as fast as hummingbird wings. "You've brought the law to our doorstep?"

Gabe held up a placating hand. "This isn't about you or the family. It's about Kenna."

"Oh, Kenna. Sweet Kenna. Of course, if it's about her, come in." She stood back, revealing the same small foyer with the same decor from his childhood.

On an entry table sat figurines of Mary and Jesus along with the family Bible. Not only did his family live a life in opposition to Gabe's faith, but they were hypocritical in their pretense of being strong Christians. Their philosophy? Go to confession on Saturday, then resume sinning as if nothing had happened. After all, why change when they could go back the next weekend and be forgiven again?

"Keep going, Gabey." His mother's continued use of his pet nickname bothered him, but they wouldn't be there long, and there was no point in bringing it up. "To the kitchen."

He led the way down the hallway to the only room his father had no desire to control, and where his mother felt most at home. The floor was covered in wall-to-wall, indoor/outdoor carpeting with a green background and huge orange flowers, a blast from the seventies his grandmother had installed when she'd owned the home before them. The avocado green appliances he remembered from his childhood were still in place. Not surprising. His father didn't believe in improving things as long as they worked or could be repaired.

Gabe pulled out one of the rusty-orange vinyl chairs for El, and she took a seat. He sat next to her.

His mother smiled at them. "I just made a fresh pot of coffee. Would anyone like a cup?"

Gabe hoped he wouldn't be there long enough to even drink a half cup. "Not for me."

"No thank you," El said. "But thank you for asking."

Disappointment overtaking his mother's expression, she brushed her hands over her worn clothing and turned to pour coffee in her favorite white mug that he'd given to her for Mother's Day just before he'd learned his family members were all crooks. Another stab to his heart for what he was doing to his mother, but he couldn't live the life they did or condone it.

She brought her coffee to the table and sat across from them. Cupping her hands around the mug, she looked at Gabe. "What is it you want to know?"

He wouldn't waste time and there wasn't a good way to tell anyone about a murder, so he came right out with it. "Kenna was murdered on Friday night. Her daughter was with her and she's missing."

His mother gasped, eliciting the response he'd expected. She'd always liked Kenna. After all, Kenna walked him to school and gave his mother more freedom. More time away from his father. Time when she could follow her own agenda, not his.

She released her cup. "What happened?"

"We're still piecing that together," he said. "But she was found floating in Lost Lake after having been strangled."

"Oh. Oh. Oh my." She clutched a hand to her flowery button-down blouse. "That poor dear. Who would kill her?"

"We were hoping you might have an idea," El said, heading into an area that Gabe hadn't wanted to go with his mother.

"Me? I try to keep up with what's going on in the neighborhood, but once her family moved away, all I heard was that Kenna is a daycare teacher, and she has a young daughter."

"Do you know where her parents live now?" El asked.

"Last I heard they'd bought a home near Gold Beach. Some sort of senior living or retirement village. Something like that. I remember because we're about the same age as her parents, and it's hard for me to believe we could be considered old enough to retire."

Could they even retire? There sure wasn't a 401(k) or retirement plan for criminals. Neither of them paid into Social Security either, so they weren't eligible for those payments, but he kept his thoughts to himself. Knowing his dad, he was still in the thick of things and socking away money for old age.

The back door opened. Dread flooded Gabe's body like a bad virus. He swiveled his chair. Not his dad, but almost as bad. His brother, Brad, stepped in. He resembled Gabe in many physical ways. Hopefully not in the cruelty that was often found in his eyes, a true expression passed down from their father. Neither of them had forgiven Gabe for walking out on the family business.

Brad scowled. "So, the prodigal son has returned."

Their mother jumped up and rushed over to Brad. "He didn't come back to the family, if that's what you're thinking.

He came to tell me Kenna has been murdered, and her little daughter is missing. They need to know how to contact her family."

A flash of pain crossed over Brad's face, and he gripped the counter. Gabe had always believed his brother had a crush on Kenna back in the day. His reaction could be a confirmation of that.

"When did this happen?" he asked, his voice strained.

"Friday night. She was strangled and left face down in Lost Lake."

He tightened his grip on the counter. "What was she doing there?"

Odd question for him to ask, especially when he didn't know anything about her these days. "She was afraid of something and was on her way to see me."

"But you don't know what it was?"

Another odd question.

"No, do you?" Gabe asked.

"Me?" Brad's tone mirrored his mother's surprise. "Why would I know what Kenna was afraid of?"

"Because you know what's going on in the criminal underbelly around here. If it somehow invaded her life, you'd know about it."

Brad removed his hands and shoved them into his pockets. "If you're here to insult me and the family, you might as well leave."

"We're just here for the current address of Kenna's parents," El said.

"And who are you? Law enforcement by the looks of it. Otherwise, I don't know why a beautiful woman would dress like a nun in today's world."

"Brad!" their mother said. "No need to be rude."

"No worries." El smiled. "He's right. I think of this as my

uniform. Do you know where Kenna's parents are, Mr. Irving?"

"I'm sure Mom told you they moved to a retirement village in Gold Beach."

"She did, but she didn't have an address."

He stood looking at El, and Gabe could almost see the thoughts pinging through his head. "I can probably get that for you."

"You being helpful? That's a first." Gabe studied his brother for a few moments to see if he had an ulterior motive. "How would you get their address?"

"I know the couple who bought their house. They might have a forwarding address in their paperwork. Sit tight. I'll go ask them." He spun and rushed out the door.

"He's always willing to help." Gabe's mother said with pride as she returned to the table.

As usual, his memory of his brother was far different than his mother's. "He seemed bothered by hearing about Kenna's murder."

"Of course he did," his mother said. "He might come off as a tough guy, but he's very sensitive."

A snort came to the surface, but Gabe swallowed it and stood. "Unless you have anything else to offer regarding Kenna and her family, we'll be going."

Her eyes widened. "But what about the address?"

Gabe fished out a business card from his pocket and laid it on the table. "If Brad gets it, have him text me at this phone number."

She got up slowly. "You sure you can't stay, son?"

"Not as long as even one person in our family is still involved in criminal activities."

His mother glanced at El.

"Don't worry, she knows about the family business, and

she's not here to do anything about it," Gabe said. "Like we said, she's here to get information on Kenna."

El stood and handed her business card to his mom. "Please let me know if you learn anything else about Kenna and her murder. Or where Lucy might be."

His mother nodded vigorously. "I doubt that I'll hear anything, but you can be sure if I do, I'll call you."

"Goodbye, Mom." Gabe barely got the words out through a closing throat. He rushed for the front door, assuming El was following him. He whipped it open and charged down the steps. On the sidewalk, he turned for a brief last look at his mother, but his emotions overwhelmed him, and he couldn't stay there.

Battling tears, he fled to El's car. The locks clicked open from her remote key fob. He dove inside as if closing the door would protect him from his pain. Stop him from going back up that walkway to hug his mom. To consider connecting again with his family.

El got behind the wheel and started the engine, but looked at him instead of shifting into gear. "Is there anything I can do?"

"Drive. Just drive and get away from this house." He stabbed the address into the GPS for the daycare center where Kenna had worked. "Follow directions. Takes less than five minutes."

He looked out his window, but not at the house. He would totally lose it if he saw his mom standing there upset and confused. Maybe crying. He never wanted to hurt her. His reaction told him he still loved her and still hated what had happened between him and his family. And most importantly, proved he hadn't really made any progress in leaving it behind.

El reached out and gently touched his knee. "I'm here for you if you need to talk."

He gave her as much of a smile as he could find, then looked back out the window. She was proving more and more to be the woman for him.

But how in the world could he ever follow his feelings for her when this baggage still had such a hold on his life? A question he didn't need to ask.

The answer was obvious. He couldn't.

11

El approached Little Pines Daycare, but she might as well have been on a distant planet. Children's laughter rang out behind tall wooden fences at the single-level building painted in bright colors. She had zero experience with children or in a daycare center. Not that she didn't love or was afraid of children. For years she'd worked in her church's nursery and their summer camp. Something that had fallen by the wayside after Victoria had gone missing.

Let it go. You need to focus, not think about the past.

Thankful this place provided weekend care and was open on a Saturday, she stepped through the vivid aqua door that Gabe held for her. The small, welcoming lobby had calming blue walls filled with child-friendly decals. They'd mounted a plaque hanging on the wall thanking the center for partnering with Safe Harbor. A small desk with two chairs took up most of the space, the wall behind filled with framed certificates of excellence for this daycare.

A redheaded woman wearing a director name tag that read *Bonnie Wilson* sat behind the desk and looked up. Recognition dawned in her expression, and a broad smile crossed her face. She was cheery and welcoming just as

Gabe had described, but nothing like the woman Kenna had said she worked for.

"Gabe!" She shot to her feet. "It's been a while since we've seen you."

Gabe nodded. "I've mostly been visiting on weekends when Lucy doesn't come here."

Bonnie frowned. "I know Lucy loves to have you pick her up, but she's not here today."

Gabe didn't seem to be able to find the words to go on, so El held out her credentials and introduced herself. "I'm sorry to tell you Kenna was murdered on Friday, and Lucy is missing."

Bonnie fell back into her chair. She opened and closed her mouth. Repeated. Then shook her head and tears began to fall. "I can hardly believe that. She was the sweetest, most loving teacher and an awesome mother. Who would do this to her?"

Eager to make Bonnie feel more comfortable, El took a seat in the chair across the desk. "We were hoping you might be able to answer that."

"Oh, well, you're wrong there. I don't have any idea who had anything against her. But then I didn't know much about her personal life. She seemed to be stable, and she certainly wasn't into anything illegal. I mean, she passed her background check and all, but I guess she could've been doing something and has never been caught." Bonnie shook her head hard, her curly hair whipping around. "No. I don't believe that. Not Kenna."

Interesting that she went to talking about something illegal, but El could understand the thought process. "What about other staff members? Did she get along well with them?"

"Perfectly. In fact, we vote for the daycare's head teacher every year, and they voted for her the last three years. They wouldn't do that if she wasn't someone special."

Gabe sat next to El. "Did she have any issues with parents?"

"No. They all loved her, too." Her eyebrows drew together. "What about Lucy? I hate to be blunt, but do you think she's still alive?"

Gabe nodded. "We have nothing to suggest she isn't, and we're proceeding that way."

"That said—" El paused and shifted in her chair. "—we'd like to look at any personal belongings Kenna kept here. Lucy's too."

"Sure." Bonnie stood. "Follow me."

She unlocked the door to the classrooms, and they followed her down a hallway with closed doors on each side. A window in each door and a larger one next to the doors allowed people to look inside the classrooms. Open lockers painted a vibrant red were lined up in the hallway.

Bonnie passed the younger children's classrooms to stop outside the four-year-old room. Kenna's name was proudly posted on a nearby bulletin board. She'd filled the remaining space with children's colorful drawings.

Bonnie entered the childless room and went directly to a desk sitting in front of a closet door. "The children are on the playground. They'll be outside for another fifteen minutes. It would be good if you were gone before they came in and asked questions."

El wouldn't be hurried through her search, but she could focus and be efficient. She withdrew gloves from her pocket and sat down behind the desk. She thoroughly searched every drawer, not finding anything Kenna might've brought from home or hidden, like her journal. She looked at Bonnie. "Is it unusual for a teacher not to have anything personal in their workspace?"

Bonnie shook her head. "Unfortunately, turnover in teachers and aides is high. They often don't stay long enough to bring items from home. Kenna is an exception to that, but she kept her personal life separate, so not bringing anything here makes sense."

El understood keeping her private life private, but she did that because she wanted to hide her guilt. Did Kenna have something to hide, too? Something El needed to talk with Gabe about?

She glanced at him. Found his expression surprisingly neutral, so she turned back to Bonnie. "Did you ever see her with a journal?"

"No, but that's not surprising either. She wouldn't have any time in the classroom to journal while the children are here. She would've had to do it on her breaks or lunch, which she tried to spend with Lucy or helping out a struggling teacher."

Gabe's phone dinged. He grabbed it from his pocket and stared at the screen. "My brother came through with the address."

El stood. "Let me check the closet, and we can get going on that."

The space revealed shelves filled with construction paper, paint, crayons, and other daycare necessities. Still, El looked between and behind everything, through open boxes, continuing until she was confident Kenna hadn't stored anything personal except a sweater.

She took the sweater off the hook and turned. "I'm assuming this belonged to her."

"Yes." Bonnie's eyes creased, and her eyes glistened with tears again. "I can't believe she's gone."

Her emotional response raised a similar response in El, but she had to remain in control. "Could you take us to Lucy's things?"

"Her cubby's right down the hall." Bonnie took a tissue from the box on the desk and mopped her face before fleeing to the hallway. She stopped in front of a locker holding Lucy's name in large, colorful letters. A small section held pictures and clothing. A larger one had hooks for coats and backpacks.

Gabe retrieved a Bluey-themed backpack from a hook.

"Oh, gosh." Bonnie blinked a few times. "Parents often leave things behind. Not Kenna, but they were in a hurry to leave on Friday. She didn't say why, as usual, and I didn't ask."

"We might as well clear everything out." Gabe reached for the artwork, and a stack of clothing with a small blue sweater on top.

"Sounds like you don't think Lucy will be coming back," Bonnie said.

"Kenna wanted me to take custody."

"She thought the world of you and so does Lucy." Bonnie nibbled on her lip. "Since you don't live here, I'll disenroll Lucy, but there'll always be a place for her here. If something changes, let me know."

Bonnie started for the exit, and Gabe followed.

El caught up. "Did Kenna pay tuition or was it free for working here?"

"All teachers get free tuition for one child after they've been employed for ninety days. A perk to try to keep teachers on staff."

"Did she ever seem to need money?"

Bonnie frowned. "Almost all of our staff need money. I wish I could afford to pay more. But she didn't seem desperate, like asking for an advance on her paycheck or anything like that. And Lucy never seemed to go without anything. Kenna was always able to pay for special field trips Lucy's class took."

Could mean her murder wasn't money-related.

"Could we get a list of students along with their contact information?"

"Sorry, no can do. Privacy and all. You understand."

"I do, and I'll get a warrant for that information."

"A warrant says I'll have to provide it, but I'll also have to tell the parents. I don't want them to worry, so it would be wonderful if you could avoid the warrant."

"Understood." El really did understand and didn't want to upset the parents or children unless necessary. "I'd like to interview your staff. Would now be a good time?"

"Actually, not really. It would be best if you could come back and talk to them during their break times so we don't disrupt care."

El didn't like the answer, but she understood that as well. "Is there someone on staff who Kenna was particularly close to?"

"As I said before, she kept her personal life separate and didn't really connect."

"Okay." El got out her business card for Bonnie. "I'll let you know if I'll be returning for those interviews or with a warrant. If you think of anything helpful, you can reach me at any number on my card."

Bonnie turned the card over to study it before looking back up. "Can you let me know when you find Lucy and when Kenna's funeral is scheduled?"

Gabe nodded and swallowed hard. "Sorry to be the bearer of such bad news."

Bonnie crossed her arms. "I can't imagine having to tell the rest of the staff and parents. Oh, and the children. The poor children. It'll be a huge blow to all of them."

"Thanks again." Gabe quickly pushed outside and held the door for El, then came alongside her as they walked to the car. "You buy anything she said?"

"I feel like there was some truth in there, but the question I have is, when was she putting on a show for us or telling the truth? After what you said about the staff not getting along with her, if we did come back to interview them, she might tell them what to say to us."

"Do you think she has anything to do with Kenna's death and Lucy's disappearance?"

"I don't know. This one's got me puzzled. I noticed the many awards in the lobby saying this is a highly respected daycare, so I have to figure something good is happening here. But is there something illegal going on underneath? I don't know. And if there is, is it connected to Kenna? I don't know that either."

"Let's get Hayden to dig deep on Bonnie and this place. Hopefully, he'll find information to help clarify our questions." After getting in the vehicle, he grabbed his phone and started thumbing the screen.

She suspected he was sending the text to Hayden.

His phone dinged. "Hayden will get started with our request right away."

"Thanks." El buckled her seatbelt. "So Brad confirmed Kenna's parents live in Gold Beach?"

"Yeah, in a retirement village like my mom said." Gabe shoved his phone into his pocket.

"Are you up for seeing them now?"

He scowled. "Not something I really want to do, but we need to do it."

"I'll text the deputy who's coming to pick up the evidence that he can meet us before we talk to them."

El sent a text then got her vehicle on the road, her palms getting sweaty. She loved her job. She didn't love doing a death notification call. One of the most difficult parts of her job. It was easier with two officers present, but today her partner was a man with very strong feelings about Kenna's parents.

The interview would be similar to the one with his parents, at least in the emotional stakes for Gabe. Her too, as she watched him suffer even more. She wanted to take his pain away, or at least talk to him about it so he could find some release before his emotions exploded. But he went through Lucy's backpack, holding each item as time ticked slowly by.

Fifteen miles in, she glanced at him. He'd placed Lucy's backpack and papers on his lap, the sweater resting on top, and he was holding them close. She really couldn't imagine his pain now, but if they were to lose Lucy too…

She wouldn't let that happen. They needed to work harder. Smarter. Do something extraordinary to find her. They'd already passed the golden window when finding a child alive was more likely. Golden window or not, she would choose to believe Lucy was still alive and proceed with that in her mind and heart. And she needed Gabe to be able to focus.

Talking it out should help. "That was hard."

He nodded, but didn't speak.

She wouldn't give up. "Kenna leaving the backpack when it was out of character for her adds to the theory that she wanted to get to you quickly."

He gave a single nod. "Unfortunately, we're no closer to finding out why she stopped at the lake instead, and if she knew her attacker. I was really hoping we would learn something from one of the people we talked to today."

"Me too, but the day isn't done. Don't get your hopes up for her parents. Being estranged from her, I doubt they'll have anything to give us."

"Other than heartburn, you mean." His mouth turned

down. "But I won't lose hope. Not while my team is still working the investigation. We've been known to pull off things others can't. When we get back to town, I'd like to meet with them and review their tasks. Hopefully they found something to help."

El didn't hold out any hope for such a thing.

Not because she didn't trust their abilities or think they wouldn't find any leads. But if they'd discovered anything related to Lucy, they would've called or texted Gabe by now. Still, with his mood, she wouldn't mention that.

Instead... "Their help could make all the difference for us."

He swiveled to look at her. "Don't think I've missed your concern about how I'm feeling. It's always helpful to know someone cares. I appreciate it. But you. How are you doing? I know this investigation is bringing up memories from your past."

She'd been captivated by him for sure, but this concern for her emotional well-being added to her impression of a kind, considerate man. Still, she didn't much want to talk about Victoria or how it was impacting her. That wasn't fair to him. She expected him to talk to her, but she wouldn't share.

But maybe if she did, he'd open up more. "I won't lie and say it's not bothering me, but I'm trying to work through it. Seeing you struggle with the loss of Kenna, and Lucy missing, minimizes anything I'm feeling."

His fingers curled into Lucy's sweater. "I thought I'd be prepared for something like this, especially with my family's business. In fact, I've imagined what it would be like to lose one of them to violence. But none of that has prepared me for losing someone I love deeply."

"I won't pretend to know what it feels like. I don't even

fully comprehend losing my birth parents. When I was taken away from my mom, I was too young to really even understand what loving her meant. Now, if something happened to my adoptive parents, that would be a different story."

"It's an all-consuming pain that I wouldn't wish on anyone."

"But we'll all experience it at some point."

"Yes, assuming everyone loves someone."

"Isn't love something we all search for? Even the most unstable person wants to be loved."

He nodded.

She probably shouldn't make this more personal, but they'd been together for some time now, and she felt a need to discuss it. "You know, we have a lot in common in this area."

"How so?"

"This mutual attraction we've been fighting forever that hasn't gone anywhere. If I'm reading it right, we both avoid relationships. I mean, I'm certain about myself, but can't be as certain about you."

"You're right. Now that you've met my family you can probably understand why."

Confused, she glanced at him. "You mean because they aren't loving?"

"It's all about their criminal activity. No matter what I do, I can't get away from my past. It's like a shadow following me, and anyone who knows where I came from rarely trusts me completely."

"But Kenna did."

He nodded.

"So why don't you believe someone else can?"

He shrugged.

"You're a man of faith. Do you ever hear that still small voice of God telling you to open your heart to others and trust Him with what happens?"

"Yes, do you?"

"All the time."

His challenging gaze held hers. "And do you listen and respond the way God wants you to?"

She jerked her focus back to the road. "I've tried, but I've never succeeded long-term. My issues always come back. Or should I say, I let my issues come back."

"Same." One word, but the pain ran deep in his tone.

She pulled to a stop at an intersection and looked him in the eye. "What if we tried together?"

He tilted his head. "You mean, follow these feelings and get together then help each other overcome our issues?"

"Yes." She held her breath in case he found the suggestion too disgusting to even contemplate.

"I'd be glad to try. Not until we find Lucy, and Kenna's killer. But afterward..." He gave her a trembling smile.

She squeezed his hand, then directions from the female GPS voice came over the speaker.

El let go of their personal discussion and pressed on the gas to enter the little town where Kenna's parents lived.

She drove past small houses and an almost nonexistent downtown with a grocery store, drugstore, and bank. Her heart had grown lighter than the situation called for. Gabe had done that in his willingness to pursue a relationship with her—someone who had done the most horrific thing in failing a young child in the past—and yet he wanted to be with her.

This is You, isn't it, God? I know it's not me. Not in my humanness could I ever let go of my guilt for even a moment to entertain someone being able to love me. Maybe You're telling me to put that guilt behind me once and for all. That I'm forgiven and have a clean slate going forward. Maybe that I don't even need forgiveness because it was an honest mistake. But I do need forgiveness for the many years I've let guilt lead me and avoided choices You had for me. Please let that stop today and let my heart be open to Your leading.

12

———————

Shocked, Gabe paused on the sidewalk outside the unkempt and rundown single-story home in the neighborhood full of high-end homes. Something had changed in the James family.

This place didn't at all resemble the well-manicured and maintained property where Kenna had grown up.

Gabe aimed to find out what was going on. He rang the bell as El joined him, after saying goodbye to the deputy who'd met them to pick up the evidence from Kenna's house.

Mrs. James pulled the door open. Or at least he thought it was her. She had once been as beautiful as Kenna, but her skin sagged as wrinkles crawled like a road over her face. She wore a gray jogging suit, the sweatshirt stained on the front with what resembled splotches of coffee. Odd. Women in the neighborhood used to envy her fashionable wardrobe.

She eyed them both, no recognition of Gabe's identity dawning on her face.

"If you're here to sell or preach at me, don't bother. I'm not interested." She started to push the door closed.

El held out her credentials. "Are you Mary James, Kenna James's mother?"

Mrs. James scowled. "Yeah, but not like I've seen or heard from the ungrateful girl in years."

El cringed. "Could we come in for a minute, please?"

She planted a hand on her hip. "This about Kenna? She must've done something really bad to get you here."

"Please, can we come in and talk about it?"

Mrs. James shifted on her feet. Ran her gaze from one to the other. "Fine. But I'm busy, so only a few minutes. And before you say anything about that girl, I won't bail her out. Just so you know."

She made room for them to enter and backed away. El pushed past her like Speedy Gonzalez, as if she was afraid Mrs. James would change her mind. Gabe followed, wondering if the woman would act any differently when she learned Kenna had died.

Gabe recognized the traditional beige sofa he'd watched movies from with Kenna, but it was now worn from years of use. As he sat next to El, he looked around the room. The same furniture he remembered from his childhood filled the space painted a calming blue. Dust covered most of the wooden furniture and water rings underneath were too numerous to count.

Mrs. James plopped onto a faded blue easy chair with a matching ottoman. She propped her bare feet up. "Now what is it you want to tell me?"

El slid to the edge of the sofa and laid her hands on her lap. "I'm sorry to tell you this, Mrs. James, but Kenna was found dead on Friday night."

Mrs. James shifted her feet to the floor and sat upright. "Dead. But how?"

"We're investigating it as a homicide."

"Homicide, huh? I knew that girl would come to no good."

Gabe sucked in a sharp breath. What a horrible way for a mother to talk about her daughter. "Stop right there. Kenna led an exemplary life and was a terrific mother and role model. You've spoken badly about her far too often over the years, and you can't possibly be blaming her for her own death."

Mrs. James sniffed. "You seem to know a lot about her, but who in the world are you?"

Gabe squared his shoulders. "Gabe Irving. Kenna's friend since first grade."

"You?" She blinked several times. "You're that scrawny kid who hung around her all those years? Don't tell me you finally got her to fall for you and you got married. That you're the father of the kid I heard she'd had."

Just like this woman to misread everything. "I've never had a romantic relationship with Kenna and never wanted to. But I was honored to be her best friend and be there for her in lieu of you and her family. Especially to help with Lucy, even though she's not my daughter."

"Well, isn't that sweet?" She gave him a snide smile. "What happens to the kid now?"

El cleared her throat. "She's currently missing, and we're looking for her. But I assure you, just like we'll find Kenna's killer, we will find Lucy."

"And then what? You're not expecting her to live with me, are you? Because I'm too old to be raising a little kid."

Way to show concern for the missing grandchild. Still, Gabe had hoped she would say something like this, and he wouldn't end up in a custody fight over Lucy. "What about Mr. James? Might he want custody?"

"He passed away three years ago. Lung cancer." Her tone was level, no emotions.

Did this woman even have a heart? She couldn't, with the way she spoke about the loss of her husband.

He cleared his throat. "Kenna's will designates me to take custody of Lucy, and I'm glad to do it."

"Well then, I guess we're done here." She started to get up.

El held up her hand. "I'd like to ask you a few questions about Kenna."

Mrs. James narrowed her eyes. "You can ask all you want about her, but everything I know I've heard through the grapevine."

El didn't look daunted. "I first need to ask where you were on Friday evening."

"That's rich." She shook her head. "You think I killed her. What reason would I have to do that?"

"I don't know, Mrs. James, but could you please tell me where you were?"

"Stop calling me Mrs. James. It's Mary." She crossed her arms and glared at El. "Friday night my group gets together to play cards. I was the host that night so plenty of people saw me."

"What time did you meet?"

"We started with a light dinner at six and played until ten o'clock. Then because it was at my house, a couple of my friends stayed to help clean up. Was probably close to midnight by the time they went home. Is that good enough for you?"

El held out a small notebook and pen. "Please write down their names and contact information so I can confirm."

After a dramatic eye roll and sigh, Mary took the pen and pad and started writing. She got out her cell phone and scribbled down phone numbers before shoving the book back at El. "Is that all?"

El poised her pen above the notepad. "I don't mean to pry at such a sensitive time, but do you have any idea who might've wanted to harm Kenna?"

"Like I said, I didn't know much about her other than what was on the grapevine. I'm sure you heard the rumor that she was involved in drug trafficking."

"What?" Gabe couldn't control his shock, and his outburst made Mary jump. "Kenna was no more involved with drugs than I am."

Mary pressed her hand over her hair much like a cat would try to flatten their fur when frightened. "Maybe so, but it's the word on the street."

Gabe stood and stared at her. "I can assure you that I'll find out who started such a terrible rumor and make sure it's corrected." He looked at El. "I think we're done here. At least I am. She hasn't changed a bit in all of these years, and I doubt she can be very helpful."

Still holding her pen over the paper, El got up slowly. "It would help if you could give us a name or two for who shared this rumor."

"Sure." She raised her chin and stared back at Gabe. "You don't have to look any further than your family. They know the drug trade and who's involved in it. And they're more than happy to share information."

Gabe stormed to the door, but El didn't follow him.

"Is there someone I can call for you?" she asked Mary, "A friend or family member who can come be with you?"

Gabe didn't wait for the answer, but pushed out the door and onto the sidewalk, where he pulled out his phone and dialed his brother. "Are you spreading a rumor that Kenna was involved in drug trafficking with you?"

"First of all," his brother replied in a deadly calm tone. "I have nothing to do with drug trafficking. If Kenna did, I know nothing about it. And even if I did know something like this about her, I wouldn't tell anyone else."

Gabe wished he was looking his brother in the eye to see if he was telling the truth. He'd always been able to catch Brad in a lie. "You're trying to convince me you're a choir boy now?"

"Didn't say that. Just said I'm not involved in drug trafficking, and I respect Kenna's privacy."

"Your concern for my friend is new. Since when do you care about not spreading any gossip about her?"

"Since I spent a lifetime dodging gossip. Not an easy thing to live with."

A noise behind Gabe, had him turning.

El left the house and walked toward him. He held up a finger and took a few steps away for privacy. "You know the way to stop it."

"You mean the way you did? Run and hide?"

"I'm not hiding. You all know where I am. But yeah, man, I ran away from it as fast as I could, and I've never regretted my decision." Didn't mean he hadn't suffered because of it. As the memories came back, Gabe cleared his throat. "If you want, you can leave too."

"Where would I go, and what would I do at my age?"

Shocker of all shockers, he sounded as if he was actually considering it. "You could start by coming to live with me, and we'll figure out what you'll do from there."

"After all we've been through, you'd let me stay with you? That's hard to believe."

"If you leave that life behind and go legit, I'll do everything I can to help you."

Silence filled the phone for a long moment. "I'll think about it. And I'll ask around to see who's spreading the rumors you heard."

"Thanks. Mary James mentioned it to me, and she said not to look further than my family."

"I don't know who she still talks to around here, but I'll find out and let you know."

Feeling better about his brother than he had in a long time, he ended the call and pocketed his phone. He joined El, but with Mary watching and listening to them from her open front door, he didn't speak until they got into the car.

The moment the doors closed, he shared his conversation with his brother. "I might be a fool to believe him, especially that he might want to change. Guess that says I've never given up on them."

El sat silently for a moment. "It's like our relationship with God. He's our father, and He never gives up on us no matter what we do. Once we turn away from our sins, He's right there where we left Him with open arms and ready to forgive us."

"Yeah. I guess you're right. I'm not sure I can open my arms just like that with Brad. I'll need to see some evidence that he's changed before I can welcome him that warmly."

"I get it. It's that whole trust thing that we both need to change. Even more difficult because of our time in law enforcement." She let out a long breath. "But maybe that's just an excuse. An excuse not to be like Jesus."

Gabe stared at Lucy's backpack. "Could be, but I don't think it is in a missing-child investigation. We wouldn't be doing our jobs if we didn't suspect everyone connected to her. And in this case, that would include my brother. Maybe my whole family."

~

In her cubicle, El sat behind her desk and relaxed her shoulders. She'd been trying to hold them up since before dawn to look like she knew what in the world she was doing. She'd been surrounded by people all day. People asking questions. People wanting answers. People looking to her to find this missing child and a killer loose in their community.

And now, after dropping Gabe off at his vehicle, she was blessedly alone in the detective bullpen. Sure, other areas of the office weren't closed for the night, but staff in her department had gone home to grab some sleep or were working in the field.

But was it a good thing to be alone? Or would she let difficult memories come back and raise doubts about her abilities? Bring back the guilt that had barely stayed at bay? Or would she trust God? Trust He knew what was best for her, and that no matter what happened in this investigation, His will would be done.

"Oh, man. So much easier said than done," she whispered to the dark and empty place.

She couldn't waste any more time thinking about what that might mean.

She signed into their department's system. Her first task. Check the electronic murder book to see if anyone on the team had logged any developments. Several calls had come in from the public claiming they'd seen something Friday night, but Ulrich had already investigated and ruled them out. Also listed were the names and addresses of people deputies had talked to, but nothing indicating a lead. The only other item noted was the boat cushion belonging to Howard Mason, and she needed to update the log on that.

Took her a couple of hours to record the day's incidents, but she finally finished and pushed her chair back to slide across the aisle. She entered the cubicle dedicated to their ViCAP terminal. Trying to summon positive thoughts, she entered her password.

The screen unfolded in front of her, and she typed in

search parameters, starting with a wide base. She would move to more specific factors if needed. She entered location details, starting with the state of Oregon. Next, she added *female strangulation* using the same two methods used to kill Kenna.

She sat back while the computer churned, looking for any matches.

The search returned four investigations in the past three years. More than she'd expected to locate. She printed a list, then added restraints, like specifically textured zip ties with a serrated or ribbed inner surface.

A circle churned on the screen as the system thought again, this time returning one investigation from seven years prior. Not in their area but in Bend, a city in central Oregon, more than a six-hour drive from Lost Lake, which made it less likely to be their suspect. But not impossible.

The telltale lobby door squeak sounded and footsteps approached. El swiveled to see Mina headed her way. She was still dressed in uniform minus her cap. Weariness clung to her like a wet blanket. She rested an arm on the corner of the cubicle. "Any luck?"

"Maybe. Four strangulation cases in our state matching some of our criteria and occurring in the past three years. I figured if I went back further than that, it might not be related to our investigation. But if none of these pan out, I can go back further."

"Did they use zip ties?"

"Not the ones I mentioned, but a Bend investigation, seven years ago, involves unusual zip ties for restraints. Problem is, the murder was so long ago, and it occurred in Bend. I'll dig into it, but I don't know how related it'll turn out to be."

"But it's a start."

El nodded. "I was about to print out the information to review at home tonight."

Mina's big brown eyes narrowed. "I appreciate you working all hours of the day, but go home and get at least a couple hours' sleep. You won't be any good to others if you don't take care of yourself."

El nodded but didn't commit to anything even though Mina was right. But how could she sleep when a child was counting on her to bring her home? They'd passed the critical twenty-four-hour period. If she didn't do her job, and they hit forty-eight hours, they would have to begin preparing for worst-case outcomes.

Memories of reaching that timeframe with Victoria swamped her mind. The change in attitude among the investigators and team. The parents. The news media. Sorrow. Disappointment. Gut-wrenching.

El curled her fingers into a tight fist. She wouldn't let that happen again. She just couldn't.

Mina pushed off the cubicle. "I'd like to schedule a team update at ten a.m. I'll contact everyone on the investigation."

"Could we push it a couple of hours? We should have forensic results from Sierra, and maybe I could get her to come to the meeting to update us."

"Let's say noon then. It's probably better anyway. It'll let anyone who wants to attend a worship service have time to go. I'll arrange box lunches for everyone."

Right, tomorrow was Sunday. El had lost track of days and didn't want to take time from the search to go to church, but starting the day with God would be the most important thing she could do. She'd make up the time by working all night.

"I'll text Sierra," she said. "See if she has time to meet with us. I'd also like Gabe to attend."

"Sierra giving us results is great, but Gabe attending a department meeting is highly irregular."

"Nothing regular about this situation. Not when a child is counting on every one of us." El took a breath, allowing her boss time to think this through. If she said no, El would be forced to remind her of the many ways she'd let the Lost Lake Locators help them in the past.

"If things go south here, my relationship with Nolan will have people calling my actions into question. But you're right. We need Gabe. He can be there."

"Great. I'll tell him. Can Jude attend, too?"

"Fine." Mina shifted her duty belt. "Home now. Sleep."

"You should do the same thing."

"Oh, don't worry. I just stopped in to check a few things." She squeezed El's shoulder. "Don't let me find you out here when I'm ready to leave."

El started texting Sierra to avoid making a promise she might not keep. Despite the time of day, Sierra responded promptly.

We'll have results by then. Glad to join you.

Excellent. We'll provide lunch.

See you then.

El's phone rang. Gabe's name flashed on the screen. He said he would call if the team wanted to meet with her tonight. She answered quickly.

"Any luck with ViCAP?" he asked.

"Maybe." She explained what she'd located. "I'm printing the files now to review when I get home."

"Want some help?"

Did she? She'd already spent way too much time with him today, and if he came to her place, the setting would be far more intimate. She would meet with him at the office, but Mina wouldn't be happy about El not taking her advice to go home.

"Please," he said, the desperation in his tone cutting into her. "I won't be able to sleep tonight anyway, and two heads are better than one."

She still wasn't ready to say yes.

"Besides," he continued, "won't you want to see Hayden's report on Mason?"

No fair. He knew she did. "Can't you email it to me?"

"I could, but I think it would be better if we reviewed it together." His words were a suggestion, but his tone was firm as concrete.

No way she'd convince him that working together wasn't a good idea, and there was no point in arguing. "Give me an hour then come over."

She ended the call, instantly regretting giving in. She would have to be more on guard than ever, because finding Lucy was far more important than thinking about a potential relationship with Gabe.

13

Gabe knocked on the front door of El's house, thinking it resembled her in many ways. She wasn't square and boxy like her small ranch, but she was no-nonsense. No frills. Basic, like the colors she wore even off duty. Not that he'd seen her off duty more than a couple of times. She certainly didn't dress flashy, but fit in well with her nondescript house, painted a simple green and white.

The door swung in. El stood before him, her hand on the knob and her hair hanging wet to her shoulders. Ah, they thought alike and she'd showered too. He'd not only needed to wash away the crime of the day, but to eliminate the cobwebs in his brain for a long night ahead.

She'd dressed in a rust-colored sweater and baggy jeans, her bare toes poking from under the hem. She looked far more casual than he'd ever seen. Soft and curvy and way more approachable. A good thing, and yet not a good thing.

He steeled his resolve to keep this evening all business and held out a pizza he'd grabbed on the way. "I didn't have time for dinner and figured you might not have either."

Flashing a generous smile that went straight to Gabe's heart, she leaned toward the box and inhaled deeply. "Bless you for thinking of that." Apparently unaware of her effect on him, she spun. "Follow me, and I'll get some plates and drinks."

She led him into the combined living-dining room. "Have a seat, and I'll be right back."

Before he could ask her about the many moving boxes in the room stacked to the ceiling, she went into the kitchen. He placed the pizza on her glossy white table and set the reports he carried next to it, then sat in one of the green velvet chairs. She'd decorated the place in oranges, greens, and mustards, totally different from her work wardrobe.

Surprising. Maybe he didn't know her as well as he thought he did. Nah. He knew the important things. Maybe not her decorating style, but the person deep inside. Still, what was up with the boxes? There were even more in the living area.

She rushed into the room, carrying green plates, napkins, and a pitcher of water along with two glasses.

"So, the moving boxes," he said and reached for the pizza box. "Coming or going?"

She quickly laid things out. "Neither."

"So, you just moved in then?"

"I've been here for almost a year but haven't had a chance to finish everything." She poured the water. "The job, you know? Takes up all my time, and I pretty much only sleep here."

"But you had time to paint, right?"

"Not me. Hired a painter to do the walls before I moved anything in. Figured if I didn't have time to finish the place the way I wanted, I'd at least have something that made it look like it was mine."

"I like your choice of colors."

"Thanks. I'm a big mid-century modern fan, and it took me a while to find a house that fit my aesthetics."

He opened the pizza box and pushed it closer to her. "I didn't know what kind you liked so I got pepperoni. Figured it's easy enough to remove if you didn't like it."

"I love pepperoni." She grabbed two large slices and put them on her plate, then dropped into the chair across from him. She chomped off a large bite and pointed at the documents he'd brought. She swallowed. "That Hayden's report?"

He'd also grabbed a few slices, one of which he'd taken a large bite from, and nodded. Before he could swallow and say anything, she reached for the report and started reading.

Her head popped up. "Mason was a retired police officer?"

"Twenty-five years on the force in Seaside Harbor."

Her eyes widened. "Your and Kenna's hometown," she said more to herself than to him. "Then Faye has a better chance of finding his fingerprints in the database and giving us a concrete ID."

"Unless his department chose not to enter officers' fingerprints in the database."

"Right," she said. "Do we have any indication he knew Kenna?"

Gabe polished off his first slice. "Hayden didn't find anything to connect them, but he'll keep after it."

"Living in the same city as Kenna means there could be a chance he knew her. If Faye gets a positive confirmation on his prints, I'll notify his daughter tomorrow. Hopefully, she can shed some light on any connection to Kenna." El bit into her pizza. She chewed and got a faraway look in her eyes. "It's odd that he lives near the ocean and owns a lake property."

Gabe tapped the report as he grabbed more pizza. "Wasn't meant to be his full-time residence. Just a fishing getaway he bought about a year ago. Maybe he liked freshwater fishing better than saltwater."

"A year ago, huh? He was probably the one who cleaned up the boathouse. I would've started with clearing out that house. Even if it was only a lake home, how could he possibly stay there?"

"You said it didn't seem like anyone lived there. Maybe he camped on the property instead."

"We didn't find any evidence of camping, but it's another question for his daughter." Her eyes lit on something in the report, and she snatched it from the table. "Says here Mason made a few substantial bank deposits this past year."

Gabe swallowed the last bite. "Hayden's searching deeper to locate the payment source."

"Could mean something to our investigation, or he could simply be getting a single payout for contract work or something like that."

"Again, more questions and zero answers." He turned his attention to eating and powered through several slices of pizza.

She picked at hers.

He got it. It was often hard to eat in a murder investigation. He didn't have that problem. Especially if it was a juicy burger. But now with a full stomach, his mind focused in on Kenna. He shoved his chair back to get up. He stretched his tired muscles in his back and shoulders, then walked the length of the room and back.

El stepped in front of him. "Looks like you should be home getting some shuteye."

"I might look exhausted. I am, but with Lucy still missing, I won't be able to sleep. I'll just lie there and think about the condition she might be in. I'd rather stay here and start looking at your ViCAP investigations."

"Okay, sure," she said. "But at least take a quick break with me."

"I don't—"

"This isn't up for discussion." She took his hand and tugged him toward her sofa.

He relented and followed her. She sat and drew him down next to her. He expected her to let go of his hand, but she took it in her other hand and turned it over to study. "I know we're putting our personal stuff with each other aside for now, but that doesn't mean I can't tell you how much I feel your pain. I didn't know Kenna, and I don't know Lucy, but I do know if you care this much about them, they're both special."

Her kindness was nearly his undoing, and he had to look at the ceiling and count to ten before he could speak. "I can't imagine life without my best friend, and I refuse to imagine it without her daughter."

"How do you feel about raising Lucy?"

"I haven't had much time to think about it, but I'm honored that Kenna wants me to do it. Scared to be a parent too, but terrified we won't find her, and I won't get a chance to try."

She tightened her fingers on his. "We'll find her."

"I don't know how you can say that with such confidence. You know even better than I do that each passing day means the outcome might not be as we would hope."

"Then we should pray about it again. Trust that God will bring her home to you."

"There's that pesky word *trust* again." He leaned his head back against the couch. "If anything, I'm heading the opposite direction. Seeing my family today didn't help."

She turned his head to face her. "Do you trust me?"

Her eyes were wide with expectation and maybe, just maybe, the same strong feelings he had for her. He'd never wanted to kiss a woman as much as he did right now. He cupped the side of her face.

She pressed her cheek against his hand. Her skin was

soft against his rough palm. But then she lifted her head, her eyes filled with questions. She hadn't forgotten about what she'd asked him.

He wanted to answer right away. To say, "Of course I trust you. No doubt." But he didn't know if he did. He just didn't know. And as long as he couldn't give her the answer she wanted, he couldn't kiss her and lead her on.

14

———

Gabe shoved to his feet in the bedroom's small sitting area and paced past his worn leather couch he'd owned since college. He'd been home for two hours, tried to get some sleep, but as predicted earlier, he'd failed.

He reviewed all the reports and data again until his eyes glazed over. Including the strangulation cases El had found. But as they'd concluded together, none of them were actually similar enough to warrant further investigation right now. He didn't give up, but no matter how many times he flipped through the pages, he couldn't make these investigations match theirs simply because he wanted—no, desperately needed—a lead.

A loud knock sounded on his door, and he spun to look at it. Living at a former inn, he knew no one came to his door in the middle of the night, other than one of his teammates who also lived in the building. "Come in."

The door opened, and Jude poked his head in. "Figured I'd still find you up. Want some company?"

"Yeah, sure."

Jude stepped into the room and quietly closed the door.

"Please tell me you're here to give me a lead?"

Jude's shoulders slumped. "No, nothing like that. I just finished putting up *missing* posters and fliers all over town and in Seaside Harbor and saw your lights on. Wanted to check in on you."

Gabe had passed his bad mood on to his buddy, who was only there to help. Not acceptable. "Hey, man. Your work could provide the lead we need. Sure, there's an Amber Alert out, but people get their information in many ways."

Jude settled on the couch as if he planned to stay for a while. "I want to do more, but we keep hitting roadblocks. I don't get it. We've never struck out this much in an investigation."

He didn't have to tell Gabe that. "Maybe the forensics is our key."

"We have—"

A high-pitched alert on Gabe's phone stopped him. "Hold that thought."

He tapped the alert for an email with the subject of *Developed Photos*. "Speaking of forensics, the text is from Sierra. Pictures from Mason's camera are in."

Jude jumped to his feet. "We can view them on the big screen in the conference room."

"Good idea," Gabe said, already on his way to the door.

Pumped now, they jogged the short distance down the hallway to the former dining room.

Jude dropped into the chair behind the computer assigned to this room. "Airdrop the files to the network, and I'll get them on the screen."

Gabe uploaded the pictures, not surprised to see his fingers trembling as he tapped his phone screen.

Jude's fingers clicked over the keyboard. "Got them."

Gabe straddled a chair at the head of the table, working

hard not to hold his breath as Jude put an array of pictures up.

"Say what?" Gabe leaned closer to the screen. "Why does Mason have pictures of Lucy's daycare?"

"No idea, but it could prove his murder's connected to Kenna's."

Gabe kept staring at the pictures. "Give me the next set of pictures."

The photos shifted to a black van parked across the street from the center.

"Van is black." Gabe squinted at the screen. "Could be the vehicle that ran Kenna into the ravine."

"I'll zoom in to see if there's any front-end damage."

The photo enlarged, and Gabe searched for any sign of damage. "I don't see anything, but the camera angle blocks the vehicle's right side. Could have damage that we can't see."

"Agreed." Jude looked up. "The photos are clean. No dates or markings to tell when they were taken."

"Maybe they were shot before the ravine crash," Gabe said. "Looks like a person in the driver seat. See if you can focus better on him."

Jude played with his mouse and computer keys, sharpening the picture. "There's a guy there, all right. Looks like he's holding binoculars."

Wishing they could make out more of the guy's face, Gabe rested his arms on the chair back and propped his chin on them. "You think this guy is watching the daycare and Mason was watching him?"

"Looks like it." Jude rubbed his jaw. "But why?"

"The six-million-dollar question." Gabe peered at the photo. "Can you make out the license plate?"

"First four characters. 974M."

"That's what I see too." Gabe grabbed his phone and called El.

"Gabe," she answered, far too alert to suggest she'd been asleep.

He put her on speaker. "You see the email from Sierra?"

"Just heading into the office to run the van's plates. We can only make out four digits, how about you?"

"Same, but they're enough to generate results that we should be able to narrow down through process of elimination."

Why in the world would she waste time driving to her office? "Can't you do it from your car?"

"More efficient to be at my desk to print out a list of potential candidates. Then I can use the computer to start narrowing them down."

"Can I help?"

"Sure."

The answer came far faster than Gabe had expected. "Jude is here with me. Mind if I bring him too?"

"That might be helpful."

"Be there in fifteen." Gabe ended the call and looked at his buddy. "You in?"

Jude grinned. "Thought you'd never ask."

Gabe shot to his feet. "On our way out, we need to get Hayden searching for a connection between Mason and the daycare."

"Agreed." Jude clicked the mouse a few times then stood. "I might be okay as the team's technical backup, but he can run circles around me."

Gabe didn't disagree with that statement. He charged for the door, beating Jude. Together they raced to Hayden's room. Gabe pounded on the door until his teammate answered.

Hayden rubbed his eyes. "Do either of you know what time it is?"

"Yeah. Two a.m.," Gabe replied. "Your usual prime work time."

"Why're you sleeping anyway?" Jude asked.

"Long day."

"Got enough in your tank to run one of your famous algorithms?" Gabe explained their discovery. "Not only run the van's plates but look for a connection between Mason and the daycare."

Hayden perked up. "I'll fill the tank up with some coffee and get started right away. It'd help me make connections if I had a list of kids enrolled in the daycare."

"No can do," Gabe said. "We tried earlier to get one from the director. She refused, claiming client privacy. I'll ask El to request a warrant, but don't hold out hope. It's not likely we have probable cause to get one. I'll also ask the director if she knows anything about the van."

Hayden stifled a yawn. "I'll let you know the minute I find anything."

Gabe bumped fists with his teammate and jogged out of the building, Jude hot on his heels. After they both settled in his truck, he pointed it toward the sheriff's office located in Seaside Harbor, the county seat.

Jude glanced across the pickup cab at Gabe. "I'm shocked El agreed to your help so easily when she was adamant about you staying out of the investigation at first."

Gabe could feel Jude's focus on him, but he didn't look at his buddy. He was fishing for information Gabe didn't want to share.

"Something change that you want to tell me about?" Jude asked.

Gabe should know his teammate would keep pressing him until he answered. Persistence was one of the hallmark traits of every member of the team and why they'd succeeded on all of their investigations so far. Even so, he answered, "Not really."

Jude shifted in the seat to face Gabe. "'Not really,' as in, something hasn't changed or you don't want to tell me about it?"

"Tell you about it."

"But you will, right? I mean, we don't keep secrets from teammates."

Gabe groaned. "Sometimes you guys are as determined as the local gossips."

"We *are* investigators after all." Jude chuckled. "But seriously, did you reach some sort of professional or personal truce?"

"Personal," Gabe admitted, since he couldn't lie. "You know we've got a thing for each other, right?"

Jude snorted. "Bro, the whole world knows."

Gabe looked at him and rolled his eyes. "Anyway, we agreed to pursue it, but tabled it until after we locate Lucy and find Kenna's killer."

"Congrats, man." He gave Gabe's shoulder a playful punch. "That's great news. I'm glad to see you both found a way to get past whatever was stopping you."

"Trust me." Gabe was shocked at the raw emotion in his own voice. "We didn't put that aside. If we don't figure it out, this could fail big time."

"What's your issue?"

No, Gabe wasn't going there. Thankfully, the sheriff's office was just ahead.

He glanced at Jude. "That's a story for another day. Now we need to focus on that van and what it means to finding Lucy before time runs out."

That put a silence in the cab for the duration of the drive. Gabe parked near El's vehicle and didn't wait for Jude.

He slipped off his seatbelt and rushed up to the front door, where he texted El to notify her they'd arrived. Jude joined him. He should probably be thankful a third party was with them. Their conversations were less likely to drift to personal issues.

She came to the door. His heart lurched

Calm down. This is a business meeting. Nothing more.

"Perfect timing," she said, pulling the door in and standing back. "My search returned nine vehicles, and you can help me narrow down the list."

Gabe shared a quick look with her, but he couldn't read her expression and he wouldn't ask. "After you, Jude."

"Whoa, who knew you could be polite at this time of day?" Jude laughed.

And they could count on him for comic relief, too. Gabe was in no mood for humor, but he appreciated his teammate's help and forced out a laugh.

"C'mon," she said to Gabe. "Get inside so I can make sure the door latches. Wouldn't want to violate security protocol."

He stepped past her, catching a whiff of her citrus-scented shampoo or lotion. She pulled the door closed with a reverberating click and followed the same process with the lobby door leading to their bullpen.

He trailed her scent through the open pen to her cubicle.

"The vehicle list." She handed a paper to each of them. "Let's split the list. Gabe, take the first three. Jude, the next three. And I've got the last ones. Search the internet for anything that connects them to Kenna, Mason, or the daycare. Feel free to sit at one of the desks, but I can't give you access to our computers or network. You'll have to use your phones."

Jude rubbed his hands together. "I guess that ends my diabolical plan to hack your network."

Gabe pinched the bridge of his nose.

"Okay," Jude said. "I get it. Lay off the jokes. Just trying to lighten things up."

"I appreciate it, but it's falling flat for me." Gabe looked at El. "Can you email this list to Hayden so he can work it too?"

"On it." She settled into her desk chair.

Gabe took that as a sign she was done talking with them. He nodded at Jude then moved to the nearest cubicle, where he made sure she was still in his line of sight. Jude slid down onto the floor and crossed his legs. He was often more at home on the floor. Probably frustrated his perfectly mannered mother.

Time ticked past as they got to work, Gabe feeling every second of the urgency to find Lucy. Instead of helping to focus him, he found it hard to concentrate.

You can do it. For Lucy. For Kenna.

He entered Mason's name, but it returned nothing. He typed in the second name and the third with the same parameters. No link connecting them.

He tried again, this time, entering all three potential vehicle owners with Kenna's name. Another bust. Then Bonnie's name. Lastly, he typed in each name with the daycare as the second factor. Nothing.

Pressure mounted. Weighing down on him like a two-ton vehicle pressing on his chest.

He glanced at El. She was concentrating on her screen. Jude, too.

They hadn't given up. He needed to keep at it. But doing what? Maybe simplify and enter only the individual owners' names for background information.

He typed in his first guy, Ronald Ryker. The search returned a long list of links, the first one from Multnomah County in the Portland metro area. The story was titled, "Ronald Ryker Charged With Assault With a Deadly Weapon." Gabe read the story then rolled his chair into the aisle.

"One of my guys might have a record. An internet story says Ronald Ryker was charged with assault with a deadly weapon. Allegedly attacked his wife when she planned to leave him."

"Could be related, I suppose, but what connection might he have to the daycare?" El's eyebrows knitted together. "It might help if we list why we think the van driver was watching the place."

Jude's narrowed gaze didn't look promising. "I'd rather not say this, but my first thought is some perv making plans to abduct a child."

Gabe really didn't want to consider that motive. Especially not as it related to Lucy. But Jude could very well be right.

El swiveled her chair. "Might be a father who doesn't have custody of his child, keeping an eye on him or her."

"From what Kenna told me, Lucy's father doesn't know about her, so that one doesn't fit our situation," Gabe said.

"Fair point." El stared at the floor then her head snapped up. "What if one of the other parents called the cops, and they were watching the place for the same reason Mason had eyes on it. Unfortunately, we don't have any idea what his reason was."

Jude uncrossed then recrossed his legs. "What if someone was watching the employees. Like a jealous spouse or boyfriend."

"Could be a private investigator for the same reason," Gabe said. "Or they could have any number of reasons to be keeping eyes either on the children or the staff."

"In that case, the van should probably come back with a business name instead of a person," El said. "But if it's a small company, the guy might be using his personal vehicle."

"Maybe the daycare owner hired this guy to watch the center for some reason," Jude said.

Gabe shoved his fingers into his hair, wanting to pull it out. "Too many possibilities."

"I'll pull up Ryker's record." El rolled back to her computer. "Only one Ronald Ryker in the state with an assault with a deadly weapon. He was charged in 2019. It's a Measure Eleven offense and the conviction carries a mandatory minimum sentence of seventy months in prison. No possibility of parole, probation, or early release."

Gabe quickly did the math in his head. "Means if he kept his nose clean in prison, he should've been out and could possibly be the man who killed Kenna."

"He's also a former Marine," she said. "He could've learned how to strangle someone in the service."

"Then we need to find Ryker like stat!" Gabe's phone rang, and he checked the screen before answering. "Hayden, you're on speaker."

"I ran all of your names in an algorithm of probabilities of the most likely to commit a crime." Either caffeinated or excited, his words tumbled over each other. "Ronald Ryker comes out on top due to a felony charge and military background. I know you'll want to talk to him. I'll email all of his details including his last known address, then do a deep dive on him."

"Thanks, man," Gabe said. "Anything on the other guys?"

"Lots of things, but nothing I think you'll find helpful. Still, I'll compile a summary and email that too." He ended the call.

Gabe looked at El and Jude. "Looks like our direction is clear. Once Hayden completes his deep dive, we go question Ryker."

"And while we're there," Jude said. "It would be good if we could get a DNA sample from him to compare to the fetal tissue result when it's available."

"It would be purely voluntary at this point," El said. "If he agrees, it could tell us he doesn't think he's the father."

Gabe met her gaze. "And no other evidence would be as clear-cut of a connection to Kenna than DNA."

15

Sunday morning, and El didn't want to sit around not when Faye had just texted to say the boathouse victim's fingerprints officially matched Howard Mason, the retired police officer. El wanted to race over to interview his daughter, Talia, but attending church with Gabe and his team was a priority for all of them. Then she agreed to a quick breakfast at the inn to fuel up for a day that promised to be packed with activity.

"This is *not* happening." Hayden pounded the table where he'd been eating and working on his deep dive. "Ryker moved to Phoenix to live with his mother when he got out of prison eighteen months ago."

Gabe frowned at his teammate. "Doesn't mean he couldn't have been the person watching the center."

Hayden let out a long breath. "Actually, it does. He re-offended within a week of his release and is a guest of the Arizona State Prison Complex. His black van is now registered to his mother in Arizona."

"We can strike him off as the person watching the daycare then, and as a suspect in either of our murders," El recapped, though she hated to say it. "But I'll have Ulrich follow up with the mother to be sure his van is physically at her residence and not left here with a friend who might be driving it."

Gabe shoved his chair back hard enough for it to hit the wall, then turned his attention to El. "You ready to go? We might no longer be interviewing Ryker, but hopefully Talia Mason will give us something to go on."

"Ready." El put her dishes in a bin on the food table to be washed. "Thank you for breakfast, Reece. It was wonderful."

"You don't have to be working an investigation to come by." Reece smiled.

El glanced at Gabe to get his reaction, but he was scowling as he started for the door. She couldn't determine if his mood was due to striking out on Ryker or because she'd been invited to come by for breakfast at any time.

Nor did she ask him on the drive to Talia's house. He buried his face in his phone, doing what, she had no idea. He only put it away when she pulled to the curb in front of Talia's two-story home, painted a very deep gray and boasting weird contemporary angles. They took the sidewalk up to the door in silence, too.

Gabe pounded as if his life depended on it.

A woman answered right away. "What can I do for you?"

El would never pick this woman out in a crowd to be Howard Mason's daughter. She looked nothing like her father. Petite, blond, and blue-eyed, while he was burly, brunette, and had brown eyes.

El identified herself and handed her a business card. "Are you Talia Vogel, and is your father Howard Mason?"

"Yes." She took the card, but not without hesitating.

"I'm sorry for bothering you on Sunday morning, but could we come in for a moment?"

Talia cast a suspicious look in their direction. "Is it about my dad? Is that why you asked about him?"

"It's best if we come in and talk about it." El took a step to enter, basically forcing Talia to move back.

She did, then escorted them to her light-filled family room with contemporary furnishings that fit the exterior of the house.

El and Gabe took seats on the sleek leather sofa, and she broke the difficult news to Talia.

Talia gasped and stared wide-eyed. She started sobbing and tears flowed freely. She took a cleansing breath. "Tell me it's not true."

"I'm sorry, but it is," El said to this woman whose life she'd changed by this visit. "Fingerprints confirm his ID."

Talia swiped at her tears with the back of her hand. "I can hardly believe this happened now when he'd retired. I'd prepared to hear this while he was on the job but not now. No, not now. My father murdered."

"I'm very sorry, Mrs. Vogel." El got out a clean tissue from her pocket and handed it to her. "Do you have any idea who would want to harm him?"

"Call me Talia." She sniffled hard and gave her nose a thorough wipe with the tissue and seemed to find some internal strength and raised her shoulders. "He was a police officer for twenty-five years. I would imagine there are any number of people who might want to harm him."

"How about since he retired?" Gabe asked. "How long has that been, and is there anyone who he wasn't getting along with?"

"He quit working about a year ago. He wasn't Mr. Personality with an easy-going, fun-loving demeanor, and I suspect he's had altercations with people since then. No offense, but he had that sharp, observant, assessing person-ality cops have. Not one to trust easily."

"No offense taken." How could El be offended when many law enforcement officers fit that profile? Herself and Gabe included.

"We've discovered he'd taken photos of a black van outside of Little Pines Daycare," Gabe said, thankfully moving them forward. "Do you have any idea why he might be taking pictures there?"

"Yes, but..." Her gaze suddenly went wild, roaming the room as she shook her head. "You don't think this has to do with what happened to him, do you?"

"We don't know," El said. "But it's a line of inquiry."

Talia clasped her hands together in her lap and took several deep breaths, seeming to find that internal strength again. Strength El suspected came from being the daughter of a police officer who could die in the line of duty at any time. "His death might be my fault. My daughter, Natalie, attends the Little Pines Daycare."

The connection between Mason and Kenna, but...

Gabe slid forward on the sofa and locked his focus on Talia. "Please tell us how you think her attendance there could be related to your father's death."

"About two weeks ago, a black van was parked across the road. A man inside was watching the daycare." Talia shivered. "I brought it to the director's attention. She agreed it was suspicious, but she said there was nothing she could do about it because the guy wasn't doing anything illegal and wasn't on their property."

"What did you do?" El asked.

"Two days later, when I arrived at the daycare, he was still there. So I turned around and went home with Natalie. Then I called Dad and asked him if he would keep an eye on the guy to see what was going on." She twisted her hands in her lap. "I vowed to keep my sweet little girl home until that van was no longer there. I mean, Natalie might've loved Kenna as her teacher so much that she begged to go to school every morning, but I wouldn't risk Natalie's life."

The second connection. Maybe they were finally getting somewhere.

Eyes alive with interest, Gabe shifted even closer. "Kenna James was Natalie's teacher?"

"Yes, and her daughter Lucy's in Natalie's daycare class. They're great friends."

Not ready to break the news of Kenna's murder yet, El asked, "What did your father find?"

"Not much. The first day, he got the van's plate number and tried to get his former partner to run it for him. But he was on vacation, and none of the other officers were willing to stick their necks out for him. So he approached the driver to ask what he was doing. The guy went off on him. Told him to mind his own business and leave him alone or else. My dad said he thought the guy was carrying so he backed off and returned to his truck but stayed that day until the man left. He tailed him for a short time but lost him in traffic."

"Did it sound like he might've been mad enough to kill your dad?" El asked.

Talia's eyes widened. "I suppose he could've been, especially with the way he went off on my dad."

"What happened the next day?"

"Dad took a bunch of pictures of the van that he would develop in his darkroom. He also said when the director arrived that morning, the guy jumped out and confronted her. They were far enough away that he couldn't hear the whole conversation, but he did hear him say at the end, 'We need her to come through for us, and you're gonna make sure that happens.'"

El shared a look with Gabe. His expression said the

same thing she was thinking. What in the world did that mean?

No way to tell at the moment, so El turned her attention back to Talia. "What happened after that?"

"Dad went back the next day. The van wasn't there. He stayed all day, and the van never showed up. Then he checked on and off for the next few days. Still didn't see the guy. So we figured it was safe for Natalie to go there and Dad stopped watching the place."

"Did he ever get his former partner to run the plates for him?"

Talia shook her head. "He took off for his lake house and never mentioned it. The van guy never showed up again so I figured it wasn't important anymore."

"Have you talked to him since he went to the lake house?"

"He called me Tuesday morning to say he had more work to do there than he thought and would be staying for a couple more days." She got her phone out and flipped through the screens. "He called at eight minutes after ten."

"And you didn't hear from him after that?"

She shook her head and set her phone on her lap. "There's no cell service at the cabin. He has to climb a nearby hill to get a signal. Means he rarely called or texted. If I needed to get a hold of him, I would have to call or text and wait for him to check his phone."

El added the time to her notebook. "Did he ever take a laptop or tablet with him to the cabin?"

"No. No way. The cabin was for fishing and only fishing. He has a tablet basically for checking email and playing games. He would never let email interrupt his life and wouldn't take the tablet to his sanctuary."

Her story fit with what Hayden had located.

El prepared herself for the bomb she was about to drop.

"I'm sorry to have to tell you, but you mentioned Kenna James. Her body was found in Lost Lake. She'd been strangled."

"Oh, oh..." Talia raised her hand to cover her mouth. "Do you think her death is connected to my father's?"

"Uncertain at this time," El said. "With his connection to the Little Pines Daycare, I'm beginning to."

"When that man was threatening the director, do you think he might've meant to get Kenna to come through for them?" Talia asked. "But she didn't, and they killed her?"

"It's possible, but this is the first I'm hearing of her knowing you and your father, so I haven't had a chance to even consider it."

"Poor little Lucy." Talia twisted the tissue in her hand. "How is she taking this?"

"We don't know," Gabe said. "She's missing."

"Missing?" Her mouth parted. "But what happened?"

"We believe she either wandered off from the lake or someone took her."

"Oh my, that's not good. Not good at all. The poor sweetie." Talia ran a hand over her face. "I can't believe this. It might be connected to my dad, all because I asked him to look into that van."

"Don't blame yourself for any of this," El said. "The person who took your father's life is the one responsible."

"Can you tell us more about his lake house?" Gabe asked. "Have you ever been there?"

"Yes." She shuddered. "I refused to go back until he got that place cleaned out, but now... I should've taken the opportunity to spend time with him."

"But he was willing to stay there in the condition it was in?"

"No. He always brought his travel trailer with him when he planned to spend the night."

"If he's been staying there for some time, any idea why his trailer wasn't there?"

"No, that's odd. If it isn't, I don't know where it would be." Talia nibbled on her lip. "All I know is I'm sure he wouldn't stay in that house."

"Did he have a dog?" Gabe asked.

"Yes, a little beagle called Spotty. Got him when he retired, and he went everywhere with Dad." She gave a wavering smile. "They were so cute together."

A beagle was a fitting description for the dog that had died in the house, and his death fitting for a more brutal killer. El's gut churned with nausea.

Talia flashed her gaze to El. "Don't tell me something happened to Spotty, too."

"I'm sorry, but one of the stacks of televisions fell on him." El hated to be the bearer of bad news again. "He didn't make it."

Talia winced. "Oh, the poor sweet thing. Natalie will miss her Pop Pop, but she'll miss Spotty just as much." She clutched her arms around her stomach. "What in the world is going on? Are we in danger, too?"

"Highly doubtful. But until we can learn more about the man in the van, I can't give you one hundred percent assurance." El wasn't about to tell her how they'd struck out with Ryker and were back at square one. "Did your father carry a Zippo lighter?"

"Dad? No, he didn't want to get lung cancer and was anti-smoking all the way. Besides, he said he only had room in his pocket for the knife his granddad gave him. It really wasn't much more than a penknife but he carried it all the same. If you find it in his pocket, can you make sure I get it?"

El nodded, but couldn't agree to hand it to her. Especially when her father had been stabbed, and they didn't have the murder weapon. "Once the investigation is over. Do you know if your father loaned his boat to someone?"

She inhaled deeply. "Not that I know of, but he really didn't talk about his lake property much. Ever since I was a little girl, he always hoped I would love going fishing with him, but honestly, it bored me to death." She looked up at the ceiling. "Now I wish I'd cared about what he wanted and spent as much time with him as possible."

An emotion that so many people who lost a loved one expressed, but one that El wouldn't linger on.

"I'd like to have a look around your father's place. Do you have a key you could give me?"

"I'll get it for you." Talia hurried away.

For the first time, El noticed the sound of Natalie playing in the other room. "I'm guessing it won't be easy to tell her daughter about her grandfather."

"Letting someone know a loved one died is never easy, is it?"

"The hardest part of the job."

As if reinforcing the difficulty of learning a loved one had died, Talia returned to the room, tears once again rolling down her cheeks. She held out the key, but didn't speak, and grabbed her tissue from her pocket to dab at her eyes.

"Is there anyone we can call to be with you?" El asked.

Talia shook her head. "I just texted my husband to come home. He'll help me tell Natalie. Since Dad retired, they got to spend a lot of time together. Maybe he hoped she would go fishing with him."

"Thank you for your time, Talia. You have my card. Call me if you think of anything that might help."

"I'll see you to the door."

She rushed ahead and had the door open and waiting by

the time they reached it as if by getting rid of them, the news they'd brought would go with them.

"Oh, before I go." El stalled Gabe's progress at the front door. "When you take your daughter to daycare, it would be great if you asked other parents if they recognized the man in the van."

Talia lifted her hand from the doorknob to wipe away tears. "Of course, but I don't know when we'll be going back. Not with funeral arrangements and things to settle."

"I understand, but if you learn anything, you have my card." El didn't linger, but went straight to her vehicle, before she let her emotions for this family get to her.

Gabe followed and slid in. "You look uneasy."

She glanced at her watch. "We don't have enough time to search Mason's place before the update meeting. But a sick feeling in my gut says when we get there, we'll find something his daughter won't like and neither will we."

16

Gabe wanted to punch the wall outside the meeting room. He wasn't eager to go inside and tell them they hadn't come up with anything helpful this morning, but he had to. Even if El had gone to the restroom and wasn't at his side.

He stepped inside the large conference room and searched for an open spot at the table. Mina sat at the head, Ulrich on her left, her admin on her right, and Jude next to her, his hands on the table, twiddling his thumbs. Deputy Ewing and Massey from the crime scene had taken places at the other end of the table. Everyone had helped themselves to the box lunches and water bottles on a long table at the head of the room.

El marched in. "Grab some lunch before we sit."

He followed her to the table, where they both picked up a box and a drink. She took the open seat by Ulrich and pointed for Gabe to take the chair next to her. He'd planned to sit by Jude, but leaned across the table and bumped fists with him, and then sat next to Deputy Ewing on his other side.

"Hey, man," Gabe greeted, and nodded at Massey.

He gave him an agreeable nod while chewing. Gabe had

expected them not to like an outsider, a PI nonetheless, attending a law enforcement meeting, but maybe it didn't bother them.

Sierra breezed into the room. She held a tall cup of coffee in one hand and a laptop along with papers under her arm. "Sorry I'm late. All-nighter, and I had to stop for coffee."

"No worries," Mina said. "We appreciate your willingness to come in person to update us. There are sandwiches on the table if you'd like one."

"Thank you, but I plan to have lunch during an update meeting with my staff." Sierra sat next to Mina's assistant and set her items on the table.

Mina stood and introduced everyone. "Sierra still has a big job ahead of her so we'll start with her update."

"Oh, thanks." She took a long pull on her coffee then passed a report down the table. "This investigation has an unusually large number of evidence pieces, and it's growing. So I've created a list of the items we're processing."

Mina glanced at the report, then looked up. "This is most helpful, thank you."

Sierra gave a sharp nod. "In an effort to save time, I'll power through this list and review the evidence by the crime scene where we located it. If you have any questions, please stop me."

"Don't worry." Jude picked up a sandwich thickly stuffed with roast beef. "I don't think anyone in this room is too shy to interrupt."

She chuckled. "I know you're all dying to get the information from Kenna's phone so I'll begin there. The good news is our electronics expert is confident he can retrieve the data. Bad news, the phone has to dry out. Could take seventy-two hours or so before he can access it."

"You're right," Mina said. "We do want that information,

like yesterday. What about fingerprints or DNA on the phone?"

"We only recovered one person's fingerprints. Kenna's."

"How do you know they're hers?" Deputy Massey asked.

"All daycare workers in a licensed facility in Oregon are required to be printed. We also recovered DNA from the phone, but it would only be an assumption to say it's hers." She picked up her coffee cup again and drank as if her life depended on it.

She cleared her throat. "Now to other DNA. Most of the samples we recovered will complete at around four o'clock today. That would be for items where the samples were easy to extract DNA. For samples where it's more difficult to extract, we'll have results tomorrow at the soonest."

Deputy Ewing groaned.

"Hey, don't knock it," Ulrich said. "It'd take the state lab weeks to finish, and we all should be thankful for Sierra taking on our investigation."

Red crept up Sierra's neck. "No thanks needed. Fortunately, we have Lucy's DNA from her ID kit for comparison. Any sample with a Mitochondrial DNA match to Lucy would mean the sample very likely belongs to Kenna. We're also testing the adult toothbrush from Kenna's suitcase found in her van."

She picked up a copy of the report she'd handed out. "On to fingerprints. In addition to Kenna's from the daycare, we have Lucy's, thanks to her ID kit."

Gabe put down his turkey sandwich and leaned forward. "Were you able to match any to them yet?"

"Yes, several. The only prints on the unicorn and bracelet belonged to Lucy. The shoes held prints from three people. Lucy, Kenna, and unidentified, i.e., not in the databases. The car seat had four unique prints for Lucy, Kenna, unidentified again, and the third one matched your prints, Gabe.”

“That makes sense. I’ve moved her seat plenty of times and as a former state trooper, my prints are in the system.

Sierra nodded. “We’ve also recovered DNA for these items along with the pink sweatshirt found in the car seat. Processing will complete today for all of them. None of the blood evidence will be ready until tomorrow. In the meantime, we ran blood types so we can compare to Lucy’s ID kit. For reference, Lucy is type O. The blood on the car seat is type A.”

Jude dropped his bag of potato chips on the table and brushed off his fingers. “If I remember my high school biology, type A blood is compatible with type O and the blood could belong to Kenna, as it means Kenna could be Lucy’s mother.”

“Correct,” Sierra said. “All depends on the father’s blood type. Blood found on Kenna’s shirt and hand was type B, likely her killer’s.”

“But not Lucy’s father,” Jude said. “Parents with types B and O could not have a child with type O unless the father carried an O gene as well.”

“Correct again.” Sierra smiled at Jude.

He leaned back and preened. “All in all, the typing is something to go on now, but we still have to wait for the DNA for any certainty.”

“That’s right, but it might give the investigation a headstart,” Sierra said. “Next, the footprints cast on the beach. The small footprint matched the brand for the recovered child’s shoe, but the soles didn’t have a distinctive wear impression and could belong to another child with the same brand of shoes. The larger footprints are a men’s size eleven athletic shoe. Our staff is searching national shoe databases to find a match to the sole to try to identify the shoe's brand and model."

"But it won't help if you don't have a suspect to match it to, right?" Massey asked.

She smiled at the young deputy. "Very important point to keep in mind. We also lifted fingerprints and DNA from the boat cushion—uncommon underwater, but conditions helped. DNA results will take longer."

She paused for a moment as if expecting more questions, then continued. "The dock is public, and we recovered an overabundance of fingerprints. We had to prioritize resources and delay the dock prints, but a dedicated tech will be assigned to them tomorrow."

El wrapped up the remaining half of her sandwich. "It's surprising you found techs to work on the weekend at all."

"We have amazing staff." Sierra smiled. "One last thing about the dock. We also located a small sample of type O blood by a protruding nail. Likely a minor prick, not a significant loss. But it's enough for DNA and we typed it as O, a potential match to Lucy. If DNA matches too, we could confirm as soon as tomorrow that not only were her shoe and bracelet on scene, but she was too."

Mina let out a slow breath. "With the bracelet and shoe present, we're working with the assumption she was there, but it would be good to have official confirmation."

Sierra nodded then glanced around the room. "That's the end of the beach evidence. Any other questions before I move on?"

"Pretty straightforward," Mina said.

"Okay, then on to the ravine. The screwdriver is first on your list. Multiple latent prints from the same person belonged to Kenna. We found two distinct DNA samples, both of which will complete tomorrow. We typed the blood from the tip, and it's type B, likely the attacker."

She took another draw of the coffee. "Moving on to the van. My team used the FBI's automotive paint database to narrow down the paint sample to a Ford Transit 350 Passenger Van."

"Perfect," Gabe said. "Having the make and model should help us narrow down suspect vehicles. If we hadn't already discovered Ryker was incarcerated, he owns a Chevy Express, so this information rules him out."

El slipped her chocolate chip cookie out of its sleeve. "Rules out any of his buddies who might be driving it too."

"Forensic evidence can both help and hinder," Sierra said. "Next is the blood near Kenna's van and on her hand. Unfortunately, we don't have the DNA yet, but the blood is type B."

"It's not Lucy's." Relief rushed through Gabe like an out-of-control river in a flash flood. At least she wasn't out there bleeding or badly injured. One less worry.

El shared a relieved look with him then let out a long breath and slumped in her chair as if deflating. Gabe completely understood. He wanted to do the same thing, but he hung in there for her sake.

Sierra looked around the attendees. "That's all we've recovered so far at that scene. On to Howard Mason's property. You already have the camera photos. Let me know if you need Nick to enhance them. The Zippo lighter had unknown prints, and the prints don't match the coffee mug from the house. However, those matched former police officer, Howard Mason as we expected."

El sat forward, her gaze fixed on Sierra. "The lighter might not be his and could belong to the killer."

"I hate to burst your bubble," Jude said. "But the water churned up by a boat's wake could've carried the lighter into the boathouse, and it could belong to anyone."

"You're right. That's a possibility we have to keep in

mind." Gabe usually appreciated Jude's take on things, but in this case, he hoped his buddy was wrong.

"We've only started processing his property, and more may turn up," Sierra said. "DNA in progress for the mug should return today. Lighter tomorrow or later. Now, the boat. We lifted prints for Kenna and Lucy, and several unknown prints. We also recovered a good quantity of type B blood. DNA is running for that and samples from several additional areas. We'll have it to you tomorrow."

"Confirms Kenna and Lucy were in the boat," Gabe said. "And gives credence to our theory that the boat was used to transport them from the ravine."

El met his gaze. "And if you believe the type B blood we recovered is the killers, then that likely puts him in the boat."

Gabe shuddered at the thought of Kenna and Lucy in a small boat with the killer, but had to let it go.

"Next are items found at Kenna's place. The pregnancy test held only one clear-cut set of fingerprints that belonged to Kenna, but we recovered multiple DNA samples and should have the results after four. The news on the jacket isn't as good. Despite several hairs on the fabric, it's proving to be difficult. We need hair with follicles attached to determine DNA. None of the samples qualify. We'll continue to process the jacket for touch DNA, but a date for those results is unknown. We'll also check for prints, though fabric doesn't yield as many liftable prints."

"You haven't mentioned the fetal tissue sample," El said, her expression tight.

Sierra took a long breath. "DNA is very straightforward in this situation. Hopefully, we'll have results by four o'clock today. The blood is type O."

"Does this help us figure out the blood type for the father?" Gabe asked.

"Unfortunately, no."

Gabe gritted his teeth. He'd hoped to find out the father's identity by now, but they would have to wait for the DNA results.

Sierra closed her computer. "Of course, once we complete the work, you'll receive a detailed written report, but that's all I have for now."

No one spoke up.

Mina stood and held out her hand. "Thank you, Sierra, for the thorough update and for handling our evidence so quickly. I know you have a lot of priorities."

"Nothing more important than finding this little girl."

The others mumbled their thanks, including Gabe, but his thoughts soon turned to what they'd learned today that could help them other than that Lucy hadn't suffered a life-threatening injury at the crime scene. That was news for sure. Big news. News that encouraged him.

But one fact hadn't changed. They still had no idea where she was being held captive, and with every lead that didn't pan out, time in which to find her alive ticked by faster and faster.

17

———

El stood and stretched. She appreciated Sierra's information, but it really didn't move them any closer to the truth. However, once the DNA came in, the game could change in a moment.

Gabe had gotten a cup of coffee from the table and returned to his chair. He had a pensive look on his face the whole time, so she didn't bother him. She followed his lead and grabbed a cup after Jude finished pouring his.

"Hey, sorry if I seemed rude when I made my comment about the lighter."

She shook her head. "You were only speaking the truth."

"Sometimes when I speak the truth, I speak it a little hard and it gets me in trouble." He grinned.

"No trouble here. I appreciate your help."

He glanced at Gabe. "You've spent a lot of time with Gabe. He says he's doing okay, but is he really?"

"He's hanging in there. Doing the best he can with Lucy missing and his best friend murdered."

"He really loved Kenna. We always wondered why they didn't get together, but I guess they never had that kind of interest in each other."

"It's sad that he's never found someone."

"That's the way things go. But he's got you now."

She couldn't keep her mouth from hanging open. Had Gabe been talking to others about her? Or had she been so obvious about her feelings for him? Did everybody in this room see it? She thought she'd been hiding them. Maybe not, and she needed to do a better job to keep Mina from yanking her off this investigation.

"Don't look so horrified," Jude said. "We all think you're great, and he'll be blessed to have you as a partner."

Heat rushed up El's face, and she didn't know what to say.

Thankfully, Mina gave a solid clap of her hands. "Let's get back to it."

Jude squeezed her arm and gave her a soft smile, a side of him she'd never seen before. She'd been told it was there, but now she knew for sure.

"You're a good friend, Jude. He's blessed to have you, too."

They shared sincere smiles, then headed back to their seats.

Gabe's gaze tracked her all the way back. "What was with the intense conversation with Jude?"

"I'll tell you later when we have more time."

Mina stopped at the head of the table. "I assume you've all read last night's latest reports and are up-to-date on our findings."

Gabe looked around and everyone was nodding.

"Good, thank you for keeping current when you're already working such long days." She turned her attention to El. "Go ahead and start with your morning interview."

"We talked to Talia Vogel, Mason's daughter." El swallowed to erase residual feelings for the family. "She last spoke to her father on Tuesday just after ten a.m. which fits with our timeline of his murder. She also explained why her father was taking pictures of the daycare center." El gave a brief summation of the story Talia had told them.

"So this may or may not be related to our investigation," Mina said.

El nodded. "We need to get someone out to the center to question staff and parents about the van, but thinking they might be more open with Ms. Vogel, I've asked her to talk with them too. Problem is, she might not be going back to the center for a while."

"I'll assign someone," Mina said.

El waited for any questions, but when no one spoke, she moved on. "She also confirmed the deceased dog probably belonged to her father. The vet I contacted completed the dog's necropsy right away. As suspected, he died from crush injuries, and he's been dead for several days."

"Doesn't mean Mason's killer tipped the TVs onto the dog," Jude said.

"Correct. Unless the killer admits to doing it, we may never know if it was on purpose or an accident." El shifted in her chair. "Also, you all saw the results of my ViCAP search. Now that we have the make and model for the van that ran Kenna off the road, we can review this list to see if any of them are even applicable anymore."

"I'd be glad to do that," Ulrich volunteered.

"You got it," El said. "Another point Ms. Vogel made was that her father's death could be related to his time as a police officer. Someone who had a grudge finally settled the score."

"She could be right," Mina said. "But we could be talking a large group of people with a grudge against him. If we go down that route it could take us into a deep rabbit hole, and we don't have the resources for that right now."

"I agree," Gabe said. "I could task my team with that, but they're still working on more promising leads."

"Then we put it on hold for now." Mina shifted to look at Gabe. "Any update on the actual zip ties?"

Jude looked at Gabe. "I got this. We worked with Dr. Briggs to match pictures of Kenna's wrist and ankle bruises to zip ties that could've been used. We've tracked them down to one manufacturer."

He reached into his pocket and pulled out a black plastic tie. He slid it down the table to Mina. "Take a look. Specialty nylon cable tie with the exact pattern to Kenna's bruising. Mid-length. Not the cheap kind either. Industrial grade."

Mina frowned. "Meaning?"

"Meaning," Jude said, "whoever used the tie didn't grab it out of a kitchen drawer or buy it at a big box store. This came from a worksite. Probably stolen. Or we're looking at someone who knew what they were doing and has his own supply."

"Can these be bought in retail stores in the area?" Ulrich asked.

Jude shook his head. "They're military-grade serrated ties designed for heavy-duty industrial or military use and can only be purchased by companies or the government."

"Then how did you get one?" Massey asked him.

"We contacted the manufacturer, who put us in touch with a local worksite using them, and they were more than happy to give us a few."

Ewing perked up. "So if our killer didn't work on a construction site or wasn't in the military, this murder would have to be premeditated to have the time to obtain these ties."

"I don't know," Massey said. "Could be an employee of the manufacturer."

"Could be, but the company is out of Massachusetts, so probably not as likely."

Mina turned the sample over in her hands. "Good work. This, along with the army jacket, could point to a suspect in the military or former military."

"*CHAMP* on the lighter could be a military call sign or nickname, too," Ulrich said.

Mina looked at Gabe. "Any luck on finding a connection for the engraving to our suspects?"

"Not yet," Gabe said. "Hayden still has several algorithms running. So far nothing, but he said to be patient as they could still return results."

"This murder confirms the theory I shared yesterday," Jude said. "This is more than a domestic killer. Domestics don't usually create additional victims the next day."

"Hold up," Massey said. "What exactly do you mean by domestic killer?"

"Someone who commits homicide within their immediate household. Or a person they share an intimate relationship with, like a domestic partner, or boyfriend or girlfriend."

Massey shook his head. "As a rookie, I have a lot to learn."

Jude looked around the group as if waiting for additional questions. No one spoke, and he continued. "Mason likely knew something, or he was involved with Kenna's murder and had become a liability. Now the offender is trying to control the fallout, not just commit a single act of violence."

"I, for one, am buying into this." Gabe gave his teammate a look of approval. "What else can you tell us?"

"We've seen the killer is capable and organized, but something about this situation is now forcing him to act again quickly. He doesn't like it. The strangulation was controlled and personal in Kenna's murder. The body disposal was planned, but the second murder? Stabbed, leaving a knife impression that can be traced? Possibly rushed. That doesn't match and looking for a pattern with him might be impossible."

"So we have a killer on the loose who is unpredictable and highly motivated to avoid capture," Mina stated. "And he could have a small child in tow."

"Exactly," Jude said. "And I hate to say this, but at some point, she could become a liability he isn't willing to entertain keeping alive any longer."

The room became absolutely quiet and no one looked like they were going to speak.

Gabe couldn't stand the quiet. What Jude had said was probably the truth, but Gabe couldn't sit there and dwell on it. He had to move on. "Hayden's other algorithms are for individual background information on Kenna, Mason, and his daughter. So far, Kenna is who she says she is. No surprises."

"Also, now that we know Mason had a phone," Jude said, "Hayden will try to get the call log."

El looked at her boss. "I'll give you his number. Can you make a formal warrant request?"

Mina nodded. "Anything else on Mason? Like social media?"

"Hayden confirmed Mason didn't have any social media accounts," Gabe said. "Not unusual for a former police officer. He didn't locate accounts for other electronic devices either."

"His daughter said he had a tablet," El said. "But he rarely used it except for email."

Jude nodded. "We've been checking library computers, and we canvassed the neighbors. Libraries were a dead end, as were neighbors. Our dog walker is the only one who even knew Mason's name. One did say they saw him pull out of his driveway towing a travel trailer a few days before he died, but they weren't certain of the day."

"That's right," El said. "His daughter confirmed he usually stayed in that trailer at the lake house, but as you know, it wasn't there."

"Why?" Mina asked. "Did the killer take it? Did Mason move it somewhere, and if so, why? Could be very important questions to answer."

"Other than putting out an alert on it, which I did after the interview," El said, "I'm open to suggestions on how we could find it."

"Notify the public," Ulrich said. "Put up fliers. Contact the newspapers, etcetera."

Mina looked at her admin. "Can you handle that?"

The petite young woman smiled. "I'll get right on it after the meeting."

Jude cleared his throat. "One last thing I want to update everyone on. Hayden worked on the potential boyfriend picture found at Kenna's house yesterday. There isn't enough of a face for his facial recognition tools to work. He did say Nick at the Veritas Center had better equipment and might produce a different result, so he forwarded the information to Nick."

Mina stood. "We don't have any strong leads, and many of our early leads have dried up. Could be time to go back to square one. Rebuild a minute-by-minute timeline. Since people often remember new details, reinterview family, friends, witnesses. Look for inconsistencies in statements that no longer line up. Reassess whether the case is truly an abduction or something else."

"I can get started on that," Ulrich said.

Mina gave a thumbs up to her detective then peered at Jude. "Could you work on a behavioral and psychological profile of Kenna James, including an analysis of her habits, routines, online behavior? Look at possible offender types, opportunistic versus targeted for this crime."

One swift nod was all Jude offered. Everyone fell silent and continued to stare at him.

El cleared her throat. "Our biggest win right now would be to get those phone records we've requested. Tracking people's last phone calls or texts can provide major leads."

"Then let's get out of here, people, and get this done." Mina looked around the table, pausing longer on Jude than the others.

El had no idea what was going on with him, but he must've had a bad experience in the past and didn't want to put himself out there with a detailed profile. She wanted to respect that. Especially since she was going through the same thing, but Lucy needed him, and as the lead investigative officer, El would have to find a way to get him to come through for the sweet little girl.

The drive to Howard Mason's place had been quiet and introspective for the first ten minutes, but Gabe had a bunch of questions he wanted to ask El before they arrived. No time like the present.

He glanced at her, posture perfect as she sat behind the wheel. "What do you think the guy in the black van meant when he said, 'We need her to come through for us, and you're gonna make sure that happens'?"

"We can speculate all we want, but the statement's too vague to draw a solid conclusion." Her answer had come quickly, as if she'd thought it through already.

Gabe wasn't ready to let it go. "You're probably right, but let's say this is related to Kenna. That she's the one who had to come through for him. What could he even be talking about?"

She flashed a quick look at him. "I know you don't want to believe the rumors of her involvement in drug trafficking, but if she was involved, he could've been alluding to that."

She was right. He didn't want to think that. "If that's true, and I'm saying it's doubtful, the daycare director had to be involved too or she would've reported him to us."

"Maybe not. It wouldn't be unheard of to funnel drugs through a daycare with or without the director's buy-in. It's a place people trust and one that sees constant movement of adults, their bags, and vehicles. Makes it a very effective front or conduit for criminal activity."

"But not activity that Kenna would be involved in. I'm certain of that."

El fired a questioning look his way, but didn't say anything.

He would move on for now. "What about the missing travel trailer? What do you make of that?"

She shrugged. "Stolen like the boat, maybe. Hopefully, we'll find something at Mason's place to help with that question."

The GPS voice announced their destination on the right in a middle-class neighborhood with smaller and older homes that were well maintained and the lawns manicured.

She leaned forward. "Looks like we're looking for the blue duplex ahead."

She parked in front and didn't waste any time, but charged up the sidewalk. Gabe appreciated her sense of urgency. Lucy had been gone for thirty-eight hours by now and every minute counted.

Gabe trailed her steps to the two-story duplex with faded blue paint and overgrown shrubbery. She had to give the door a hard bump with her hip to get it to open. The pungent odor of marijuana seeped out. The inside of the small place smelling even worse.

"Okay, not what I expected a former police officer's house might smell like." El pocketed the key. "But it's legal here, and he's free to smoke it or take it in any formula he wants as long as he doesn't get on the road or commit a crime while under the influence."

Gabe stepped further into the dark living room, the only light inching from the edges of closed blinds. He went to the long coffee table, stacks of papers piled high on top. He clicked on the overhead light then dropping onto a couch, he put on his disposable gloves.

El sat next to him. "If things go our way, he was working on these papers right before he died."

Before she could touch anything, her phone rang. She answered. "Ulrich. Putting you on speaker with Gabe, too."

Gabe rested the stack of papers he'd picked up on his knees and sat back to listen. Unless he had an urgent question, he would keep quiet.

"Just got the report on Mason's autopsy," Ulrich said.

"Interesting timing, since we're sitting in his duplex."

"Yeah. Dr. Briggs said he died somewhere between three and five days ago. Beyond that, we'd be looking more at estimates than facts."

"Until we can get his phone processed, we can assume he was still alive on Tuesday around ten a.m. when his daughter talked to him. Did Faye find his cell?"

"In his pocket, but that means it spent a few days in the water. Still, I'll pick it up and get it to Sierra today. Maybe it'll give us vital information we need."

"Let's hope," El said, but looked disappointed. "What was the cause of death?"

"Multiple stab wounds to vital organs including his heart. The wounds are about two centimeters wide on the surface, and the knife was most likely a single-edged blade. Probably somewhere between half an inch and an inch across."

"A single-edge blade makes me think of a kitchen or pocketknife. I didn't see any knives in the kitchen at the boathouse property, but I'd like you to check that out. Did she find a pocketknife on Mason?"

"None in the inventory. You thinking that could be our murder weapon?"

"His daughter described it as more of a penknife that he carried with him every day, but it's possible."

"Then where is it?" Ulich asked.

"We'll keep an eye out for it here. You go back to the crime scene to look for it and other knives."

"Will do but there's one more thing. Mason had lung cancer. Dr. Briggs says his lungs showed advanced cancer. An extensive spread. She wouldn't speculate on the time he had left, but it wasn't long."

"Wow." She shared a look with Gabe. "How terrible for him, but how it affects our investigation remains to be seen. Call me after you finish searching the crime scene again." She thanked Ulrich and ended the call.

"Crazy when his daughter said he didn't smoke to avoid getting cancer and then he does," Gabe said.

"Knowing he didn't have long to live could make it easier for his family to accept his death."

"Maybe, but death is final, no matter how it comes." Feeling Kenna's loss, he turned to the papers on his lap and started thumbing through them. "These are doctor's reports and internet research about Small Cell Lung Cancer."

"So he knew he was dying." El grabbed another pile of papers.

"Mason highlighted lines that say it spreads fast and initially responds well to chemotherapy. Problem is, it quickly becomes resistant and returns. Survival rate is really low."

"Exactly like Faye said." El tapped the papers on her lap. "His will and a trust, recently signed. The cancer would explain why he set these up."

"Those might not make the loss easier for his family to bear, but at least it'll save a lot of hassles regarding his estate." Gabe moved onto another pile. Surprised by the top page, he looked at El again. "You have to see this." He handed her the document.

She studied it. "A Craigslist ad for his travel trailer."

"Explains why it wasn't at his lake house."

Gabe fanned out the pages on his lap. "He listed many more items for sale."

She continued to hold the travel trailer posting in her hand. "The cancer is a strong motivator for selling his possessions. Maybe he was getting ready to spend more time with his family instead of fishing, or he could've been getting rid of stuff to make it easier for Talia after he died."

"This could also explain the large deposits in his checking account." Gabe continued to flip through ads for other items and pulled one out to give to El. "For his boat. Maybe our killer responded to the ad and met Mason at his boathouse with the intent of stealing it. Maybe even killing him so he didn't have to pay."

"Or maybe the murder was a spur-of-the-moment thing and he took the nearest boat, killing Mason when he tried to defend it."

"You could be right, but in that case, why go into the house and kill the dog?"

"I can't explain that, other than he might not have done it. Could've been an accident and the dog jostled the bottom television, sending the stack tumbling. I'd much rather believe that than that we're looking for a man who'd kill a defenseless dog."

Gabe nodded and stood to look around the room, searching for any electronic devices, and failing. "If Mason kept emails he received for the boat sale, Hayden could potentially find the prospective buyers' real identities."

She waved the pages at him. "We need to get this info to him after we finish going through these piles and maybe that'll be enough for him to go on."

"I'll start searching for Mason's tablet."

She set the papers on her lap. "I can request the data from Craigslist, too, but it'll take a warrant, and companies like Craigslist are notoriously slow in providing users' information."

"No kidding, but we have to chase the lead down, no matter what it takes." His gut said if they found the buyer for Mason's boat, they'd find Kenna's killer and Lucy's abductor, but maybe he was oversimplifying things.

"I'll do my best," she said, "and I can be pretty persuasive."

Something else she didn't have to tell him. He'd witnessed it firsthand.

They separated, starting their house search in painstaking detail and in silence. Finally, finding nothing—including the tablet—they had to admit defeat and headed for the door.

El's phone chimed. "Text from Sierra. She sent the new DNA results to my email."

Gabe glanced at his watch. Nearly five. Time had slipped by while they were searching.

El quickly thumbed through a few screens, her hand trembling. "Here we go. She starts with Kenna's toothbrush and compares it to the other DNA. It was found on her cell phone, Lucy's pink sweatshirt, the car seat, the toy, and the shoe. At the ravine, it was all over the handle of the screwdriver and in her prints from the boat. And last, on the pregnancy test, the other DNA on that item is still processing."

"Really nothing new. It's only confirmation of what we suspected."

El nodded. "Next, she lists Lucy's DNA, also found on the sweatshirt, the car seat, the unicorn, the bracelet, the shoe, and her prints on the boat. But here's a new one. It was in the small blood sample recovered from the dock by the nail."

Important news, but... "That confirms Lucy was there, but did Sierra find any other suspect's names?"

"They located Mason's DNA on the boat, but not on the Zippo lighter. She says that belongs to an unidentified suspect whose DNA was also collected from the car seat, the child's shoe, the blood outside Kenna's van, and on her hand, plus on the screwdriver. No other unidentified DNA except on the boat."

"So we're looking for one suspect for all three crime scenes."

"It also clearly tells us the boathouse is connected to Kenna's murder and Lucy's abduction."

He squared his shoulders and met her gaze. "Then I need to get my team to work harder to find a connection between Kenna and Mason."

"Finally." She lifted her chin. "We have that elusive lead that could bring us the identity of Kenna's killer and Lucy's abductor."

And Gabe could only pray that the abductor had not ended Lucy's life.

18

A sharp sound pulled El from her fitful sleep. Something was wrong. She had to act. Now!

She grabbed her phone from the nightstand and rolled to the other side of her bed. Plunged off the mattress, hitting her shoulder hard on the floor. She reached for her gun safe in the bottom of a nightstand, willing her fingers to stop shaking enough to tap her code into the keypad. Thank goodness the safe was set to stealth mode. Wouldn't do to have an intruder hear her awake and moving. A quiet sigh slipped out as she curled her fingers around her favorite SIG Sauer P365 and seated a cartridge.

Letting out a breath and inhaling another, she dialed 911 and took a quick look at the time on her phone. Quarter after two. Middle of the night.

"Nine one one. What's your emergency?" The confident yet soothing female voice came over her phone.

"This is Detective Elaina Lyons. Someone's in my house." She quickly but clearly gave them her address. "I'm inside and armed. I need immediate backup."

"Copy that, Detective Lyons. Are you safe right now?"

"Yes, I'm in the bedroom. Suspect's in my living room searching for something."

"Understood. Units are en route. Do you know if there's more than one intruder?"

"Sounds like only one."

"Stay on the line, Detective. Help is on the way. Keep yourself secure and don't engage unless necessary."

"I'm holding my position but won't be staying on the line. I have another call to make." She hung up before the dispatcher challenged her decision. She dialed Gabe.

"El?" he answered, sounding tired, but not as if he'd been asleep.

"Someone's in my house. Not sure what they're up to. I've called 911, and I'm in my bedroom behind my bed."

"Is the door locked?"

"No, but I don't want to risk him seeing the door close. I'm hidden, and I'm armed. I should be fine until backup arrives."

"Stay safe and in control. I'm on my way." He ended the call.

He said exactly what she hoped for. Not that he could actually be of help. Patrol should be here before him.

A siren sounded in the distance.

Frantic rustling of papers in the living room followed.

She laid her phone on the floor and aimed her gun over the bed.

She listened.

Waited. Heart racing.

Running footsteps. The flash of a person moving past her bedroom. Headed for the front door.

She counted to ten, waiting to see if another intruder followed.

She hit ten. Bolted around the bed to her doorway. Paused for a minute. Her phone. She didn't have pockets in her pajamas, and she wasn't about to let go of her weapon to carry it with her.

Heart pounding loudly in her head now, she stepped out, then cautiously cleared the living area.

Empty.

She made her way to the front door. To the edge of the porch. Peered around the heavy support column.

There he was. Tall, six feet or so. Wearing a gray hoodie with the hood up, jeans, and athletic shoes. Bolting down the sidewalk. Just reaching a corner. He barreled to the right.

She caught sight of her laptop and some file folders under his arm, but he was too far gone for an effective foot pursuit. Thankfully, a patrol car raced toward her from the opposite direction. She shoved her weapon in her waistband and rushed over the grass to the curb. The deputy stopped and lowered his window.

Good, Deputy Price. Someone I know.

"Intruder bailed," she said, her voice shaking. "He's on foot. Headed east from here. Turned south at the corner. Uncertain if he's armed, but didn't see a weapon."

She described the suspect and backed away from the car to stop Price from wanting to talk further when he had all the information she could provide. He took the hint and floored the gas pedal, flew to the corner, then careened around it. She wished she could've ridden along with him, but she wasn't on duty or in uniform. If something terrible happened, it would reflect poorly on not only herself, but Price, too. She wouldn't do that to him.

Her nerves consumed her whole body, and continuing to stand seemed impossible. She dropped to the grass and breathed slowly as she'd told victims to do in the past. She'd handled many intruders and some home invasions and believed she'd understood what the victim was going through. Now she knew. She'd been wrong. Way wrong.

From the other direction, a black pickup flew down the street. *Gabe.*

His brakes squealed as he stopped on the other side of the road. He jumped out and raced across the street. She put the caring in his expression at the highest DEFCON number.

He reached her and looked down on her, that intensity still present, but he'd mixed caring and compassion in equal measures.

Her heart fluttered.

"Are you okay?" Sounded like anger tried to swallow his words.

"Fine. Intruder's gone. Raced away on foot. Deputy Price went after him." Tears pricked her eyes.

Stop it. You're a detective. Be strong. She looked away, trying to stop herself from falling apart and letting the tears flow. She failed.

He dropped in front of her and enveloped her hands in his.

The warmth of his skin was bliss against hers, but even with his support, her hands shook uncontrollably.

"Aw, sweetheart, don't cry." He released her hands to draw her into his arms. "I'm here now. It'll be okay."

She reveled in his touch, loving that he thought if he came to her rescue, she should believe everything would be okay. And really, if he were by her side in life, wouldn't everything be okay? Sure, they'd have problems. Maybe lots of problems. But with a strong, honorable Christian man like Gabe at her side, she had twice the strength of one human.

Couple that with God, and they couldn't lose.

He continued to hold her, and she let him do so longer

than a resilient detective should. But she was also a woman. Something she'd tried to ignore in life far too often.

She drank in the feel of his arms for one last moment, then pushed free. "I knew before I called you that you would come."

"Well, yeah, I would've shown up for a stranger, but for you? I would've battled any natural disaster you can name to get here."

"Makes me want to have you in my life all the time," she said, and held her breath, unsure how he would take her comment.

He leaned his forehead against hers. "Same for me. Sometimes it takes something this terrifying to set priorities."

"Without a doubt we need to pursue what's going on between us after the investigation is over."

"I can hardly wait, and I'm going to kiss you, if that's all right."

Oh yes, what she'd wanted for a long time.

She placed her hands on both sides of his face. "More than all right. In fact..." She couldn't wait and drew his head down, pressing her lips against his before he had a chance to initiate the kiss.

He groaned and tightened his arms around her, pulling her even closer. The kiss started out tame at first, but he deepened it, and she relished every second. She wanted it to go on and on again. To be close to him. Dare she even think about being married to him?

But she wasn't one for public displays of affection. No one had come out to see why there were sirens, but someone was probably watching out a window. Price would return. Another deputy might be responding to her distress call. Potentially catching them together.

She wouldn't embarrass herself or them. She inserted

her hands in the small gap between them and pushed against him, wanting to stop when the space grew. But she did the right thing and kept pushing.

He blinked a few times and breathed deeply. "I didn't want that to end."

"Me either, but Price could be on his way back, and I can't afford to have a story about our PDA go around the department. You either, if you want to maintain your business's professional image."

He ran his hand through his hair. "I should've thought of that, but when I finally saw you were okay, I couldn't think."

She couldn't talk about this anymore without flinging herself back into his arms. "We should go inside and see what the intruder was up to."

He helped her to her feet. "Do you know if he took anything?"

"He has my laptop and some files," she said, turning toward her front door. "So if Price fails to apprehend the suspect, I'll need to get on the phone to my IT department. I have a challenging password, but if a thief's a pro and cracks it, then connects to the internet, the tech staff will see it."

Gabe nodded. "Allows them to trace the connection and lock it down or wipe the drive to stop him from getting to any data including our investigation."

"That's correct." She stepped inside. "Depending on what we know at that time, we'll have to decide if we want them to track it before they do anything. We might not want them to alert the thief before we can catch him."

She flipped on the overhead light in the living area, and he followed her. She stopped at the dining table now devoid of the investigation files she'd worked on after her dinner with Gabe. "It doesn't look like it matters if we wipe the electronic files for this investigation. He took all of my notes and a copy I made of the murder book."

"You made a copy of that?" He didn't even try to hide his surprise. Maybe he thought their department didn't allow it. Many didn't, but she was a stickler for following protocol and didn't violate department rules.

"I do keep copies. I'm not proud of my reasoning, but every day in an investigation, I have to end the day by reviewing what other people working the investigation have added to the book."

"The control thing. You need to make sure they're doing the work to your satisfaction."

She nodded. "Like I said, I'm not proud of it, and I need to change, but there you have it. Thanks to my foolish control, the intruder has all of the details for the investigation."

"We'll talk about the control thing later so you don't blame yourself for this, but we need to find this person ASAP."

Thinking more clearly now, she scoured her brain for a solution. "My security feed. Let me grab my phone from the bedroom." She raced through the house to pick it up and scrolled to the security app as she walked back to the living room. "That's odd. The feeds are live, but blacked out and no notifications."

"Likely not an electronic glitch then. You think he covered the camera lenses?"

"Maybe the doorbell, but he would've needed a ladder to reach the other ones. That's why I mounted them as high as I could."

"You stay here. I'll go check it out."

"Perfect," she said. "It'll give me time to get dressed."

He spun to exit. She followed him but veered off to her bedroom. She quickly put on one of her usual work suits and tamed her hair into a bun. Not hearing Gabe in the other room, she even took a moment to brush her teeth.

Back in her living room, her phone rang right as Gabe returned.

She held it up. "It's Sierra. And if she's calling at this time of day, it has to be important." She connected the call. "Sierra. Gabe's here, and I'm putting you on speaker."

"Good, "she said. "The results came in for the fetal tissue sample. I thought with Lucy missing you'd be working and want to know right away."

Gabe stepped closer to the phone. "You have a match in the database?"

"Not exactly," Sierra said.

"Then what?" Gabe's urgent tone seemed as if he were trying to push her along.

"First, you should know it was a boy."

Learning the gender of the baby made the loss more real. El watched Gabe to see how he handled it.

His shoulders slumped, and he stared blankly at the wall.

"Second, the sample matched two men in the database." She paused, and El heard her draw in a long breath.

The suspense was killing El, but after Gabe's reaction to the baby's gender, she wouldn't push Sierra along, but would be patient for her to reveal the name. Still, she gripped the edges of the table as she waited.

"I'll send a report with both of the names," she said, "but I think the one you'll want to know about, is you, Gabe. It's a familial match to you."

All blood drained from Gabe's head and the world spun in circles. He might pass out. He grabbed the phone from El's hand as if that would make a difference. "What do you mean a match to me?"

"The findings are consistent with a first-degree relative," Sierra said. "A parent, child or full sibling. We refined it using gender. Male. Your dad's in the system too, and it's a match to him as well."

"Then why focus on me?" Gabe asked even though the real question he should be thinking is why would one of his family members be involved with Kenna?

"Because we refined it further using age. Even if the DNA sample didn't give us an approximate age of thirty-three, your father isn't likely capable of having more children. This left the only other male relative in our database."

"Me," Gabe said. "But I can assure you, I'm not the father of the child."

"Do you have another male relative in this age range who doesn't have a criminal record?" Sierra asked.

Gabe's mind whirled with the news, but though he could hardly believe it, he immediately knew the answer. "My brother, Brad."

"Is he your only male sibling?" Sierra asked.

"Yes." Gabe's hand shook so badly he set the phone on the table before he dropped it.

"Then it looks like your brother is the father of Kenna's child," Sierra said matter-of-factly. It sounded like she'd put a megaphone to her phone, and her statement roared through Gabe's brain.

He took a moment to catch his breath and come to grips with what she was saying.

His brother, Brad. A relationship with Kenna. Father of her baby.

No. He couldn't believe it.

"This can't possibly be." Gabe pulled out a chair and sank onto it, leaning his elbows on his knees and taking in more oxygen. "Kenna detested my family's criminal

behavior as much as I did. There's no way she'd be in a relationship with Brad."

"I apologize if this offends you," Sierra said, "but it might
not have been a consensual relationship."

"That could make some sense," El said. "Perhaps the
voicemail she left you was that she was afraid of him, and he
used the baby to get her to stop at the lake to talk to him."

"And he killed her? My brother killed my best friend?"
Gabe shoved a hand into his hair. "No. No. Don't tell me
that. I couldn't possibly live with that."

"I'm sorry, Gabe," Sierra said. "But just because he's the
father of the baby doesn't mean he killed Kenna. Whether
you like it or not, they could've been in a relationship."

"She's right." El looked at him, concern flooding her
expression. "Is there anything else, Sierra?"

"No. Looks like I've done enough damage for the day. I'll
get back to you as soon as other results come in."

The phone went dark, matching the color of Gabe's
heart right now. He didn't know what to do. What to think.
Other than that he wanted to hurt his brother in the
worst way.

He jumped to his feet and grabbed his keys from the
counter.

"Where are you going?" El asked.

"To see my brother."

"With the mood you're in, I don't think that's a good idea.
Not to mention, it's the middle of the night." She pushed in
front of him, blocking his way.

Didn't matter. He could simply step around her, or with
his strength, easily force her out of the way.

"I'm sorry, but I have to. There's no other choice." He
sidestepped her and charged toward the door.

"What about this?" she called after him. "What about
the break-in? The violation of my private space?"

The anguish in her voice stopped his feet, his hand on the door handle. What was he doing? Bailing on the woman he'd come to love, just for a little revenge? Something the Bible warned against, and it wouldn't bring Kenna back. Bring any peace.

Or help find Lucy.

And he certainly couldn't leave El here on her own. Not after the break-in. Sure, she was a law enforcement officer and had proved tonight that she could handle herself, but this could've gone the opposite way in a flash. His time as a state trooper told him that. Bullets were fast and deadly, and stoppable only when wearing a protective vest, and that wasn't even a certainty.

He rested his head on the cool metal door.

Please help me give up this desire for revenge. You see the big picture. I only see the little piece in front of me, and I can be prone to jump to conclusions. As if this is news to You. Let me respect El enough to wait until the time she decides we should talk to my brother.

Calmer now, he pushed off the door and strode back to her. She remained in the same place, and he rested his hands on her shoulders. "I'm sorry I let my selfish need for revenge take over. How could I even have considered leaving you? Can you forgive me?"

"Already done and forgotten." She beamed a smile at him.

His heart took a tumble. "Not only do I want to be here for you, but I'd like you to bunk in the guest room at the inn until we catch the intruder. In fact, it would be a good idea to stay with us until we find the killer. Maybe even Lucy."

She chewed on her lower lip. "I appreciate your offer, but I'll be fine here."

He must've frowned because she gently pressed the

muscles on the sides of his mouth. "You really want me to stay there, don't you?"

"I do, but I'll respect your decision."

"That means a lot to me." She studied his face. "Since it's important to you, I'll stay at the inn."

His turn to send a smile her way, but then he swept her up in a hug and held on tightly. "You and Lucy are the most important people in my life. I need to keep you safe and find Lucy."

"Detective Lyons." A deep male voice called out from the doorway.

"That'll be Price." She broke away from Gabe, her gaze shifting to the door. "In here, Price. Come in."

He stormed their way as if intending to arrest them and stopped in front of her, his hands resting on his duty belt. His mannerisms reminded Gabe of Barney Fife from the old *Andy Griffith Show* that he used to watch with his mom when he was little. But if he was a bumbling deputy like Fife, El didn't let on.

"Sorry, ma'am," he said, his southern drawl stronger on the word *ma'am*. "Suspect's in the wind. Got a partial on his plates and dispatch is running it now along with the make and model of the vehicle."

"Text me the details," El said before Gabe could ask for it. "My number's correct on the department roster."

"Roger that." Price rubbed the back of his neck. "Would now be a good time to take your statement?"

Was it? Not by the looks of El's troubled expression, but then she straightened her shoulders and nodded. "I'll make a pot of strong coffee. Have a seat at the table, and I'll bring it in when it's ready."

She started for her kitchen, open to the family room.

She was putting on a good front for the deputy. The only thing Gabe wanted her to do right now was to climb in bed at the inn and get some sleep. But it didn't matter what he wanted. He couldn't postpone the statement. He could help her make the coffee, though.

He trailed her into the kitchen with walnut cabinets and stainless-steel appliances. Her back to him, she was grinding fresh coffee beans, the nutty smell already saturating the air.

He glanced back to make sure Price wasn't watching them and rested his hands on her shoulders. "Remember, I'm here if you need or want support."

She smiled at him, this time, a genuine, glorious smile, and he could imagine a lifetime of moments together in a kitchen like this, making coffee. Not with the underlying turmoil and strife of the night, but as they went through their lives with Lucy in a house like this one.

Oh man, he'd never asked her if she would want to be a ready-made mother. That could most certainly stand in the way of their getting together. Now wasn't the time to discuss it, but they would soon need to have that conversation.

He released her shoulders and grabbed the carafe to insert under running water. As it filled, his mind drifted to his brother. To his family. To how dysfunctional they were. In many ways, he'd had a good childhood. At least until he'd discovered their so-called occupation. That hadn't taken long. Not that they'd told him, but elementary school classmates had been more than happy to tease him about it.

That wasn't the kind of life he wanted for Lucy, but she would benefit greatly from having grandparents. Not his dad, for sure, but his mother was awesome. Her only downfall was enabling the family's criminal activities and expecting him to join in.

"You filling the carafe or starting a fountain?" El gave a pointed look at his hand.

He glanced down to discover water flowing over the top.

"Sorry." He turned the handle. "Lost in thought."

She rested a hip against the counter, her expression perking up. "About?"

"Nothing important."

"Is that true or do you not want to share it with me?"

"I do want to share it with you, and I will, but now isn't the right time." He tipped his head toward the living area. "Especially not with a deputy waiting for you."

Gabe looked in Price's direction. He was lost in his phone, the screen reflecting off his face.

She squeezed Gabe's hand. "I know things aren't good tonight, but I feel like it's set my priorities and brought us closer together."

"Agreed." He clung to her hand, but needed to clear his brother's name before this could go any further. "I'm not trying to pressure you, but how soon before we can interview Brad?"

She arched an eyebrow, but didn't speak.

"Honestly, I respect your skills and experience, and I'm good to do whatever you say."

"You said you suspect him of killing Kenna, but when you think about it now, do you really believe he did?"

"He's been a criminal all his life," Gabe said. "But I'd like to think murder wasn't part of his ethos."

"And if you believe what Jude had to say, then we would think if a boyfriend killed her, it would be an unplanned rage-filled incident. Sure, the strangulation could've been anger-induced, but everything else points to a more controlled incident."

He nodded as he was starting to believe she was right. But was he buying into it because he didn't want to believe his brother was a killer or because he really believed in his innocence?

How could he know? How could he separate family from his work even though he was no longer part of their lives?

The very reason he needed El to make the decision on how and when to approach Brad.

"Do you think he's holding Lucy?" she asked.

"Again, I don't think kidnapping is in his wheelhouse. I know criminals escalate, but they don't usually go from petty burglary to murder and kidnapping without something in between."

"True, but if he did kill Kenna, and if Lucy saw him do it, then he couldn't let her go."

"So what do you want to do?"

"Get a warrant to search his place before we talk to him and tip him off that we know about his involvement. We don't want him disposing of any evidence. Until then, we hang back. He doesn't know we're on to him, so I doubt he'll flee. Means there's no need to track him down in the middle of the night."

"Sounds like a plan," he said as the coffeemaker gurgled its readiness.

He respected her strategy, and he would abide by it, but there was no way his brain would quiet down and let him sleep tonight. Not only because of his brother, but because he wanted to be sure no one broke in to hurt El.

He certainly hadn't backburnered finding Lucy, though. Time was ticking down, and his drive to locate her pressed harder on him than ever.

Even if it meant accusing his own brother of murder and kidnapping.

19

———

The inn's guest room carried a faint lavender scent, very calming after the trauma El had just experienced. Gabe put her suitcase on a bench at the end of a plump bed covered with a soft, beige comforter and holding large fluffy pillows in immaculate white cases.

Feeling very much at home, El almost sighed, but sudden fatigue took over her body, and she collapsed on the sleek sofa. By the boxy design, she expected it to be uncomfortable. It was. Not the entire cushion, but a hard object protruded beneath her. She scooted down a couple of feet, and the cushion was plump and comfy.

Alert now, she got up. "There's something hard under the last cushion."

Gabe knotted his forehead. "None of us would put anything under there."

She started to lift it up, but the sofa didn't belong to her. "The room has obviously been cleaned after your last guest, but maybe the last person who stayed here hid something there. Who stayed here last?"

"Kenna and Lucy. Last weekend." He started toward the sofa and flipped up the cushion.

A thick journal lay on the frame.

El stared at it, her heart starting to pound. "It's green with a big black cross on the front exactly like Mrs. Z. described."

Gabe reached for it.

"Wait." El dug in her suit pocket for disposable gloves and handed them to him. "You don't want to ruin any forensic evidence."

As he slipped his fingers into the gloves, he cast her a sideways look. "You always happen to have gloves with you?"

"Once a detective, always a detective." She smiled. "But seriously, you never know when you'll need them, so I make sure I have a pair in all of my suit jackets."

Gabe sat, placed the journal on his lap, and lifted the cover.

El sat next to him. "Can I make a suggestion?"

He looked at her. "I'm listening."

"Let's start at the back to read her final entries. That should give us her most current movements and help us find something to go on."

"Good point." Gabe flipped to the back and laid the pages open on his lap.

She scooted close to him so she could read the entries too.

Gabe tapped the second page under the words *Safe Harbor*. "She mentioned Safe Harbor. It's a group home that she told me she volunteered at. She never said much about it other than they cared for difficult kids."

"There was a plaque hanging in the lobby thanking the center for partnering with them."

"That's probably how she got involved." He turned the page. "She worked as an admin on evenings and weekends. She says she had access to enter bills into the financial system, to vendor lists, and some internal emails."

Not surprising," El said. "Her house was super organized, so I can imagine her doing this."

Gabe flipped the page again. He stabbed his finger against the paper. "Someone saw her making a copy of records. Threatened her then threatened Lucy."

Now they were getting somewhere. "Probably why she put the locks on her doors."

"But if she was in danger for this, why hide the journal instead of coming to me? She sat right here talking to me, and she knew about it, but didn't say anything."

"Maybe if she stumbled onto something illegal, she thought if she reported it, she would be safe."

"Yeah, I could see her thinking that." He punched the arm of the sofa. "If her death had something to do with this, and she'd told me what was going on, she'd still be alive. Lucy would be safe."

"I'm sorry, Gabe, but on the bright side, this is our best lead yet. Stronger than your brother by far." She regretted having to continue, but Gabe had to know where this was headed. "If these people did indeed threaten her and Lucy, then perhaps they had second thoughts on simply making threats, and decided to kill her."

El couldn't think of any better place to be at the moment than the Lost Lake Locators' office, where Gabe had zero reservations over waking his teammates at four a.m. to discuss the journal. He'd given them a five-minute warning to get dressed and book it to the meeting room. Five minutes later or less, they stumbled into the room, none of them grumbling.

Reece immediately started brewing coffee. Then as everyone else sat stretching and rubbing their eyes, she pushed through the swinging doors into the kitchen. No one questioned her actions. They must all expect her to provide food. She'd chosen to be the mom of this group, and loved doing it. In El's mind, it equaled herding a group of unruly toddlers, and she didn't envy her position.

Gabe claimed a spot standing at the head of the table and quickly shared details about the journal. "Hayden, we need you to do a deep dive on Safe Harbor. New Tide Foundation, too. They fund the home."

"I'll get started right away." Hayden opened his laptop, which was seemingly always in his presence.

"You're thinking this is the reason Kenna was killed," Jude said. "That she saw something she shouldn't have and got caught making copies of whatever freaked her out."

"We do," El said.

Jude eyed Gabe. "You're usually the devil's advocate, but since this is your investigation and you're too close to it, I'll step in. We're talking about a group home here. A place where struggling children found a safe harbor, just like the name suggests. Whatever Kenna discovered wasn't likely a reason to commit murder."

"You could be right." Gabe returned his teammate's penetrating stare. "But if you read the journal entry, you'll see she's very convincing about this being a big deal."

"I agree," El said. "And we should treat it as such unless we find evidence that disputes it. After Hayden does a deep dive, we'll begin by interviewing people involved in both organizations."

Hayden poked his head up for a moment. "I can already tell you both organizations are very well thought of in the social services community. Silas Tinsley is the director of

Safe Harbor, and local philanthropist and entrepreneur, Jonas Trent manages New Tide."

His findings further raised doubts that these men could be involved, but El agreed with Gabe. They couldn't let this slide.

"We can't go see them before business hours." Gabe picked up a marker. "Now would be a good time to review our suspects and set priorities accordingly."

"Wait," Hayden said as his fingers continued to fly over the keyboard. "I need a little more direction here. We know Mason's murder is connected to Kenna's through DNA, and his granddaughter was enrolled at the center where she worked, plus he had the encounter with the guy in the black van, but I've failed to find anything else. Do you want me to include them in the Safe Harbor/New Tide search?"

"He could be linked to them," El said. "Even Bonnie could have more of a relationship with these organizations other than supporting them through her daycare."

"Okay, I'll look for that." Hayden typed something into his computer. "And while I've got your attention, I'm getting close to obtaining a call log from Mason's phone and finding real names for the buyers on Craigslist. I should be getting Mason's bank statements sometime today, too."

"Thank you," El said. "Anything we can—"

"Hold up! Breaking news coming in." Hayden's eyes lit up. "There are rumors that Bonnie had an affair with one of the center's parents, ending her marriage."

"Who?" El asked.

Hayden kept his gaze pinned to his computer. "Guy's name is Carl Acosta. He's been flirting with the edge of legal since he got divorced a couple of years ago. Been pulled in for questioning on two burglaries but never charged. No consistent address. No consistent job. No custody of his daughter and has no planned visits. It's up to the wife to grant them. And by the way, the big news is his kid attends Little Pines Daycare."

"I don't suppose it says whether he owns a Ford Transit."

Hayden shook his head. "Easy enough for me to find out while you all plan."

Gabe looked at El. "You think he was watching the daycare to get a glimpse of his daughter?"

"Seems possible to me. That means Bonnie knows him, and we need to question her again." El glanced at her watch. Five a.m. "It'll have to wait until the center opens."

"If it helps you decide what to do," Hayden said, "Acosta does own a Ford Transit from a carpet cleaning business he couldn't make a go of."

Before El could reply, her phone rang. She glanced at the screen and then at Gabe, who was sitting across from her. "It's Ulrich. Has to be important if he's calling this early."

Gabe rushed over to sit next to her. She tapped the speaker button. "I'm with the Lost Lake Locators and have my speaker on. I can find a private location if you want."

"No need," he replied with certainty. "They should hear this, too. A credible witness called in to say she just saw a man with a little girl who looked like Lucy."

"Where?" The word erupted from Gabe's mouth.

"At the entrance to Silver Mist Trail. They were starting down the path, and she was coming back from her morning run. The man pulled his stocking cap down lower and glared at the woman, so she slowed to take a good look at the child. The child whined and said she wanted Mommy, but he shushed her, saying they were going to Mommy now. Then they took off down the trail."

"Dispatch SWAT," El said with no hesitation. "I'll meet you at the trailhead."

"Already done. Mina deployed them as soon as we verified the legitimacy of the call." Ulrich's tone rose. "Caitlyn Armstrong's the witness's name. She's waiting for us there."

"We can be there in ten minutes." She ended the call.

Before she could even look Gabe in the eye, he was on his feet. "C'mon, let's move."

"Not so fast. This is a law enforcement op. I can't have you in the middle of it and risk not being able to prosecute this guy because we allowed a civilian to participate."

"What about tailing you?" Jude asked. "Couldn't we both follow close enough to see what's going on, but not close enough to be in the fray should something go down?"

El didn't have time to sit and ponder his request. Not when time ticked down to finding this man and child still on the trail. "Ride with me. I'll call Mina on the way, and she can decide."

"Fair enough." Gabe jerked a thumb over his shoulder. "Let us grab our vests, and we'll meet you at the car."

"Sounds good."

As observers, they wouldn't need their vests, but if it made Gabe feel better to put one on as if he was in the rescue and take-down, she wouldn't stop him. They all needed to do whatever they needed to do to find this child alive.

Gabe and Jude made their way past the witness sitting and bobbing her knee, a uniform deputy seated at her side. Gabe started down the unlit trail behind the SWAT team made up of six additional deputies including Mina, El, and Ulrich in the mix. The trail wasn't an official one like he'd expected to find as part of this highly groomed park. It was nothing more than a dirt path packed down hard in a hilly forested area, really only wide enough for two people to walk at a time.

But deputies hauling gear, their rifles at the ready as they advanced on the trail, had to move single file. Gabe and Jude, packing only their handguns, took the rear. Gabe wished he was carrying his semi-automatic rifle, but he wouldn't be allowed to use it even if he did have it.

Their restrictions could discourage him, but he wouldn't let them. Not after Mina had cleared him and Jude to participate, but only by taking up the rear. If the suspect and Lucy were found, they would stand back while law enforcement rescued her. The most important point was rescuing Lucy. Secondary, making sure the charges held against the creep who had taken her.

"I feel naked with only my sidearm," Jude whispered.

That got him a sharp look from Deputy Price. Mina had instructed everyone to use hand signals only, but Jude was ever the maverick. Marched to the beat of his own drum. That only worked in a law enforcement environment if you were an exceptional officer, which he'd been at the FBI.

They continued to move silently up and down the dark trail. An owl hooted in the distance, wind rushed through the trees, but otherwise they were surrounded by silence. The moon hung behind heavy clouds, the morning sun just thinking about rising above the horizon. It would be helpful if they could turn on their headlamps, but they couldn't alert the suspect to their approach.

The leaders rounded a curve and disappeared. Price suddenly flipped up his arm like a stop sign.

Gabe and Jude came to a stop. Had they spotted something? Was it go-time? Time for him to hold Lucy again?

His body flushed with a heavy emotion he'd never experienced. Fear for Lucy? Thankfulness for finally finding her?

He didn't know what it was, but he didn't like it. Not when it weakened his knees, and collapse seemed imminent.

El appeared at the curve and made her way back to Gabe. "Abandoned cabin ahead," she said, her voice low. "Could be where they have Lucy. Mina is taking a close-up look now, and we'll breach the building, but this is as far as you go until we clear it. Understood?"

Gone was the woman he'd come to love, replaced by the strong detective. In control and in charge. Expecting agreement and cooperation. Nothing else would do.

He gave a sharp nod, and honoring the directive to be quiet, he hopefully transmitted his respect for her in his expression.

"I'll come back for you when you can join us."

He nodded again.

She looked at Jude. "This goes for you, too. No cowboy moves. Lucy's life could depend on you following directions."

Jude gave her a salute. He didn't do it in sarcasm, but respect.

"After Mina formulates a plan, we'll go in as soon as everyone's been instructed. The path ahead doesn't have any cover. If you want to keep tabs on the op, you can slip into the underbrush on the south side, but make sure you aren't seen."

Gabe nodded again.

Surprisingly, she squeezed his arm. "If Lucy is here, we'll bring her home alive. I promise."

Gabe's knees weakened more, but he forced his shoulders back in an attempt to look like he was in control. No way he wanted her to send him packing. He gave a thumbs-up.

She released his arm and spun, then disappeared once again around the curve.

Gabe leaned close to Jude. "We wait until they move, and then we get that better look."

"You know it." Jude gave one of his mischievous grins that he always had when they were about to see action. As an FBI agent and profiler, he hadn't often had the need to draw his weapon. As much as he appreciated the gravity of finding someone like Lucy, he also liked the adrenaline rush that came with rescuing them.

The deputies moved ahead and rounded the curve. Gabe quickly slipped into the trees and underbrush. He wanted to plunge in and forge ahead, but he couldn't risk being seen and ruining the op.

He moved cautiously; branches scraped at his arms and face. So what? Minor compared to what Lucy had suffered. He kept going until he reached a place where he could see ahead but not be seen. He lifted the night vision binoculars hanging around his neck and zoomed in on the structure huddling in a small stand of trees.

Abandoned didn't begin to describe the place. Rotten wood threatened the integrity of the structure. Cedar siding split and was hanging by nails, looking like it wanted to take the cracked windows down with it. The porch slanted at an angle as if waiting to fall off the front. A surprisingly sturdy-looking red metal roof sat on top of it all.

Gabe could easily imagine the matching interior in what looked to be a one-room cabin. Anger for Lucy raged in his gut. How could anyone force a little child to live here? The uncertainty. Her fear. Had she been restrained all this time? Too many days for such a young child. For anyone.

He should've found her sooner.

Jude laid a hand on Gabe's arm and telegraphed strength through his expression. What would Gabe do without his teammates? He might not have his traditional family at his side, but he was part of a family nonetheless.

One who had seen him through years of trials. They would see him through this one.

Gabe nodded his understanding at Jude and turned back to the cabin, his anger receding a notch.

Mina didn't stand around, but rifle shouldered, sights on the target, led her team up the steps. At the door, she took her place to the right.

El took the left side. Ulrich stacked behind Mina. Two of the remaining deputies split between each side. The last one, a large burly guy, approached the door.

Mina signaled for the team to move forward. Though the door was so ramshackle it looked like a strong breeze would take it down, a deputy turned and kicked it in.

Wood splintered, and the door disintegrated. They charged inside.

In a matter of minutes, the SWAT team members spilled back out of the building, jogged down the steps, made a circular sweep of the property, and stopped out front.

"All clear," one of the deputies shouted, and the team lowered their rifles.

El stepped down to the porch, her rifle at rest. She shook her head.

Gabe's heart fell, and he clung to the nearest tree branch to stay upright.

Did this mean Lucy and her captor weren't in there?

Most likely.

Why, Father? Why? Why must this little girl continue to suffer?

El waved Gabe and Jude ahead.

"Sorry, man," Jude said as they slipped out of the brush. "I really believed she'd be there."

Gabe's disappointment nearly overwhelmed him, and he couldn't speak so he simply nodded. He focused on his anger to get his strength back as he strode across the grass.

He took the porch steps two at a time and entered the one-room cabin. Someone had lit an oil lamp, and a soft glow revealed a rusty metal bed with a mattress covered in a surprisingly clean white sheet. Pillows had clean cases too, and the blankets looked new.

The back wall held a small kitchen, the other side, a wood stove with a fire smoldering inside. There was a faint smell in the room that didn't seem to fit with a secluded cabin, but he couldn't place it. If anyone else noticed it they didn't say anything.

He glanced back at Jude. "You smell that?"

"Musty smell common to closed-up cabins?"

"No, it's something else. Maybe chemical. The owner could've stored something here in the past."

Gabe approached El. Jude matched him stride for stride. "Fire says someone was here not long ago."

She nodded. "My guess is our suspect came back to get anything incriminating then bolted right after the witness saw them."

Carrying a single piece of paper, Mina joined them. "Check out the window before you go. There's a child's handprint there, and we found this."

She held out the paper and displayed rudimentary stick figures. A man, woman, and child, and an indistinguishable blue object at the child's feet.

El leaned closer. "The red hair coloring for the mother and child couldn't be a coincidence."

Gabe pointed at the blue blob. "This is your true give-away. Lucy thinks Bluey is real, and she wants him to come live with her."

"So she was here," El said.

"And she's alive!" Gabe's gaze burned with fire.

"At least she was when the witness saw her," Jude said and looked at Gabe. "Sorry, man. Someone had to say it."

"Then we need to find her now!" El's words exploded as if she couldn't contain her increased drive, raised by just missing Lucy. "We need to take a good look around. See what else we might find."

"You don't want the whole team tromping through here and potentially disturbing evidence," Mina said. "I'll take Ulrich and SWAT with me. Ulrich can interview the witness so she can go to work. You can get in touch with her later if you have follow-up questions."

"Thank you," El said.

"I'm not needed here so I should head back." Jude looked at Mina. "If I can catch a ride, that is."

"We can drop you off." Mina pointed back at the picture. "Obviously this is Lucy and her mother, but who's the male figure?"

"Gabe's hair coloring matches the picture," Ulrich said.

"Could be me, I suppose. Not as an actual father figure or Kenna's partner. We made sure Lucy knew I was just a friend." Gabe looked around the group. "My brother, Brad, and I look a lot alike and the fetus DNA is probably his."

Mina gaped at him. "Your brother?"

El nodded. "Sierra called early this morning with DNA results from the fetus. He's most likely the father of Kenna's unborn child. I would've updated the murder book but this call came in."

"Have you talked to him yet?" Mina asked.

El shook her head. She told them about discovering the journal and Safe Harbor. "I want to evaluate his potential role along with the suspects from the charity."

Mina gave her a nod of affirmation. "You need to tread lightly with New Tide. It's a highly rated charity, predominantly supported by Jonas Trent."

"We already know about his involvement," El said, and looked at the others. "He's the big-time developer and town philanthropist with a lot of political clout. Including having the power to get a deputy fired if he doesn't like one of us."

"Sheriff too, and I'd like to stay employed," Mina said. "He and his wife were never able to have children, so they adopted two boys from Safe Harbor maybe five or so years ago and want to help so-called throw-away children to find families."

"Good to know," El said.

The intel about approaching cautiously probably mattered to El, but Gabe's team could push Trent for answers.

Mina folded the picture and put it in her pocket. "After you finish this scene, get the murder book updated ASAP, and let me know how you decide to proceed before you do. I don't want a surprise call from either of these guys complaining about being questioned."

El nodded and stood back to let Mina and Ulrich depart. The SWAT team had remained outside. Deputy Price had been assigned to secure the scene and was getting crime scene tape and stakes to cordon off the outside. That left El and Gabe alone together. He hadn't had a chance to process what had happened yet and didn't know what to say to her.

"Be right back." She stepped onto the rickety porch.

He knew her heart ached for this dead end and no Lucy, and some fresh air might be good. And maybe he could help out with her obvious disappointment.

Question was, how did he comfort her when the child he deeply loved continued to be missing and in extreme danger?

Only one way to find out. Step outside and try to help her.

20

Gabe was wrong. El wasn't wallowing in her disappointment. She was staring over the railing, her phone to her ear, and talking with the electronics expert at Veritas. Gabe just caught the tail end of their conversation, but it sounded like they would have Kenna's call information by the end of the day.

She turned and held up her phone. "That was Nick Thorne from Veritas. Kenna's phone dried out, and he promised to have data to us by the end of the day."

"Great news."

She responded with a sharp nod. "Let's search this place and hopefully we'll find evidence that will help too."

Seeming all business right now, she marched past him and inside. Maybe that was how she'd chosen to hold her emotions in check. He should do the same. He followed her, but paused at the threshold. There it was again. That faint, chemical edge in the air. Not strong. Just wrong.

He moved deeper into the room, eyes scanning every surface.

A sharp hissing sounded from the woodstove area. Also wrong.

"El, I—"

An ear shattering *whump*, cut off his warning.

A flash slashed across the room. The white-hot streak of orange flames hit the wall and raced up.

"Get out!" He kicked it into gear, grabbing El's hand on the way to the door, pulling her along.

Eyes wide, El slowed a fraction. "The evidence!"

"Doesn't matter right now." He tugged harder to get her moving faster.

Flames raced across the ceiling above. The air filled with an acrid smoke.

El coughed. Gabe couldn't let her succumb to the smoke. He pulled harder on her hand.

They burst through the front door. Hit the rickety porch.

El stumbled. Fell to her knees, her breathing tortured by the smoke pouring out of the door behind them.

Gabe scooped her up. Tossed her over his shoulder. Smoke burned his chest, but he wouldn't quit. He leapt from the porch.

"Fire," he yelled at Price, who was gaping at the cabin.

Price spun. Dropped the tape and charged away.

Gabe was hot on his heels. He pounded across the grass. The heaviness in his chest begged him to stop, but he kept going. Didn't stop until he believed they'd run far enough in case the outside propane tank exploded. It would take five minutes or more for the fire to heat up the propane, but better safe than sorry when building materials could fly fifty feet or more.

He settled El on the ground and gulped in deep breaths. Coughing out the smoke. Then breathing and coughing again. But all he could think about was sweeping El up in a hug to make sure she was fine. He couldn't, wouldn't touch her with Price standing nearby.

Rapidly breathing, eyes watering, she spun to look at the

building. "The evidence. Fingerprints. DNA. Our suspect was probably all over that place, leaving valuable evidence behind, and we're missing out on it."

Gabe finally cleared his lungs and could breathe again. "Could be why he set a delayed ignition fire. Cleaning the place before he left would take time, and he needed to get away before the fire drew anyone to the scene."

She flashed a look at him. "Then he wasn't trying to kill anyone. He just wanted to cover his tracks."

"That's my take. And I have to say, he might be experienced in arson, because he didn't use a common accelerant like gasoline. We would've smelled that. He used something that smelled sweet."

"Yeah, I noticed the odor, but didn't think it was a problem." Anguish dulled her eyes. "I should've thought the scent was out of place and looked into it."

"But why? None of us followed up on it. It's not your fault."

She shook her head, looking like she didn't believe him.

Would she accept the blame and feel guilty for this, too?

"I need to report this to Mina and get a fire crew out here." She stepped a few feet away and got out her phone.

Gabe turned to Price. "You okay?"

"Fine," he said, but scrubbed a hand over his face. "Never seen anything like it. From building to blazing inferno in minutes."

Gabe nodded.

A second blast ripped through the air. Deeper, heavier. A fireball rolled off the side of the structure, and something metal screamed. He didn't think, just dove toward El and took her down. He landed on his elbows to spare her from taking his weight. Pain radiated up his arms—nothing compared to what El might've felt if the metal had reached her.

He rolled free and took a quick look at the cabin area. The blast had kicked debris across the clearing, splintered boards scattered, and a twisted chunk of metal lay farther off, half-buried in the dirt.

Eyes still wide, El rubbed her hands up and down her arms. "What was that?"

"The propane tank," he said. "The reason I made sure we moved this far from the building."

On her side now, El inched closer to him. She glanced in Price's direction. His gaze was fixed on the cabin as if fearing another explosion.

She took Gabe's hand and lifted it to her mouth for a butterfly-soft kiss. "You could've just saved my life. Not once but twice."

He pressed his lips on her hand, too. "You're way too important to me to lose you. Especially not after losing Kenna. It would kill me."

"I don't want to lose you either." She squeezed his hand and let go.

"You don't know how badly I want to kiss you right now."

"You're wrong. I want the same thing."

Price cleared his throat and started toward them.

El lifted her shoulders and sat up, her detective persona solidly in place as she faced Price. "I can hear firetrucks in the distance. Meet them at the trail entrance and escort them back here."

He took a last look at the cabin and jogged down the trail.

She turned her attention to Gabe. "We need to read Ulrich's witness report. Maybe see if she gave him additional information. If not, we'll talk to her."

"Sounds like a plan," he said.

"After that, it's time we interview Silas Tinsley," she said. "Jonas Trent, too."

"I doubt they're personally involved in holding Lucy, but one of them sent a flunky to take care of her. The person who set this fire."

"You could be right. First, we check in with Hayden to find out what background information he located on them. Should tell us if either of them has military or law enforcement experience. Could mean they've used the special chokehold before. Because if they did then...then we could find Lucy and a killer all in one clean sweep."

Three hours later, El and Gabe took seats in the hospital employee lounge, waiting for nurse Caitlyn Armstrong to join them. El had read Ulrich's report from the witness interview and wanted to leave immediately to ask additional questions, but as the lead detective on the cabin investigation, she'd had to interface with the fire department.

A good thing. It had allowed her and Gabe to give their eyewitness accounts of the fire, origination, and explosion to the captain. El and Gabe believed they were looking at arson. So did the captain. But no one in their small department was skilled in arson detection to confirm their theory, so he'd called in a state arson investigator, who would arrive in the morning.

"Did I do something wrong?" Caitlyn asked as she took a seat in one of the squeaky vinyl chairs across from them. "I mean, I told that other detective everything I know."

"Absolutely nothing wrong." El offered her a smile. "We appreciate you reporting the situation and your cooperation."

"Then why are you here?" Caitlyn began gnawing the pink lipstick off her lower lip.

"I'm the lead detective on the case, and I find it helpful to hear directly from a witness what they observed. So if you don't mind, could you tell me what happened?"

"Sure, but I can't be gone for more than fifteen minutes or I'll screw up the entire department schedule for the day." She let out a slow breath and launched into the same story that Ulrich had noted in his report.

She didn't change her story, meaning she was more than likely telling the truth. Or she could be a great liar. She might've been at the park for a different reason than running, and she didn't want anyone to know. Maybe she was having an affair and meeting in a deserted parking lot in the middle of the night. Could be one of many reasons she might lie.

El needed to dig deeper to see if she could catch a contradiction in her story. "Were there any other vehicles in the parking lot?"

She shook her head. "Just mine."

"If you don't mind me asking," Gabe said. "Isn't it kind of dangerous to run in such a remote area alone?"

Caitlyn cocked her head. "Honestly, I think the seclusion makes it better than my usual trail because not many people even know that one exists."

"So, you don't usually run there, then?" El followed up.

"Sometimes, but the trails I usually take are much longer."

A deviation from her usual routine. This could be important.

"Why this one today?" El asked.

"Got called into work early this morning. Meant I only had time for a short run." She crossed her arms. "I work in the PICU, and the babies need us. We have to be flexible with our schedules when someone else calls in sick."

She certainly was well qualified to assess Lucy's condition. Even if for only a moment. "In your professional opinion, did the child look well?"

Caitlyn released her arms and seemed to relax at the change in questioning. "She did. Her face and clothes were a little dirty, but otherwise she appeared to be well-nourished and hydrated."

"What was she wearing?" El asked, in case it might be something Gabe would recognize.

"I only remember her blue jacket. It was quilted and had something embroidered on the chest. Looked like a dog, but not a real dog. More like a cartoon character."

Gabe sat forward. "Are you familiar with the show *Bluey*?"

"Yeah, yeah." Her eyes lit up. "My son used to watch it. He's nine now. Too old for that baby stuff, or so he says." She chuckled. "I forgot all about Bluey. So yeah, that was it. It was Bluey."

"Are you sure?" El asked.

Caitlyn nodded. "Positive."

El now had no doubt the man and child Caitlyn saw were Lucy and her abductor. She looked at Gabe. His expression held the same certainty.

They had a solid lead. Now they needed to find them.

"And the man? Can you describe him?"

"He was tall. Maybe six feet. He had dark hair." She glanced at Gabe. "Kind of like yours."

"Did he also look like me?" Gabe clenched his fists.

El got it. He thought Caitlyn might be describing his brother.

No hesitation, she shook her head. "His face was far different than yours. First off, he wasn't nice looking." She clapped her hand over her mouth. "I hope that doesn't embarrass you, but you are."

"It's all good." His offhand tone contradicted the red color crawling up his face.

She wrinkled her nose. "Anyway, he had a really skinny nose with a hook at the end. I couldn't tell if his eyes were small or if they were just narrow because he was glaring at me."

El shared a pointed look with Gabe, and his hands relaxed. "Any facial hair?"

"Full beard."

"And his clothing?" she asked. Ulrich had the details in his report, but witnesses remembered things as time went on and El wanted to make sure she got every detail.

"I only got a good look at his jacket and stocking cap. The cap was black, the jacket sage green. Short. Like the bomber jackets so many people wear these days, but there was a patch on the chest. Maybe military."

El was thankful for the additional patch detail. "Was there anything else unique about him that might help us find him?"

"Hmm." She bobbed her leg. "He seemed out of place. You know, you get that feeling where he's in the outdoors, but he really isn't an outdoors kind of guy."

Although Jonas Trent really didn't fit her description, El pulled up his picture on her phone and showed it to her. "Is this the guy you saw?"

"No. No. Absolutely not."

El scrolled to a picture of Silas Tinsley. His blond, nearly white hair glistened in the light. He did have sort of a narrow nose, and he could've dyed his hair. A long shot, but she showed the picture to Caitlyn.

She shook her head. "Not him either."

"Since you do take this trail frequently, can you tell me anything about the cabin near the end?"

"That thing?" She shook her head. "What an eyesore. My running group has been trying to get the council to get that thing taken down forever. Apparently, the property is just outside the park border and is privately owned, so they can't do anything about it."

Hayden was looking into it, but he'd run into roadblocks. Apparently, the property belonged to a shell company, and he was having a hard time finding the company's legal owner.

"Then thank you for your time, Ms. Armstrong." El stood. "Could I get your phone number in case I have additional questions?"

"No problem." She rattled it off.

El put it in her phone.

Caitlyn tilted her head. "Was I right? Is this the guy in the news who abducted that little child?"

"I'm sorry, I'm not free to discuss the investigation with you at this time. But please know you've been very helpful."

"Man, oh man." She stood and shoved her hands into the pockets of her uniform top. "I wish I knew, but I understand. Call me if you need anything else."

She whisked away, her soft-sole clogs squeaking on the floor.

El looked at Gabe. "We don't have proof positive that it was the abductor and Lucy, but I think we can fairly well assume it is."

"Yeah, and I'm glad we both agree about that." Gabe pushed open a hallway door and held it for her. "I want to make sure I'm not letting my feelings for Lucy point me toward a conclusion I want to be true."

"You aren't."

He stepped up beside her. "One thing I can't dispute. The actual abductor isn't either Tinsley or Trent."

"But like you said, they could've sent a flunky or an associate to take care of things for them."

"Just think of that cabin. Could you see men in their positions staying there?"

"No, and I hate that anyone took Lucy there."

Gabe grimaced. "Me too. But hopefully our interview with these two guys will lead us to her, and she won't have to suffer in a place like that again."

El nodded and led the way out of the hospital. She agreed with him, but one thing he probably hadn't thought through was how he would tell this precious child that her mother had been murdered and her life as she knew it had now completely changed.

But now that someone had seen her, at least they could pray that would be a possibility. As lead investigator, if El made the right moves, they would find Lucy alive. Make a mistake...

No pressure. No pressure at all.

21

In a quiet residential neighborhood, Gabe followed El and Silas Tinsley up a winding staircase of a large older home now turned into a group home. They were heading to Tinsley's office on the third floor. Gabe had hoped they would catch a look at the rooms, but every door was closed. Probably for security or privacy, but it still gave Gabe a bad feeling.

Tinsley's posh office, when the rest of the place was rundown, immediately made Gabe dislike the guy. Or maybe Gabe was searching for a reason to dislike him. He looked just like the picture El had shown Caitlyn—his blond hair styled perfectly, his suit tailormade—but that wasn't Gabe's issue. He disliked the way he held his head, chin in the air, as if he were superior to everyone around him. And the fact that his office was flashy and his clothing expensive when the rest of the property needed obvious repair seemed sketchy. Maybe he should just cut his salary that paid for his clothing and use it to make the needed repairs.

He pointed to two chairs by a sleek glass desk and told them to sit when he should be apologizing for keeping them waiting for nearly an hour before agreeing to see them. A power play, or was he getting his story together regarding Kenna's death and Lucy's abduction?

He sat in a white leather chair behind the desk. "Is this about one of our children?"

"We're here to talk to you about your organization," El said, relaxing in her chair, as if this interview wasn't important.

"Safe Harbor?" He blinked rapidly. "What about it?"

"We'd like to know what exactly you do and how it functions."

"But why?"

El smiled, but it was forced. "This visit is more of a formality. The charity's name has come up in one of our investigations, and we just need to cover our bases."

"Oh." He exhaled, his thin chest sagging even more. "I was worried it had something to do with one of the children."

"Rest assured, it doesn't," El said. "Please give us an overview of this place and the charity."

"It's all really straightforward. Jonas Trent...do you know who he is?"

El and Gabe both nodded.

"You may not know he adopted two boys from here. That was when he learned we were really struggling financially and might have to close. So, he and his wife started a charity for helping children in need, but the main purpose was to designate the money for Safe Harbor."

"Who decides where the money goes?" Gabe asked.

"The board of directors, but Trent is the chairman, and they pretty much do what he suggests."

The perfect situation for a perfect storm, and Gabe was beginning to think they should be looking at Trent, not

Tinsley. "I don't suppose Safe Harbor has any income other than money from the charity."

"That's correct."

"Tell me about how these funds are funneled to you," El said.

"Simple, really. We receive quarterly checks from New Tide's accountant."

"The accountant's name?" El sat with her pen poised over her notepad.

He tapped his finger on the desk a few times, then shook his head. "What difference does it make if I give it to you? You'll find out, anyway. His name is Patrick Sloan."

"Phone number?" El asked.

Tinsley looked at his phone and gave her the digits.

She wrote them down and looked back at him. "Address?"

"I don't know exactly what it is, but he works out of the New Tide office across the parking lot."

"Who handles the money on this end?" she asked.

"Our bookkeeper. Her office is down the hall, but she only works part-time and isn't here until tomorrow." He took a long breath. Let it out slowly. "So, this is about our finances?"

"Leave no stones unturned and all of that." El smiled in a way that would relax an innocent interviewee, but Tinsley tensed. "About audits. How often are they done, and by whom?"

"We've had one. I'm not exactly sure who did it, but Jonas Trent hired an outside accounting firm and he interfaced with the auditors. I think it was maybe a year and a half ago. I can get out my records if you'd like, but I have a very busy day and would like to move on. What else can I answer?"

"You had an admin volunteer named Kenna James. Did you know her?"

"Had? Did?" He batted his eyes, and his face held either the best innocent look an actor could create or he was honestly surprised. "Did something happen to her?"

"You haven't heard? She was murdered," El said as plainly as if she were telling him Kenna went on vacation.

He startled. "Who would want to kill such a lovely young woman?"

"That's what we aim to find out," Gabe said, his tone more insistent, to try to get this guy to quit stalling and answer the question.

"But you think it had something to do with our place?" He snapped the back of his chair forward and rested his hands on the desk. "Is that why you're here?"

"If you know she was a lovely young woman, it sounds like you knew her pretty well," Gabe said. "Did you work in close contact with her?"

"I don't know if I'd say close contact, but she acted in an admin capacity, so yes, we worked together. Mostly via notes or emails, but in person on the nights I worked the late shift."

El scribbled a note on her pad. "Anyone else work directly with her?"

He shook his head. "You're not suggesting I had something to do with her death."

"No, but since you mention it, where were you on Friday evening between seven and ten p.m.?"

"Friday?" He closed his eyes for a moment. "Sorry, I'm just so stunned. I can hardly think. At the movies. Yes, I was with my family. My wife and two kids can verify that." He named the movie and gave details of what happened in it, including the ending.

He was giving way too much information, the hallmark

sign of someone who had something to hide. The guy was either giving them half answers or over-answering. Seemed like he wanted to play cat and mouse.

Fine. Gabe excelled at games, and he always played to win.

~

El walked alongside Tinsley, with Gabe behind them, as they strolled through Safe Harbor's main floor. So far, they'd seen a large living room with shabby couches, a TV, board games, and worn books. They stepped into a hallway.

El believed Tinsley was holding back, and she needed to get him talking more to trip him up if he was lying. "I appreciate your willingness to give us a tour."

"Like I said, my day is filled, and it has to be fast." He pointed at a closed door with a bulletin board mounted on the front. "Staff office. This is where the bookkeeper I mentioned works. Also, our admin volunteers."

"Looks like no one's here today."

"That's normal. We're very conscious of people with families and schedule our staff and volunteers for three- or four-day weekends whenever we can. If they do have to work on Monday or Friday, we make sure it's only a half day."

El didn't know if this was significant, but she made a note of it. "Tell me about your other paid staff members."

"We have a house manager. She let you in the door and called me. She runs the place in the daytime, and we alternate evenings, ensuring a manager's on duty at all times. There are two staff on shift at a time. One awake overnight. The other asleep, but on call. They rotate. That's all. We have limited funds. Means we have a lean, but very effective staff."

"I'd like a list of their names, addresses, and phone numbers."

"I'll get one to you, but don't be surprised if it changes the next day. Turnover in daily workers is high in this industry."

Probably even higher working in a shabby place like this for a guy like you.

"Did a man named Howard Mason work for you?"

He swung his gaze to El. "No, am I supposed to know that name?"

"Not necessarily," El said. "How many children do you serve?"

"Usually six, but we can house up to eight."

Fewer than El had thought, and it explained the smaller staff. "Does anyone from the state evaluate your program?"

"Well, of course, we had to be approved before opening and obtain a license. It's renewed every two years after an on-site inspection. Plus, we have a caseworker who visits periodically and a therapist who comes in weekly."

He bolted ahead, put his hand on a doorknob, and turned back to look at them. "This last room is for high needs or new placements. It's currently vacant and you can take a look."

He opened the door to reveal a meagerly decorated room with a dresser, single bed with the bedding folded on top, and a desk. Stained vinyl tiles covered the floor, and a white roller shade shielded the only window. All in all, a very depressing room. The only thing that saved it was the cheerful yellow walls.

"There," he said. "You've seen the main floor and my office. The first and second floors are bedrooms like this, only with two of everything. Nothing else to see, and I'll escort you to the door."

El planted her feet. "I'd like to see one of the double rooms."

"Fine," he said. "We have a vacant double on the second floor where our girls stay."

He charged back down the hall and up the stairway. He used a key card to unlock the main door. They stepped into a hallway. Once again all the doors were closed, but these were decorated with bright posters and fun pictures by the residents.

"How do children come to stay here?" she asked.

"We take placements from social services for children who most foster homes don't want to deal with. Kids who are neglected or abused or have behavioral issues. We also provide temporary placements referred by social workers."

Such a shame that these children had already been through so much then had to live in such a depressing place. If she believed donating money to the home would perk the place up, she'd do it, but she only feared Tinsley would use it for his office or his needs.

Tinsley jutted out his chin. "Are you satisfied now, and I can get back to my work?"

"Yes, thank you for the tour," El said.

He walked out the door, his pace brisk in the hallway. She followed, Gabe behind her. Three early teen girls were walking toward them, heads bowed together and chatting.

Tinsley didn't seem to notice them, but continued down the hall.

El said hello in passing and continued after Tinsley. One of them tugged on the back of her jacket, stopping her. El turned.

The girl glanced in Tinsley's direction then stepped closer and motioned for El to lower her head.

"We need help," she whispered, abject fear in her eyes. "They take kids who don't have anyone. Kids like me."

El couldn't be more shocked and didn't know how to respond.

Was this girl telling the truth?

El opened her mouth to ask her name.

"Girls!" Tinsley bellowed down the hall at them. "Move along now. You should be in class. And you, Detective, should be on your way."

"Please help," the girl whispered and rushed away with the others, who also gave El a silent plea as they passed by.

El followed them down the hall. Was this girl right? Were they actually taking kids for some purpose? Maybe trafficking them or selling them for adoption? Should she believe the girl?

She didn't know, but one thing was sure. She had to follow up. Not only for the children's sake, but because it could be related to their investigation, and the reason Kenna had been murdered.

22

Outside on the sidewalk, Gabe looked around to be sure he was alone with El. Satisfied no one could overhear them, he took hold of her arm to slow her down. "What happened back there with the girl? Your demeanor changed completely."

"That's because of what she said to me." El's troubled gaze looked up at him. "She said, and I quote, 'They take kids who don't have anyone. Kids like me.'"

"Wow!" Gabe shook his head. "Do you think she was legit?"

"She seemed legitimately scared but could just be a good actor. However, the other girls didn't say anything, but their expressions seemed to confirm what she told me."

"So do you want to follow this lead or stick with finances?"

"I'll have to refer it to social services but as for us, I don't think we have enough information to go on. For now we stick with finances, then we go back to Hayden. See what he's learned about Safe Harbor and New Tide."

He nodded his agreement with her plan when he just

wanted to charge back to Tinsley and shake him until he admitted what they were doing with these children.

El shifted to stare across the parking lot. "Since we're here, we'll try to interview Sloan and Trent."

"Lead the way," he said, honoring her decision again.

She started to cross the parking lot to the New Tide office, also a house, but this one was very contemporary.

A black van whipped into the parking lot. The front side door held the Safe Harbor logo. She turned to Gabe. "Is that a Ford—"

"Transit 350? Yeah, it is, but the plates don't match the ones in Mason's pictures."

"They could've switched plates, or they have additional vans. And we don't even know if the van in Mason's pictures is the one that ran Kenna off the road." El ended their conversation and raced toward the vehicle.

A guy with slicked back blond hair wearing greasy gray overalls and a stained T-shirt slid out.

She stepped in front of him and blocked his path. "Do you work for Safe Harbor?"

He cast her a quizzical look. "Nope, just a mechanic returning the van."

"What was wrong with it?"

He crossed his arms. "Not sure that's any of your business."

She displayed her credentials.

"Why didn't you say something?" He shook his head. "We had it in for an oil change and routine maintenance."

"No body damage?" Gabe asked.

"Nope. They keep their vehicles pristine."

If El was disappointed, her expression didn't show it. "If they did incur any body damage, would they bring the van to you?"

He relaxed his arms. "We don't do bodywork. Refer everybody out to Al's Bodyshop."

She jotted down the name in her notebook.

"Look." The mechanic grabbed a piece of paper from the seat. "I gotta go. I got jammed up in traffic and my ride will be here in a minute." He slammed the van door and started across the lot.

"One more question," Gabe called after him. "Do you know how many vans they own?"

"Not sure, but we service three of them."

"And they usually park them here in the lot?" Gabe asked.

He nodded. "Now, seriously, I gotta go, or I'm gonna get canned." He took off jogging toward the home.

El looked at Gabe. "So where are the other two? We can't go in and question Tinsley, or we'll give him a heads-up that we're looking for a damaged van, and it might disappear."

"Guess we call Al's Bodyshop," Gabe said. "But odds are, the killer wouldn't take it somewhere near here."

"When we get back to the car, I'll get the registration information for your team, and they can call around with this new information."

He nodded, and they started across the lot to the New Tide office. He pulled the glass door open and held it for her. The foyer was even more posh than the group home. A professionally dressed woman with her hair twisted up in the back gave them a practiced smile from behind the wooden reception desk.

El held up her credentials. "We're here to see Patrick Sloan."

Her smile evaporated. "Can you tell me what this is about?"

"No," El said.

Gabe assumed she hoped the one word would discourage additional conversation.

"Let me see if he's available." She punched a few buttons on her console and talked into the handset. "I will," she said, then hung up and turned her attention to El. "Have a seat. He'll be right down."

El tilted her head. "I'm a little confused and maybe you can help me. Is this foundation related to the group home across the parking lot?"

"Yes." The young woman's broad smile returned. "Most of the money we raise goes to Safe Harbor, so we're very connected."

Gabe rested his elbow on the counter. "But not legally."

She looked up at him, her smile broadening. "No. However, our chairman of the board is very involved with their director. So is Patrick."

Gabe gave her a flirtatious smile. "Friends or just involved in the business together?"

"Not just the work, but friends. Good friends." She returned Gabe's smile with a wide one, her eyes alive with interest in him. "Honestly, I don't know where Patrick fits socializing into his crazy schedule. By the time he was thirty-five, he'd already sold two startups, and venture capitalists were drooling over him and his third company when he started working here."

"Thank you, Trudy," a booming male voice came from behind them. "You've told them quite enough."

Gabe spun to see the man with the big voice but was surprised by the lean mass of the tall blond guy standing there. His sleek black suit with a tailor-pressed cut screamed taste. The gold cufflinks on his starched white shirt and his Rolex watch spoke to money, maybe ambition.

He strode with extreme confidence toward them. He

stretched out his hand to Gabe. "Patrick Sloan. Detective, what can I—"

"Sorry, man." Gabe held up his hands. "Wrong choice." Gabe's comment briefly ruffled the guy. "I'm Gabe Irving with the Lost Lake Locators, and this is Detective Elaina Lyons."

Sloan turned on a megawatt smile and fired it and his hand in El's direction. "I'm so sorry, Detective Lyons." His gaze fixed on her, looking at her as if she were the only woman in the world. "Can you ever forgive me?"

El wasn't in any way affected by his overdone charm. She maintained her professional posture and firmly grasped his hand to shake. "Nothing to forgive. Is there somewhere we can talk in private?"

His smile evaporated. "What's this about?"

"It's better if we discuss it behind closed doors."

"We can go to my office." He performed a razor-sharp pivot and marched to a door he quickly unlocked with a key card. It led into a long hallway with offices on both sides.

"So many offices," El said. "New Tide must be doing very well to need all these employees."

"Indeed." Sloan led them to the end of the hallway and swung into a doorway on the left.

The corner office. Decorated in an ultra-modern style. Glass everywhere. Expensive artwork and objects all around the room, and beautiful views of a large wooded area. The office, combined with his attire, sent red flags flying for Gabe.

Of course, if what the receptionist had said was true, he would've come to this business with money, and his pretentious display might not have anything to do with his current salary. Hayden's deep dive would tell them if that was true.

Sloan gestured with a manicured hand at a round table.

He waited until they were seated, then joined them, crossing his long legs and leaning back as if he were king.

"Now, what's this all about?" he asked, sounding as if this conversation was beneath him.

El took her time retrieving her notebook and pen. "We'd like details on how payments are handled between New Tide and Safe Harbor."

His eyes narrowed. "I'm not sure that's information I should provide to you."

"Why not? It's not like you're giving me trade secrets or anything."

"No, but—"

"I can get a warrant if I need to."

He snapped his chair forward and planted his feet on the floor. "What's this about, anyway? Why do you need the information so badly that you'd get a warrant?"

"We believe it relates to an investigation we're working on."

"That was a perfect non-answer."

"I'm sorry. I can't share information for an ongoing investigation. Please answer my question, Mr. Sloan, and stop wasting our time."

He sat back. Pondered for a while. "I guess it won't hurt to tell you. It's not like it's a secret or anything. Each month, Mr. Trent tells me how much money to transfer to Safe Harbor, and I write a check. Simple as that."

Gabe thought he was either lying or sharing a half-truth. If paying the home was so simple, why was Sloan making such a big deal of keeping it from them?

El finished writing a note and looked up. "Does the money vary every month?"

Sloan nodded. "They're guaranteed a basic amount each month, but we often raise additional funds, and that money is passed on directly to them."

"What is the basic monthly guaranteed amount?"

He scrunched his forehead. "Now that's private information, and I'm not free to share it without that warrant you mentioned."

El didn't appear flustered at his answer. "I can respect that. How about an approximation? Is it less than fifty thousand a month?"

He shook his head.

"Between fifty and one hundred grand a month?"

"On the upper end of your range. But that's all I'll say about exact finances without that warrant."

El tapped her pen on her notebook but kept her gaze on Sloan. "That's a large chunk of change annually. Tell me how you raise the money."

"Thank goodness that's not part of my job description." He laughed and swiped the back of his hand over his forehead. "But seriously, I don't know all the details. I just show up at fundraising events when I'm told to by the board of directors, who are in charge of the fundraising. Basically, that means Jonas Trent does it."

They would have to go to the top to get complete answers.

"How often are your books audited?" El asked.

"I guess it was a little less than two years ago. We don't receive any federal funds, so we aren't subjected to annual audits."

"But you do receive payments for the children from the state, correct?" Gabe asked, hoping to disprove Tinsley's statement.

"Actually, no. We're funded solely by money raised by the board."

So Tinsley had told the truth, but Gabe didn't know why they wouldn't want any money from the state. Maybe Sloan could tell them. "Why would you turn down the state's money?"

"Again, another question for the board of directors."

El eyed him in her practiced interview stare. "Which you said is basically Jonas Trent."

"I mean, yeah, in most things." He paused, his gaze darting around the room, as if looking for a way out of this situation. "But I figure the entire board makes decisions like that."

"Is Mr. Trent's office in this building?"

"He has the whole second floor."

Excellent. Gabe liked the idea of marching right up there and putting him in the hot seat next. "Do you know if he's in?"

"I saw him this morning, but it's not my job to keep track of him." He smirked. "Is that all the questions you have for me?"

"Are you familiar with a man named Howard Mason?" Gabe asked.

He immediately shook his head, his expression blank. "No. Don't know the guy. Now if that's all..."

El didn't move a single muscle toward leaving, but kept her gaze raptly fixed on his. "One more question. Do you know a Kenna James?"

"Kenna James?" He narrowed his gaze in direct contrast to his innocent response to knowing Mason. "The name sounds familiar, but I don't know where to place her."

Gabe got out his phone and flashed Kenna's picture at Sloan.

Sloan shook his head. "No. I don't think I do know her."

"She worked as an admin volunteer for Safe Harbor," Gabe said.

"Oh, yeah. That's probably where I saw her name. On an email or something."

He was hiding something. Gabe was sure of it. "But you never interacted with her in person?"

"No. Never." His adamant expression should indicate he was telling the truth, but Gabe's gut told him not to believe the guy.

El sat silently for a moment. "What would you say if I told you she was murdered Friday night?"

He sat up, his body rigid and every muscle in his face locked into place. "Well, I'd say I'm sorry that happened. Exactly what I'd say if anyone was murdered. And I'm especially sorry because she was a volunteer at Safe Harbor. I'm sure everyone over there is upset and will miss her."

El held her pen poised over her notebook. "Where were you on Friday evening between seven and ten p.m.?"

"Me?" He lurched forward. "You're asking me for an alibi? Like you think I might have killed a woman I don't even personally know?"

El's outward appearance didn't reveal any emotions. "Please just answer the question, Mr. Sloan."

He crossed his arms. "Fine. Friday night I was at our fundraiser at the Lakeside Ballroom. Tons of people can confirm I was there, including our chairman of the board."

"Jonas Trent was at the fundraiser?" she asked, for the first time showing a minor crack in her armor.

"Both of us were. Arrived an hour before it started and left a half an hour after it ended. That would be from six until midnight. That's our standard procedure so not a single donor who wants to talk to us is missed." He cleared his throat and stood. "Now if that's all, I really do need to get back to work. I'll walk you out."

He didn't give them an option, but briskly strode to the door and into the hallway.

They had no choice but to follow or wait for him to

throw them out. There was something else Gabe would like to push him on, but he didn't.

On the way to the door, El eased close to him. "He's hiding something."

He peered down at her. "Agreed. The big question is, what?"

23

———————

Sloan escorted them to the elevator and waited while they got in and the door closed. Instead of selecting the first floor, El punched number two.

"I would have hit that button too," Gabe said. "We ask to see Trent, and if they try to throw us out, I plan to make a big scene." Gabe flashed her a fiendish grin.

She laughed, and her heart lifted a bit. "I'm not sure I'm in on the *scene* thing, but if he's here, I won't leave easily." She patted her shield on her waistband. "Even if I have to use this to toss out some idle threats."

"It'll be interesting to see if your credentials impact this guy at all, or if he thinks he's untouchable."

The elevator dinged, and the doors whisked open.

"Time will tell." She stepped into a surprisingly small lobby area. The furnishings were similar to the first floor, but the receptionist was a young beauty who looked like she should be a model. Stereotyping, El knew, but her job proved that out more times than not. Still, her beliefs ensured she always tried to give people the benefit of the doubt.

At the desk, she held out her credentials. "I'm Detective

Elaina Lyons with the Lost Lake Sheriff's Department. I need to see Jonas Trent, and it's a matter of urgency."

"Oh, my! The police." She batted her heavily mascaraed and very false long eyelashes at El. "Is he in some kind of trouble?"

"No, but we believe he can help us with our investigation, and as I said, this is a matter of urgency. Can you please tell him we're here?"

"Yes, yes, of course. Right now. Hold on." Seeming flustered, she grabbed the phone. Unfortunately, as she talked, El realized she wasn't Trent's gatekeeper, and they'd have to go through his assistant.

She shared a look with Gabe, and he rolled his eyes. She wanted to do the same thing but resisted as the woman was watching her.

She ended her call. "You can have a seat if you want. His assistant will be right out."

"Thank you." El gave her a genuine smile and went straight to the seating area but remained standing.

Gabe joined her, and she was struck for the first time by how much he didn't look at home in this setting. He wore cargo pants, an ice blue tactical shirt, and tactical boots. Couple that with his dark intensity, and she was sure he was putting people off. Well, maybe not the receptionist, who kept looking at him as if he was the next Tom Cruise.

If he noticed, he didn't care. "Looks like you don't think the assistant will take much time."

"I have no idea. Just tired of sitting around. I want to take action."

"Oh man, you're a woman after my own heart." His playful little-boy grin almost distracted her from the door opening.

Almost.

The door was automated, and no one stepped out.

El's phone chimed, and she checked the text. "Message from Deputy Price. The guy who stole my computer finally turned it on, and they tracked it to a guy named Justin Ward. They went to his address, but he wasn't there so they're staking out the place."

"I'll get Hayden to do a deep dive into this guy." Gabe took out his phone and started tapping the screen.

He'd just shoved his phone into a pocket when an older woman in a formal navy suit entered through that automated door and stepped their way. From what El had heard about Trent, she expected another young and beautiful woman, but with the business he did, his priority had to be someone with solid experience.

"I'm Ms. Carlisle," she said, her voice pleasant and not at all antagonistic.

El held out her credentials and introduced herself and Gabe.

"I'm pleased to meet you," Ms. Carlisle said. "I'm Mr. Trent's assistant. Can I ask what this is in regard to?"

"I'm sorry," El said. "But the information is confidential. Just know that it's for a life-or-death investigation we're working on, and it's very time sensitive. If it wasn't, I would make an appointment when it was convenient for him."

Her tongue flicked across lips covered in the palest of pink lipstick. "Follow me."

She pivoted on her low-heel, sturdy black pumps, and marched back to the same door she'd stepped through. She flashed a card on the keypad and held the door open for them, revealing another small waiting area. "Have a seat, and I'll tell Mr. Trent you're here to see him."

She waited for them to sit, then disappeared through another door behind a desk holding a plaque with her name on it.

"I'm really starting to get irritated," El said. "But I guess I can't blame the gatekeepers. They don't know Lucy's missing and it might relate to Trent."

"Still, all I want is to bust down the door and confront him."

She gave him a pointed look. "But we won't, and we'll do our very best to handle ourselves as Christians."

"Got it," he said. "No busting down doors, and I'll do my best to have a good attitude."

The door opened, and Ms. Carlisle stepped out. "He'll see you now."

So quickly? El honestly didn't expect to get in, and wasn't as prepared as she should be for such an interview. Her usual composure took a hit, but she got it together to cross the room. "Thank you so much."

El entered his office. Floor-to-ceiling windows flooded the place with light. The décor was clean and minimalist, with dark walnut furniture,

Trent sat behind a massive desk holding three or four huge monitors running financial terminals, in a big leather chair that looked insanely comfortable.

He stood, coming to his full six-foot height. He was dressed in a formal black suit with a white shirt that set off his jet-black hair to perfection. He was like his receptionist. Model perfect. But a guy El could never be interested in. She liked hers rough and tumble. Street smart, not financial investor smart.

Gabe.

Trent came around the desk, his hand outstretched. "Detective Lyons."

She took his hand, the firm grasp almost punishing. She gave back as good as she could before she let go.

He nodded at Gabe. "Have a seat."

He pointed at a sleek leather sofa sitting below colorful abstract art.

As they sat, she couldn't help but notice the whole vibe was calm, quiet, and expensive without being flashy, just serious money and total control. The exact opposite of Sloan.

He sat in a club chair across from them. "What can I do for you?"

"We'd like information on your role with Safe Harbor." She wouldn't expose any more until she heard what he had to say.

"I should first let you know I have a personal connection to the home. My wife and I adopted two amazing boys who were being housed there. They've brought so much to our lives, and I was so impressed with the home and director that I created a foundation to help fund them. Over the years, I've been fortunate to raise enough money to allow New Tide to become their sole support."

"And you serve as the chairman of New Tide's board."

He gave one crisp nod. "My role is to provide operational guidance to the director and ensure there's enough money in the bank to keep the home running with a quality program for these children."

"Basically, you tell the director what to do so their place can get money from you," Gabe said, obviously forgetting the Mr. Nice Guy routine he'd promised to follow.

Trent fired a sharp look at Gabe before he cleared it, but in that moment, El could see him as a murderer. Or maybe she wanted him to be one, because it meant they were moving forward.

He chuckled. "I wouldn't say they have to earn their money, but the board does have certain expectations that need to be followed. I enforce those expectations."

El cleared her throat to draw Trent's attention from Gabe. "Tell us the procedure on how money is transferred to the home after the board approves the payment."

"Very simple, really. I notify our accountant to issue payment. He cuts them a check, then walks it across the parking lot to their bookkeeper."

"When you say *notify*, how is that handled?" she asked, hoping there was a paper trail to follow the money.

"We're not a big organization needing a lot of paperwork. I just make a simple phone call to Sloan. Patrick Sloan, our accountant. He handles the rest."

"And I assume he also manages all of the money that comes in from your fundraisers."

"Actually, no. Sound accounting practice dictates the person who receives the money should never disperse it. The money comes in to our donation processor, and she takes care of all the accounting entries and deposits the money. She's also responsible for recurring donations and special gifts."

"So you never touch the money, incoming or outgoing?"

"I do not," he said very clearly, as if he wanted her to take note of it. "Don't tell me you think our organization's financial procedures have something to do with your investigation. If you do, I can assure you, we employ Generally Accepted Accounting Practices and have passed every audit we've ever had."

"I see," El said. "When were your books last audited?"

"Less than two years ago."

Same answer as Sloan. Either they prepared for questions about their finances, or it was the truth. "Is the same true for Safe Harbor?"

He nodded. "And I'll be glad to provide you with the auditor's conclusions if that would be helpful."

If he was so eager to help, a red flag didn't immediately pop up, but obviously Kenna had found something in the books that got her killed. "Do you know a Kenna James?"

"Name sounds familiar," he said without hesitation.

"She was a volunteer at Safe Harbor. Did admin duties."

"Oh yes, Kenna. Sure, I knew of her. We communicated via email a few times, but I never worked with her."

"I'm sorry to tell you she was murdered Friday night."

He remained expressionless, but that didn't mean anything. He didn't have much sympathy because he really didn't know Kenna, or he didn't care enough about a lowly volunteer dying.

"I'm sorry to hear that." He curled his fingers in, buffed his nails on his jacket, then stared at them. "I guess you're not safe from crime anywhere these days."

El had to fight the anger mounting over his lack of concern or caring. "This wasn't a random act."

"Oh, wait." A look of surprise flashed across his face now. Fake or real, she didn't know as she believed he was a real chameleon and could summon up any expression any time he wanted. "You think this is connected to our finances somehow? No, that's ridiculous."

"What exactly was her role to the vendors, as a volunteer?" El continued.

"She input all of Safe Harbor's invoices due into the computer so checks could be issued to the vendors." He sat forward, his gaze fixed on El. "Don't tell me she was doing something wrong over there? If she was, no one ever suspected a thing."

Of course he tried to blame Kenna's own murder on her.

"You should probably talk to our director, Silas Tinsley," he continued. "He worked more directly with her and could provide additional information. But I assure you as soon as you leave today, I'll start an investigation into her work."

Gabe glared at Trent. "From what you tell us, all she was doing was inputting data for you, not paying out money or taking in money. What exactly could she have done wrong?"

"On the surface, I couldn't tell you. I'll have to investigate and get back to you." He gave them a patronizing smile and stood. "If that's all, I have pressing matters to attend to, which now includes checking into this young woman's work."

His dismissive tone irked El, but she wouldn't let him dismiss her before she was done questioning him. "Does a Howard Mason work for you?"

That got her first real response, a flash of surprise followed by a quick emotionless mask falling over his face. "Another name I don't know." He held his hand toward the door. "I must insist you leave now."

She stood, but didn't take a step. "One last thing. Where were you on Friday evening between seven and ten p.m.?"

"At one of our annual fundraisers. I can provide you with names and phone numbers for others who attended with me to confirm that."

Just as Sloan had told them. "I appreciate the offer, Mr. Trent. I'll get back to you if we need them."

He headed straight for the door, not looking back at them, and held it open.

The only other questions El wanted to ask him would be about the van, and she wouldn't give anyone a heads-up about that. She also wanted to question him about the girl who'd approached her at the home, but first she needed to check into the validity of her statement. She couldn't risk alerting them that she suspected that something inappropriate was going on with the kids.

Keeping her mouth shut, she crossed the room to the door. Gabe didn't seem as eager to leave and took sluggish steps behind her.

Once Trent's door had closed, she stopped at Ms. Carlisle's desk. "Thank you for all of your help. I just have one quick question for you. Can you tell me the last time Howard Mason stopped in?"

She blinked a few times. "You know I can't share any information about Howard's last visit."

Ah, but you just did.

"He's just such a great guy, isn't he?" she asked, hoping Mason's cop days had taught him to smooth-talk an assistant if he wanted to get anywhere. "You don't meet many men like that these days."

"No, you don't. I always looked forward to his visits."

"Okay, thanks again, Ms. Carlisle. Your help is appreciated more than you know." El gave her a sincere smile. Not for her help, but for confirming that Howard Mason had a connection to Jonas Trent, adding an additional connection between his murder and Kenna's.

"So Mason and Trent know each other," Gabe said after they left Ms. Carlisle's office. "Now we have a further connection between the murders."

"Question is," El said, "what does that connection mean? As a former cop, I would suspect he could've been one of Trent's goons. But then, Talia doesn't describe him as that kind of man, and he would have had to have gone against what he valued for most of his adult life."

"He was dying. Maybe he didn't have any money and wanted to leave some for Talia."

"Could be. Hayden can tell us more about Mason's finances. Otherwise, we'll have to wait for this to play out."

At the elevator, Gabe punched the Down button. "What about Trent, though? Could he be more condescending or self-serving?

"Probably, but he really was thinking only of himself."

"Do you like him for the murder and kidnapping?"

"Condescending and self-serving do not say murderer, so not at this point. He has an alibi, but I could see him hiring someone to do his dirty work for him."

Gabe stared down at his feet as they walked, then he

glanced at El. "Would it be worth it to him to kill Kenna to stop her from exposing financial fraud?"

"Good question." El thought about the interview. "He's riding high right now, and that could certainly bring him down. How far he would fall would depend on how he set up the fraud. He's smart enough to have planned for a scapegoat to take the fall. We really need more details about what Kenna found."

Gabe punched the elevator button again as if it would make a difference. "Then it's time to go back to her journal."

"Agreed."

The elevator whisked open.

El stepped on board. "First, we pay Bonnie another visit."

24

———

El didn't waste any time making the short drive to the center, where they found Bonnie sitting behind her desk.

She lifted her head and froze. Then blinked. A long exhale of air followed. "Detective. How can I help you?"

Her personable yet detached tone irritated El, but she couldn't say why. "We learned that Carl Acosta's daughter attends your center. Is that right?"

She pointed at the chairs by her desk. "Have a seat."

El opted to remain standing, and so did Gabe.

"Please answer my question. Does Carl Acosta's daughter attend here?"

"Kind of," she replied. "She's his legal daughter, but he no longer has custody, and if he shows up here, we're to call the police."

"I don't understand," El said. "He was the man in the van watching your center, and you talked to him outside the center. If you're supposed to call the police, why aren't there police reports for such an incident?"

She sighed, her breath rushing out. "All he wanted to do was see her from the van. That was why he was watching us. He wasn't a threat to anyone."

El begged to differ. "That's not your decision to make. He could've been here to abduct his daughter. But that doesn't matter right now. What I want to know is what did he mean when he said to you, 'We need her to come through for us, and you're gonna make sure that happens.'"

"Talia Vogel's dad told you this, didn't he? She had him spying on us for days." She crossed her arms. "Well, I don't have to say anything. It's personal."

"Personal or not, this is a murder investigation."

She raised her chin. "He wanted me to talk to his ex-wife. To try to get her to change her mind about his visitation rights."

"Hah," Gabe said. "You expect us to believe you when the last part of his demand sounded like a threat, not simply asking a favor."

"No. No threats." She held up a placating hand. "You're misunderstanding. He was just upset."

"Why you?" El asked. "What could you possibly do to persuade his ex to change her mind?"

She held both hands in front of her face as if she wanted to hide. "I was the reason he lost custody in the first place."

Now they were getting somewhere, and El cast a knowing look at Gabe. He gave a brief nod of understanding.

"Explain," El said.

She lowered her hands, her gaze darting about as if looking for an escape. She shook her head and let her arms fall to her sides. "We made a mistake. Spent the night together. It wasn't planned. One night he couldn't get to the center before closing to pick his daughter up, so I dropped her off at his apartment. I never do that, but he would have lost custody if he didn't pick her up, and I felt sorry for him. He invited me in for a drink. It was one of those days, so I agreed. Then we had a second drink. A third. Maybe a fourth, and one thing led to another. We fell asleep. The next morning, his daughter saw us together. She told her mother. That was all the ammunition his wife needed to get full custody."

"Will he corroborate your story?" El asked.

"I don't know, but I hope so, because I'm telling the truth."

"We'll talk to him next."

"You can't," she said quickly. "He's out of town for the week."

El wasn't sure if she should believe her or not. "Give me his cell number. I'll give him a call."

Bonnie grabbed a notepad and jotted it down then shoved the page across the desk.

El picked it up to confirm she'd noted a full phone number. "You're not to have any contact with him or try to coerce him into agreeing to your story. Is that understood?"

"Perfectly. I don't want anyone to find out about this. Can it stay between us?"

"If it has nothing to do with our investigation, I'll try to keep it quiet." El turned and marched out the door, with Gabe following. She looked at him. "Bonnie sure doesn't seem the type to have an affair."

He shook his head. "But if she was inebriated, anything was possible. And she sounds like she regrets it."

"She did seem like she was telling the truth."

"But if she's somehow involved with fraud at Safe Harbor and desperate to keep that and her affair quiet," Gabe paused, as if for effect. "Then she might've gotten Acosta to take action for her."

"Run Kenna off the road and kill her," El said. "So, the guy remains a suspect until we locate him, and he provides an alibi for the time of Kenna's murder."

Gabe hoped Acosta would answer El's phone call she made in the daycare parking lot, but she had to leave a message. Another roadblock that put a damper on his conversation with El as they drove back to the inn to review Kenna's journal.

They hurried inside, and at the conference room, Gabe got a good look at Hayden. His expression burned with excitement, bringing Gabe's feet to a stop.

Gabe poked his head in the door. "Looks like you might've found a lead."

"Good. You're back." Hayden looked up from behind his computer. "I was just going to text you."

Gabe gestured for El to join him. "Is it about Ward?"

"No, that algorithm is still running, but you'll never guess what I located on New Tide and Safe Harbor."

Gabe stepped into the room. "Spit it out."

"Please," El said, firing a corrective look at him as she entered the room.

"Sorry, man," Gabe said to Hayden. "I'm just tired of people wanting to give us the runaround and am desperate for good news."

"No problem." Hayden leaned his chair back. "I'm only at the tip of the iceberg right now. I need to go deeper to find proof, but rumors on the dark web say Jonas Trent is stealing donation money from New Tide."

El clicked her tongue against her teeth in disapproval. "I can't say I'm surprised. He's apparently devoted himself full-time to this organization, but shouldn't he be managing his business projects? After all, that's where his money comes from."

Hayden nodded. "Apparently, he's turned most responsibilities over to project managers. He only handles PR and finances. Which, according to comments, includes setting up bogus companies. Then he bills Safe Harbor under renovation costs, maintenance contracts, facility upgrades, etcetera. The projects never occur, and the payments go to a shell company he controls."

Gabe's anger rose. "What a scumbag."

She gripped the back of a chair, her eyes narrowed. "The kids are the ones who suffer. They have to live in conditions that barely meet licensing requirements. You only have to visit, and it's clear very little money is spent on upgrades and maintenance."

"I take it to mean Tinsley's in on it," Gabe said. "Trent probably pays him off to keep his mouth shut."

She shoved the chair and moved her hands to her waist. "Could also be true of the accountant. And it explains why they were able to pass audits."

"Probably the thing Kenna stumbled on," Gabe said. "She might've written about it in her journal."

"I'll look into this accountant and Tinsley, but I'm also just getting a picture of Trent's finances. He took a hit on some business investments, and he's living larger than he can afford. Could be his reason for stealing from Safe Harbor."

"New Tide's accountant, Patrick Sloan, seems to be living large, too," Gabe said. "Even Tinsley. Probably those payoffs from Trent."

"I'll get back to you on all of that." Hayden held up his hand. "Before you go, I have something else for you. Apparently, word on the street is that Safe Harbor is linked to multiple missing children cases."

El sucked in a sharp breath, and her eyes blazed with fire. "On our visit, one of the residents said as much to me. I didn't know whether to believe her or not, but looks like I should."

"Or the kids might have a beef against Tinsley or the center, and they started a false rumor," Gabe said.

"Or it could be true." El continued to burn with anger. "At this point, we need to at least consider it, and as an officer, I'm legally bound to contact social services. Which I'll do before we start on that journal."

Hayden's expression turned dark. "Sounds like the journal is your best lead. Let me know if you find anything else needing my help, and I'll keep digging here."

"Thanks, man." Gabe bumped fists with Hayden, then looked at El. "How about some coffee to go?" He nodded at the pot on the food table.

"If it makes a difference," Hayden said, "it's freshly made and not the stale stuff you often find in the afternoon."

"I don't care how or what it's made of," she said with conviction. "I absolutely would like some."

"Black, one sugar, right?" Gabe asked.

She gave him a soft smile that went straight to his heart. "Right."

"You guys are way too in sync for just...whatever this is. Cute, I guess." He stuck a finger in his mouth and faked gagging.

A quick reply was right on Gabe's lips, but his buddy was right. Gabe *had* noticed El's coffee preference. He'd noticed that and so much more over the years.

"Besides the coffee," Hayden added. "Reece left you some sandwiches in the refrigerator."

"I could eat," El said.

"I'll grab them." Gabe handed the mugs to El and pushed through the swinging door to the large commercial refrigerator that was always stuffed with fresh food. Not only had she made sandwiches, but they were sack lunches with their names on them. Made sense, or one of the guys might polish them off as a snack.

Gabe returned with the two bags. "I'll follow you."

She turned to leave, and Gabe paused near Hayden. "Let us know the minute you find anything else."

"Will do." Hayden turned back to his computer.

El hurried toward Gabe's room, where he'd temporarily hidden the journal. She'd logged it as evidence, but since they hadn't finished reading Kenna's entries, they wanted it close.

Gabe slipped past her, unlocked the door, and followed her inside.

She sat on the sofa. "Time to call social services."

Gabe went to his gun safe and listened to her give them all the information she possessed. By the time she finished, Gabe had crossed the room to sit next to her, Kenna's journal on his lap, the lunches on the table.

"Go ahead and start eating," she said. "I need to let Mina know about this, too. But please wait for me before you read the journal."

He reached for the bag with his name on it, but his favorite meatball sandwich tasted like sawdust and he set it down. El's call ended with her leaving a message for Mina.

"Could I get my lunch, please?" She set down her phone and held her hand out. "I'm sure you heard that I had to leave a message."

"Yeah." He put the bag in her hand. "But you know she'll call back."

She removed her sandwich and used it to point at the journal. "How about we start in the same section we read before, but at the beginning of that week?"

"Sounds like a good idea, but honestly, I don't think I can read more of it." He handed the journal to her. "Will you do it?

El swallowed her bite. "Are you sure?"

"Positive." He got up to pace, and he heard her flipping pages.

"This entry is a letter to you." She started blinking as if she didn't believe what she was reading.

"What?" he asked, his stomach clenching tighter. "What is it?"

She looked up, her expression tight. "You're not going to believe this, but Kenna gave us the name of Lucy's father."

Acid burned in El's stomach and she dropped her sandwich into the bag. If she felt this bad when she didn't have a past with Lucy, how would Gabe feel when he learned the father's name?

"Who is it?" Gabe demanded, standing over her.

El couldn't bring herself to say it aloud.

Gabe dropped down next to her and jerked the journal from her hands. "It can't be Patrick Sloan. The guy's a weasel. I can't let a man like that raise Lucy."

He clenched and unclenched his fists, looking like he wanted to punch the nearest object.

She tried to take his hand, but he held it away from her. "You don't know that he even wants her. He might not have any interest in her at all. Maybe this really is about the organization's finances, and he's involved. After all, he has access to the money."

"Yeah, let's focus on that. We need to get Hayden's deep dive, concentrate on any large deposits made to his bank account."

"I agree, but as much as you want to get after this, we need far more information from Hayden about the financial fraud and potential missing children to really do anything."

"You're right. He could discover that Sloan was in the

thick of things and would end up in prison with no ability to get rights to Lucy." Gabe released an aching breath. "Wouldn't it be ironic that he abducted Lucy due to the financial fraud, all the while not knowing she was his daughter?"

"If Kenna's murder is about the finances, then that's a very realistic scenario."

He fired off a text, then set his phone on the table. "There, Hayden's alerted."

She picked up the journal. "Let's keep reading the letter."

"What if she drops even a bigger bombshell?"

El wished she could get rid of the pain causing his tortured tone, but all she could do was support him by taking his hand, and this time he let her. "You have to know her wishes. I'm right here."

He went silent, a finger tracing the page. She started reading at the beginning again in case she missed something.

My dearest Gabe,

If you're reading this letter, you found my journal, and I'm in heaven with my savior. My only concerns are for leaving you and Lucy behind, and I have important information I need to tell you.

First, I want to say how very much I love you and how much you mean to me. You're the best friend any person could ever ask for and a terrific friend to Lucy too. My life has been so much richer for knowing you and being in your life. I pray that you have the most wonderful life filled with love and laughter and friendship. That you'll put your family's illegal activities behind you and realize you're nothing like them—nothing—and their baggage doesn't carry over to you. You are so far from who they are that no one would believe you came from that family. Also, I pray that you finally admit how deeply you care for El and tell her.

"She's right, you know," Gabe said, his words sounding strangled. "She knew me."

El intertwined her fingers with his and held on tightly. She had no idea he'd told Kenna about her, but that wasn't important now. Helping him heal was the main thing.

She continued reading.

Now, about Lucy. When you said yes to taking her if I was unable to care for her, I think you were just trying to appease me, but I'm taking you at your word, which I know you will uphold. I'd only pressure you to do this because I know you'll be an excellent father. You're caring, patient, and loving with Lucy, and yet you know when to discipline her and aren't afraid to do it. Everything she needs in a father.

You'll find Lucy's birth certificate in my safe deposit box where I named Patrick Sloan as her birth father. Lucy deserves to know who her dad is and receive information from him on family health histories. You can find him at the New Tide Foundation office. I hadn't seen him in years, but I ran into him there last week. He's their accountant. Can you believe that? A man I'd only ever seen one time and suddenly he's in my life again. I think that was a God moment, because he behaved as self-serving and conceited as in the past. The real ladies' man, trying to impress everyone around him.

What did I ever see in him? That's a question I've never been able to answer, other than I was in a completely vulnerable state, and he was very attentive to me. Regardless, I have Lucy because of that one night, and I would never want to give her back for anything."

"Grr," Gabe said. "I still don't like this. Not one bit and

I'll do everything I can to make sure Sloan gets the prison sentence he deserves."

"Is that the best thing for Lucy?" El asked.

"I don't know, I just don't know. I'll have to give it some serious thought." Gabe's piercing intensity left no question as to how he felt about Sloan. "What if the murder isn't really about Safe Harbor, but it's about Lucy's father killing Kenna to take his daughter away from her?"

"She wouldn't give up custody easily, so it sounds like a possibility." El would have to keep an eye on Gabe to be sure he didn't take action against Sloan before they could prove his involvement in any of this.

He lowered his eyes back to the journal.

She read on.

I asked around about Patrick, and he's still a real playboy and has no interest in getting married or settling down, much less having a child. Legally, it would be good if you got him to sign over Lucy's custody to you, but my will should suffice to prove my wishes. Should you ever want to adopt her, he would need to sign over all rights to you. Both things I think he'll do, and I pray that you'll want to do that for my little sweetheart.

I also ask you to keep my memory alive so she doesn't forget me. Tell her what I stood for and what kind of person I am. Be sure she knows that I love her above everything else and would never leave her unless I had to. In my safe deposit box, you'll find a flash drive. I've recorded a birthday message for her for every year of her life until she reaches twenty-one. Please be sure no matter who gets custody of her, that these messages are played every year on her birthday so she knows how very much I love her and wish I could be there to celebrate the big day with her.

Thank you again for being my dearest friend and for taking on this huge responsibility for my child's well-being.

I've been blessed every day I've known you, and I praise God for that!

All my love,

Kenna

El's heart swelled with emotion, and she could barely keep her tears from falling. She looked at Gabe. His head was down. She didn't want to trouble him, so she sat silently at his side. Waiting. Hoping he would let her help him.

His phone rang. He freed his hand from hers to swipe it over his eyes before grabbing the phone from the table. "Yeah?" He listened, then gave a sharp nod. "We'll be right there." He ended the call. "It's my brother," he said, stuffing his phone back in his pocket. "Says he has information about Kenna that will change our investigation and wants to meet with us."

Say what? "Where does he want to meet?"

"At the forest preserve."

She didn't like that at all. "Why such a secluded location?"

"You're a cop, and I'm a former one. He doesn't want anyone to see us together."

That made sense, but... "Do you believe he has information about Kenna, or do you think it's a trap?"

"I'd hate to believe he would set us up," Gabe said. "Regardless, I have to go, but you don't need to come with me. I don't want to put you in jeopardy."

She released his hand and stood. "There's no question in my mind. If you're going, I'll be right there at your side."

25

Gabe pulled his vehicle into the turnout near the entrance to a forest preserve owned and managed by the city. He opened the locked compartment between the seats and removed his weapon and holster.

"Do you think that's necessary?" El asked. "We're meeting your brother, after all."

Gabe seated a cartridge in his sidearm. "I don't really think he would hurt us, but it never hurts to be careful." Not thinking about it any longer, he got out and clipped on his holster, then waited for El to join him.

"Keep an eye out," he said as they started ahead on the road to the preserve.

He followed his brother's directions down a nearly hidden path through soaring pines, needles littering the ground. Under any other circumstances, he would enjoy this walk with El, but today enjoyment was one emotion he couldn't find.

They reached the designated gnarled and deformed tree, but Brad wasn't in sight.

El turned, taking in the area. "Do you think he's coming?"

Gabe shrugged. "You could be right, and he's setting us up. Let's take cover in case."

He led them to a pine large enough for both of them to fit behind the trunk.

Footfalls rustled in the pine straw.

"Someone's coming," he whispered and pointed his weapon.

Sure, the use of his sidearm was probably overkill. If he were alone, he might not be so proactive, but he wouldn't let anything happen to El.

They waited. He counted down in his head. *Five. Four. Three.*

A man rounded the curve in the path, his head on a swivel. He walked closer. Closer.

"It's Brad." Gabe let out a long breath and heard El blow hers out, too.

Gabe waited to see if anyone else followed, but convinced Brad was alone, he stepped out from behind the tree. El followed him.

His brother approached, his steps slow and apprehensive. "Hey, thanks, man, for meeting me. I didn't know if you would."

"If you hadn't called me, we would've come to see you anyway." Gabe widened his stance. "We know you were seeing Kenna."

He jerked back. "How?"

Gabe didn't even think twice before blurting out his statement. "The DNA test on the child Kenna was carrying came back as a familial match to me but we both know I'm not the father of the child. You are."

He blinked slowly, as if the information struggled to permeate his shock. "She was pregnant? How far along?"

"Twelve weeks," Gabe said. "A boy."

A wounded animal growl came from his brother, and he

looked like he might drop to the ground. "Why didn't she tell me?"

"We found a pregnancy test in the bathroom, so maybe she'd just found out," El said. "From your reaction, looks like you would've wanted to have a child with her."

"Without a doubt. I planned to leave the family business, find a job, and we were going to get married. But then she discovered Trent Jonas at New Tide was not only stealing money from Safe Harbor, but he was falsifying adoption papers, selling, and trafficking children."

Just as they'd suspected, but hearing it spoken as the truth made Gabe want to hurl. "How did Trent do it?"

Brad closed his eyes and took a shuddering breath. He flashed them open again. Gone was his pain, anger taking over. "Trent convinced a social worker he was finding good homes for troubled children who would've stayed in the system and aged out if he didn't intervene. Likely end up on the street. She bought into it and had no idea what he was really doing with these kids."

"How did Kenna find out about the kids and the money?" El asked.

"She saw several line items in the budget Trent sent to Safe Harbor. Things like program services, consulting fees, and outreach expenses. When she asked Tinsley about them, he couldn't explain them. He said they were just fees that Trent incurred on their behalf and not to question them."

"But Kenna knew they were wrong?" Gabe asked.

Brad nodded. "She looked into the companies paid under these line items, and found one for Mason Engineering, a company with the payments going to a PO box. She suspected it was a bogus company, along with the number of others they couldn't account for. The last time they made a payment to Mason Engineering, she sat outside the post office and waited for it to be picked up."

"And was it?" Gabe asked.

"Yeah, an older guy came to get the check. She took his picture and did a reverse lookup on the internet. Guy's name is Howard Mason, a former cop. She continued digging and discovered money went to other companies that didn't have employees, a website, or any online footprint at all. Turns out the payments were sent to different PO boxes at the same post office, but that's as far as she got before she was killed."

"Why didn't she come to me?" Gabe asked.

"You know how independent she can be. Plus, she didn't want to put your life in danger until she knew what was going on."

But if she had…

"Odds are Trent is behind the financial scam, and the checks went straight back to him," El said. "Probably deposited to a shell company making them virtually untraceable."

"And the adoptions?"

"Kids at the home were telling her stories about the children who were supposedly being adopted, but they weren't actually placed in the homes social services had approved. She started looking into it and discovered the same social worker signed all of the paperwork. Kenna confronted her and showed her the proof that these kids weren't being adopted but trafficked. She caved and admitted her part. I told Kenna to stop and let us get some clarity on this before she took any other action."

"She could've been risking her life," Gabe said.

"Exactly, but she said the children came first." He took a few deep breaths. "She confronted Trent. He denied it all. But said if she ever tried to bring her lies to the police, he would kill her and Lucy. That's when she went to see you. She didn't tell me she was going, or I would've gone with her."

Gabe felt his brother's pain, and for the first time in his life, he believed the guy had a heart. Hopefully, Gabe could help him get out of the family business, even if he didn't have a life with Kenna to look forward to.

"Obviously," Brad went on, "Trent or one of his goons intercepted her. Those lying scumbags stole Kenna and the baby from me. They likely have Lucy and need to pay beyond me yelling at Trent."

"You confronted Trent?" El asked.

"Of course. I told him if he got away with murdering her, I'd continue her crusade to reveal his illegal activities. He just laughed at me, so I located the social worker Kenna had tracked down. Unfortunately, she passed away in a car accident. Probably Trent's doing too."

"Why didn't you come to me when you found out I was working this investigation?" Gabe asked.

"For the same reason Kenna never told you we were a thing. She didn't want you to know about us until I'd gone legit. I figured, even if she'd died, that still stood. But I didn't make any progress in bringing this guy to justice, and figured you guys might. Besides, I have a potential lead on Lucy's—"

A gunshot rang out. Brad spun and hit the ground.

Gabe dove toward El to take her down, but she was already dropping. He landed next to her. Brad's moans saturated the quiet. Gabe rolled to look at him.

Blood seeped from his chest. Gabe pressed a hand on the open wound. Blood oozed around his hand and through his fingers. So much blood. Gabe pulled a handkerchief from his pocket and applied it to the wound, but it was soaked through in seconds. He pressed harder.

"Here, use this." El held out a shirt.

Gabe glanced over to see that she'd stripped down to a T-shirt. He whispered his thanks and balled the fabric under his fingers to resume applying pressure.

She took out her phone. "No signal to call 911."

Brad's moans were deeper now as gunshots flew overhead. "Both of you get out of here," he choked out. "It's me they want, not you."

"You could be wrong. Besides, I'm not leaving you," Gabe said, but no way he'd let El stay. He glanced back at her. She'd drawn her weapon and sighted it in the direction the bullets were coming from.

"Go," he said to her, his voice stronger now. "Find a signal. Get help. I'll stay with Brad."

"I can't leave you."

"You have to find a signal and call for help. Getting medics here soon is Brad's only chance."

As if letting her know how serious his injury was, Brad moaned again and closed his eyes.

She pressed her hand on Gabe's shoulder. "I'll go. I love you. Don't do anything crazy."

"I love you too," he said, surprised at the intensity of his feelings.

She took a long last look at Gabe and fled, staying low and darting from tree to tree.

Please, keep her safe and don't let my brother die.

His heart in his stomach, Gabe turned back to Brad, glad to see the bleeding had significantly slowed. His only jobs right now were to keep intense pressure on the wound, keep his head on a swivel for the shooter, and pray El got safely away and help would arrive before the shooter took them all out.

~

Even with the midday sun shining bright, the forest was dark and cool as El remained low and out of sight, hoping the element of surprise was her key to apprehending the shooter. She picked her way through the thick trees, quietly alerting the 911 dispatcher of their location and requesting an ambulance and immediate backup.

Nearing the shooter, she ended the call and circled behind him. The only sound was dried pine needles occasionally cracking underfoot, but still, she paused to search the area for another sniper.

Finding none, she focused on their shooter kneeling in a firing stance on a nearby hill. A large man dressed in camouflage, sporting a high and tight haircut often worn by law enforcement and military, he had a phone to his ear and held an AK-47 semi-automatic rifle at his side. Obviously the reason the barrage of bullets had ended.

If she let herself pull the trigger the shootout would end now, but she would only use deadly force if she thought they were in immediate danger. Sure, the guy had an AK-47, but it wasn't aimed at anyone right now, and he was on the phone.

She crept ahead, climbing to within ten feet of his location. He showed zero awareness of her presence so she eased even closer.

He shoved his phone into his pocket.

Was he going to move forward to ambush Brad and Gabe? She couldn't let him. She had to act. It was now or never!

"Drop the weapon," she yelled as she lurched closer. "Police."

He started to turn.

She reached him and jammed her weapon into the back of his head. "I said, drop the weapon."

He didn't respond. She poked the tip harder into his head.

"Okay. Okay. I hear you."

"Slowly put it down in front of you."

He complied. She kicked the gun out of his reach then cuffed and searched him.

Adrenaline raced through her. She'd stopped the sniper, but she couldn't relax her guard. There could be a second shooter.

"You alone?" she asked.

As she suspected, he didn't respond. Why would he? The last thing he would do was tell her if there was someone else hiding in the woods who could take her out and free him. And he likely wouldn't tell her his name either. That could come later in an interrogation room.

"Get up." She tugged on his cuffs to help him stand. "Start moving forward. Try anything funny and I fire."

She shouldered his rifle, and in case a second shooter lay in wait for them, she cautiously made her way forward. Easing between scratchy branches, she tried to protect her bare arms, but she couldn't stop with Gabe and Brad still unprotected.

"Gabe!" Not knowing if there was a second sniper, it was risky to yell, but she had to make sure Gabe knew it was her and didn't open fire. "I stopped the shooter, and I'm coming back."

He didn't respond.

"Gabe!" she called out louder.

No response.

"Looks like I got them both." The jerk in handcuffs cackled.

Was he right? Had Gabe been shot, too?

She shoved him forward, picking up her pace and bursting

into the clearing where she'd left the two men. Gabe's shoulder was covered with blood, but he was ignoring it and still pressing the other hand on his unconscious brother's wound.

She wanted to race over to him, but she had to keep control of the shooter. She poked him. "On your knees."

He dropped down.

Gabe growled at the gunman. "You better hope my brother doesn't die or you'll pay for it."

She felt the same way, but tightened her hands on the service weapon to contain her emotions as she took a longer look at Gabe. "You're bleeding."

He whipped his angry gaze away from the shooter. "I'm fine. Bullet just grazed my arm."

There was no such thing as a graze. Every bullet wound could be dangerous, but it would be like him to play it down. "Why didn't you respond when I called out?"

"I couldn't take the risk. This creep could've captured you and used you to lead him to our exact location."

That made perfect sense. "Fortunately, I took him down without incident."

The guy grumbled, and she gave him her practiced detective stink eye.

"Are you okay?" Gabe asked.

"Fine. Backup and ambulance should be here soon. I want to be sure your bleeding stopped."

"Just a scratch. I don't think there's danger of too much blood loss."

"I meant what I said earlier, you know." She risked looking away and locked gazes with him. "It wasn't just something I said in the heat of the moment. I love you, and I don't want to lose you for any reason."

Warmth and affection flooded his eyes. "Same for me, and once we find Lucy, we can pursue that to our heart's content."

The shooter made a retching noise.

She fired another round of stink eye at him. "Don't make me gag you."

"With what? You got nothing to bind his arm means you got nothing to shut me up with."

Before she could put him in his place, sirens sounded in the distance. Maybe, just maybe, all three of them would get out of this situation after all.

Gabe leaned down to his brother. "Do you hear those sirens, bro? The ambulance is almost here, so hang in there, okay?"

Brad suddenly opened his eyes. "Lucy," he said and tried to rise up but fell back. "Safe place by the water."

"What? What are you saying?" Gabe blinked at his brother and looked like he wanted to shake him, but Brad drifted off.

"Safe place by the water," Gabe repeated as he locked gazes with El. "This must be what he was trying to tell us when the shooting started. We need to get Hayden looking into any properties owned by New Tide, Safe Harbor, or Jonas Trent and near water."

"I'll go call him while you let a medic properly bandage your arm and clear you."

"I'll get a bandage, but if Hayden finds the location, I don't care if I'm cleared. I'm going in and no one is going to stop me."

She had no doubt Gabe meant it. He wouldn't be stopped by anyone. Maybe only by a bullet.

26

Backed up by the Mina-led SWAT team, and with Gabe at her side, El focused her binoculars on the decommissioned boathouse on the far side of Lost Lake. Hayden had easily located the dilapidated structure owned by Trent. The building looked like it might fall down at any time. El imagined Lucy being held captive inside, and her stomach clenched.

"I thought housing her in that cabin was bad, but this..." El lowered her binoculars and shook her head. "Can't see anything inside. I need to get closer."

"You mean we," Gabe said, his tone insistent.

"Only one person should approach the building for recon. Lessens the chance of being seen." She met his gaze. "We're lucky Mina didn't have SWAT take over and you and I are still taking lead. Let's not give her a reason to force us out."

"That makes sense, but if Lucy's in there, I'm going in. SWAT or no SWAT. Mina's approval or not. I won't do anything to jeopardize the potential prosecution of this creep, but I won't hang back either."

"Understood," she said as she knew this was the best she

could hope for with Gabe's surging adrenaline and desire to find Lucy. "As long as it's something we can successfully carry out ourselves. If I think SWAT needs to handle it, then we both stay back."

He opened his mouth to argue.

She lifted a hand. "I need you to respect my decisions, Gabe. No matter how much you want to be the one to rescue her, we have to do what's right to ensure nothing bad happens to her."

He released a long breath. "I can't argue with that. Make sure you stay in our line of sight at all times. Remember, we have a future planned together, and I don't want you risking your life."

"And here I thought I was the one who would have to tell you that." She squeezed his arm then scooted to Mina to share her plan, which she quickly approved.

"It's go-time," El whispered as she slipped past Gabe.

She drew her weapon and crept forward, staying low behind tall grasses swaying in the stiff breeze. This property was so different from the hilly forest where they'd just been. Flat land. A sharp April breeze blowing off the water. The smell devoid of pine but saturated by a strong fishy odor.

She slipped behind a nearby tree, the thick trunk giving her cover as she lifted her binoculars to scan the area. She'd already spotted the boat at the end of a crumbling dock. No one in it. Likely the boat Lucy's captor had brought her in, but El had to remain aware of it in case she was wrong.

She scanned one more time. No movement. No sound. No light. The way was clear.

The last ten feet were paved with an old crumbling brick patio. She wanted to rush over it, but couldn't risk losing her footing, so she inched up to the building. A small cracked window could give her the insight they needed.

She took a moment to catch her breath from the adrenaline rush, then raised up. Took a quick glance. Darkness, illuminated only by a shadowy light in the corner of the dry end. The only sound was water lapping against the building.

She dropped back down. Gulped in air. Rose up for a longer look. There, near the light. A shape. She squinted to make it out. A child. Red hair.

Lucy. Curled up on a small cot.

El's heart soared. She wanted to revel in it. Revel in how happy Gabe would be. But she was on a mission and had to focus. She continued scanning the space. Found a gruff-looking man but one who didn't fit Nurse Armstrong's description, lying on top of a sleeping bag on the floor. They must've changed her guard after the cabin.

He was staring at the ceiling, and Lucy was sound asleep. He'd placed his rifle under Lucy's cot. It would take a moment for him to reach the weapon. Enough time for them to gain control of him without a shootout? Maybe.

She had a decision to make. A big one. Did they go forward to free Lucy, potentially risking her life? To send in SWAT, who in their tactical gear could scare her even more than the terrible trial she'd already endured, and still risk her life?

El searched the rest of the shadowy room, looking for other people and a less dangerous option to rescue Lucy. The boathouse was empty, and the nearby door was the best entrance, but she didn't have to send in the SWAT team to scare Lucy.

Finally. Finally! They found her. Alive.

Tears threatened to block El's view. She couldn't let that happen. She willed them to stop and started back as silently as she could.

She reached Gabe and dropped down next to him. "Keep your voice under control, but Lucy's inside. She's alive."

His mouth flashed open, but before he could utter a sound, he clamped a hand over it, his eyes wide and sparkling.

She took his free hand. Bowed her head. "Thank You Father. Thank You for keeping Lucy alive. Now, let us safely bring her home where she belongs. Amen."

"Amen," Gabe said with a shaky voice. "And praise Your holy name."

El squeezed his hand and shared her plan with Mina for approval.

Minutes later, El followed the same route back to the building, this time leading Gabe behind her. Her adrenaline before had sent her heart thumping, but now it raced beyond her imagination. Exactly the same as when she realized Victoria hadn't just wandered off.

This rescue was different. This rescue wouldn't end the same way. Maybe this was El's opportunity to prove herself. To redeem herself. Either way, God had really made His wishes clear to her. He didn't want her to hold on to any guilt, and she had to let it go to have a full life.

They reached the building. She stepped to the side of the entrance, so Gabe could grab the door handle. It was a single handle with a thumb latch. All he had to do was press down and pull it open.

She nodded at him and he jerked it open, quickly moving out of the way.

Gun outstretched, she charged over the threshold. "Police! Don't move."

She lunged for the man who'd come to a sitting position. She pushed him back down and put her gun to his heart. "Go ahead and move. Give me a reason to use this."

He blinked up at her, his eyes wide, and he didn't so much as move a muscle.

Gabe raced past her and swept Lucy into his arms.

"Sweetie, sweetie, sweetie. It's Gabe. I've got you. You're safe."

"Gabe!" she cried out in her high little voice. "I knew if Mommy couldn't come, God would send you."

"Of course He did, but I'm sorry it took so long."

El couldn't risk looking at them to enjoy the reunion. She remained in place, weapon and attention fixed on the suspect, but leaned down to her mic. "We're clear. Would appreciate help cuffing the suspect."

Mina charged in, swept the place with her gaze, then put the suspect in her crosshairs. "Way to execute your plan."

El didn't take any time to revel in her praise but sat back and nudged the suspect. "On your face. Now!"

He complied, and El holstered her weapon, then slapped handcuffs on the guy. She heard Gabe explain to Lucy that he was taking her outside where the SWAT team was waiting, and she shouldn't let all of their gear scare her. They were here to help them.

"I'm brave, and I have you," she said, sounding very confident of herself. "I won't be afraid."

Her sweet voice might have rung with courage, but where would that courage be when she learned her mother had been killed? How would Gabe tell her? El would like to be there to help him if he wanted her to, but it would all be up to him.

Gabe made his way around the suspect but paused at the doorway. "I'll take Lucy directly to the ambulance. Meet us at the hospital so I can thank you properly."

"Nothing could stop me," she said, looking up at him. "You can count on that."

～

Gabe pressed Lucy's face away from the SWAT team as he crossed the brick and entered the path toward the hill where the ambulance waited. Despite Lucy's protest of not being afraid, her trembling fingers twisted in his shirt, her breath coming in short, panicked bursts. Anger for the men who did this to her grew until he thought he might explode with it.

Didn't matter. He could do nothing about it now. Not with Lucy in his arms. Still, he would make sure they paid, but for now, Lucy was his priority.

Being careful not to tangle his feet in the thick grass encroaching the path, he picked up speed, murmuring over and over again, "It's okay, sweetie. I've got you."

She'd actually stopped trembling by the time they'd reached the end of the path leading up the hill to the ambulance.

"Stop! Or I shoot the kid." The familiar voice cut through the air like a blade.

Gabe froze. He could do nothing else. They'd moved too far away from SWAT for them to see or hear what Trent had said.

"What are you doing here, Trent?" Gabe yelled. "Do you really have a gun or are you bluffing?" He made sure his voice carried over the wind and prayed SWAT heard his questions.

"That's the bad man." Lucy's fingers dug deeper into his shirt. "I heard him when he made Mommy hurt lots. A big hurt. And then he took me away and told his friends to keep me in scawy places."

Gabe slowly faced Trent to stop Lucy from having to look at him. "Are you sure, sweetie?"

"Yes. I didn't like him. He was mean."

"This is the last time he'll get near you, I promise." Gabe

would die trying to keep this psychopath's hands off Lucy, but wouldn't say it aloud and scare her.

Instead, he held her tighter and pressed his hand over her ear, so she didn't have to hear anything that was about to happen.

Trent stepped into view, handgun raised, black-clad silhouette sharp against the sky. He'd locked his eyes and gun on the child.

"Put her down," he called. "Or I swear I'll kill her."

"I can't let you take her, Trent." Gabe filled his voice with confidence. "You know that."

"Don't even think of running," Trent shouted, his anger growing. "I'll pick her off before you can move."

Gabe might have his hand over Lucy's ear, but Trent's voice was out of control, and he didn't want to risk her hearing the conversation. He lifted his hand. "Why don't you sing to yourself, sweetie? How about your favorite, Jesus Loves Me?"

Her little voice rang out with her love for Jesus, and Gabe pressed his hand over her ear again then turned his attention back to Trent. "This is all about you killing Kenna, isn't it? You made a mistake, and Lucy saw you. She can testify against you. You can't let her do that, but you don't have it in your heart to end a child's life, which is why you've kept her alive."

"Believe it or not, I didn't really want to end anyone's life. Not even Kenna's, but she wouldn't leave things alone, and I wasn't going to prison. She agreed to meet with me in my office, and I tried to reason with her, but when she wouldn't listen, I got mad. Couldn't let anybody at my office see how I felt, so I had to hold it in and let her go back to work. Then I planned. Starting with taking Mason's boat."

"You killed him too."

"So what? He'd come to the dark side to help me and was going to die anyway. What was another month or two?"

Gabe wasn't surprised by his callous regard for life. It seemed fitting with the selfish man they'd interviewed earlier. "And then you arranged for Kenna to meet you at the lake."

"And I forced her off the road. Had no idea she'd bring the kid with her. Added to my anger, and when the accident didn't do the job for me, I saw red. Grabbed Kenna by the neck and squeezed until she wasn't breathing. Took her to the lake and dumped her in. That's what she deserved, you know. She should never have messed with me."

Gabe was seeing red himself now and wanted to charge over and strangle Trent. He sucked in a breath and remained in place with Lucy, but he didn't do nothing. He took what he hoped was an undetectable look over Trent's shoulder. Movement. Shadows shifting. SWAT positioning their rifles. *Good.*

"And now we're here!" Trent shouted. "Give me the kid or I shoot. Simple as that."

"Sir, drop the weapon!" a SWAT officer shouted.

"Last warning!" another voice said.

"You don't want to do this, Trent," Gabe said, voice steady despite the adrenaline pounding through him. "It's over."

Trent's finger dropped to the trigger.

The guy just might be stupid enough to fire even with multiple SWAT weapons locked on him. A shootout seemed inevitable.

Gabe couldn't let Lucy be hit. He spun, putting his body between Lucy and Trent's gun.

Time fractured.

A single crack split the air.

"Shots fired!" the team commander called out.

Knowing what was coming, Gabe dropped to the ground, twisting as he fell, shielding Lucy beneath him.

"Engage! Engage!" the commander shouted.

Gunfire erupted, sharp, deafening, controlled. Echoes of gun reports reverberated across the quiet lakeside property.

Gabe curled over Lucy, one hand cradling her head, the other braced against the ground. "You're okay," he muttered, though he couldn't hear his own voice over the chaos. "You're okay."

Then—

Silence.

Abrupt. Heavy.

"Suspect down," someone called.

"Hold! Hold!"

Boots thundered across the brick. Hands were on Gabe, lifting, checking. "You hit?"

He shook his head, breath ragged. "No. She's...she's good."

Lucy clung to him, still shaking, but alive.

Gabe pressed his cheek briefly to her hair, eyes scanning ahead where Trent lay motionless.

"It's over," he said again, sitting up, but facing away from Trent's fallen body and placing her on his lap. "He won't come near you ever again. I promise."

She looked up at him and held up her little finger. "Pinky swear?"

He locked his little finger with hers. "Pinky swear."

Her expression turned serious. "That's a forever promise. Mommy told me that."

"And I mean it, sweetie. Forever."

"Did that man kill Mommy, and she's in heaven?"

"Yes." Gabe couldn't put off an answer she'd probably wanted for days. "She's in heaven."

"Heaven is special, but I'll miss her."

"Me too," Gabe said, trying to keep his emotions in check.

"That means I'm gonna live with you. Mommy said if I couldn't be with her, you wanted me to live with you."

"Mommy was right. I do want you to live with me."

She threw her arms around his neck and hugged him tight. Thankfully, he was already sitting or his legs wouldn't have held him.

El came charging across the bricks and fell to her knees beside him, her gaze going from one to the other. "Are you both really all right?"

"We are," Gabe said, feeling that despite the SWAT team rushing around him and the life taken from another man, his life was right for the first time ever. Something he'd wanted for many years, and finally, finally it was going to happen for him.

For them. Forever.

El couldn't take her eyes off Gabe as he shared the details of Trent's confession, but he was called away to sit with Lucy in the ambulance as the medics gave her an IV to increase her fluids. They soon departed for the hospital, Gabe riding along. Once there, she knew he would also check on his brother.

El promised to join them as soon as she could, but first she needed to question the guy who'd been holding Lucy. Mina had cuffed and secured him in the back of her car and learned he was named Justin Ward. Shockers of all shockers, he was the guy who'd broken into El's house before he took over watching Lucy from another guy.

Now, Mina sat in her front seat, door open as she checked his record.

El joined her. "He have any priors?"

Mina slipped out of the car and closed the door. "Three convictions for trespassing, reckless driving, and burglary. Not the kind of guy who would escalate to accomplice-to-murder and kidnapping."

"Trent must've coerced him somehow." El stared at the backseat window and wanted to go over and throttle the guy for terrorizing her.

Ward focused out the opposite window, making her want to talk to him even more. "I'd like to interview him. See if I can get something out of him."

"Knock yourself out. I need to cancel the Amber Alert, call the ME, and get someone out here to transport Ward."

El looked around at her fellow deputies for someone who could do the transport, and everyone on scene had been involved in the shooting and would need to remain on-site to give a statement to an impartial investigator. "You call OSP to send out an investigator?"

"First thing I did. Someone is being dispatched out of Medford and should be here in a couple of hours."

A couple of hours to sit around there and wait, twiddling their thumbs. They couldn't investigate. She shouldn't really even conduct the interview, but no one would stop her from doing that. "Okay, if I talk to this guy?"

Mina paused for a minute, eyeing El but then clicked her key fob, unlocking the vehicle.

El walked to the back door and opened it. Working hard to control her fury at this man, she waited for him to look at her. When he did, his angry glare gave her pause. Thankfully, he hadn't turned wrath like this on her the night he'd broken into her home.

"Well, Justin Ward." She tried to stay impartial and not blurt out that she knew he'd invaded her privacy. "What exactly have you gotten yourself into here?"

His glare remained firmly in place. "I didn't take the kid, and I'm not in charge of this screw-up. I was just watching her. You want Jonas Trent for all of that. He offed that kid's mother then abducted her."

After Trent's confession, that wasn't news to her, but it would be good to hear this guy's side of things. "Do you have any proof of that?"

"I was there. At the ravine and lake. Seen it all."

She funneled her anger at his lack of caring into clenched fists. "And you did nothing to stop it?"

"What could I do?" Ward shrugged. "I was sittin' there with the boat like he said. Waitin'. Then he slammed her van and crashed it right off the road into the ravine. I thought he was done, but nah...he went after her. Found her alive in her van. She stabbed him with a screwdriver, and man...he just lost it. He closed his hands around her neck and squeezed like there was no tomorrow."

"And you didn't try to stop this either?"

"I ain't stupid. I wasn't gonna get in the way. Guy's a freak once his mask drops. Looks like Mr. Nice on the outside, but underneath? Cold, cruel, and nasty. Real vindictive."

"You willing to put in writing what you just told me?"

"As long as you make sure the DA knows I cooperated." He challenged her with his gaze.

"Sounds like your previous convictions taught you how to game the system, but in this case, Trent confessed, and now he's dead, so you're the only one who'll be on trial as an accessory."

"But like I said, I only did what he told me to do." He narrowed his gaze. "Are you gonna work with me or not?"

"Not," she said. "Unless you give me a solid reason why you followed Trent's directions, other than he told you to. Or maybe give up the names of others involved. Otherwise, I don't really see how we can help you."

"What else do you wanna know, man? Trent didn't even tell me why he killed her or why he took the kid."

His uncertain expression was exactly what El needed to get additional information from him. "Tell me how Howard Mason was involved?"

"That guy? Yeah, I forgot about him. No one wanted to work with him. He was a former cop, and he thought he could boss us all around. Mason was Trent's favorite. Until he wanted out."

Now they were getting somewhere. "What exactly did Mason do for Trent?"

"He used the boat for..." He trailed off and looked away. "Transferring kids from the home to illegal buyers. But don't jam me up in this. I didn't do nothin' with those kids. Wouldn't touch something like that."

"Go ahead and tell yourself that, but if you knew the kids were being trafficked and didn't tell anyone, you most certainly had something to do with it." El tried to control her temper. "Where were the buyers from?"

Ward shook his head. "That I don't know. Trent kept it secret. All I know is Mason talked about taking his boat to the harbor and moving the kids from his boat to a ship in the Pacific. But then his eyes must've opened to what he was doing, 'cause he decided it was wrong and wanted out."

Likely the cancer. "What happened then?"

"Trent needed a boat to move Kenna and her kid to the dock, so he asked to use Mason's. The guy was dumb enough to refuse, and Trent knifed him."

"You saw all of this?"

"I ain't gonna lie. I was right there. I hauled Kenna's lifeless body and the kid to the dock. He'd already strangled Kenna. He was still bleeding from the screwdriver. Figured he deserved that and more. After that, I ditched the boat across the lake at one of those fancy weekend houses."

"You stay long enough to see when he abducted Lucy?"

"Yeah, I split in the boat, but I could see him tossing Kenna in the water, then grabbing the kid from her car seat."

"What about earlier today? Trent sent someone to try to kill me, Gabe Irving, and his brother. Know who that would be?"

"Not for sure, no, but it had to be Damon Cross, the sniper on Trent's payroll. He served as security for when the kids were transported."

"Do you know about Trent's accounting fraud?"

"Ha! You kidding? I picked up the checks and deposited them. So yeah." He laughed. "You could say I knew about it."

"Were Silas Tinsley and Patrick Sloan involved?"

"Of course. Trent needed them to turn a blind eye."

"Which one of you broke into my house and stole my computer and files?" she asked, though she already knew the answer.

"That was all me. Sorry. I gave all the stuff to Trent."

She honestly couldn't have hoped for more information from him. "And you'll give me a statement for this as well?"

"I mean, why not? Trent's dead, and he can't hurt me."

Disgusted he wouldn't assist them because it was the right thing to do, she left him without promising to seek a lighter sentence for him.

Promise. Pinky promise.

El desperately needed to talk to Gabe.

She closed the back door and made sure it was secure, then moved to a wooded area nearby. She slid to the ground, her back to a tall pine, and dialed Gabe.

"I'm so glad you called," he said before she could get a word out. "How are things going there?"

"We're waiting on a state investigator to arrive for our

statements. Once he's done here, he'll be coming to the hospital to take yours. Is Lucy doing well enough that I could sit with her for that to happen?"

"I think so. They gave her a second IV for dehydration and thoroughly examined her, but found nothing wrong, except the dehydration and fatigue. She ate a small snack, but then was too tired to stay awake. I suspect she'll be sleeping a lot the next few days."

"How long will they keep her there?"

"Doctor didn't say. He said she was in pretty good shape for what she'd gone through. Physically at least. He recommended a counselor to help her get through the emotional turmoil."

"And your brother?"

"He just got out of surgery and is in ICU. Looks like he'll make it. I had to call my mom and dad. They got here right away but basically went straight to Brad's room. Seemed like there was a rift between my mom and dad, but they didn't say anything about it."

He sounded so matter-of-fact and not at all upset over seeing his parents that El knew he'd made a step forward with them, and she couldn't be happier for him.

"So what about you?" he asked. "Now that we found Lucy alive, do you think that'll help clear away any guilt you've been feeling over Victoria?"

"I really think it's behind me now. Sure, it'll probably come up from time to time, but thanks to God, I'm moving on." She never thought she would say that.

"You sound peaceful."

"I am, at the moment. But you. How are you doing with your family?"

"Thanks to Brad's big shock, I realized family is important to me no matter what they do for a living. I still don't want to associate with them for that reason, but I can be kinder and more understanding. And, I no longer think it reflects on me."

Her heart smiled. "Well listen to us. We've both made progress."

"Progress away from our past and on the way to our future together."

Crying sounded in the phone's background.

"I have to go. Lucy just woke up from a bad dream."

"I'm praying for you both." She disconnected the call and looked around the crime scene.

The ME and her assistant had arrived while El was on the phone. Deputies sat alone in various places. The SWAT vehicle along with squad cars remained parked where they stopped so deputies could race down to the lake and free Lucy.

Everything pointed to something negative that happened tonight. But something positive happened, too. Something big. Little Lucy had been rescued. And, not as important but very significant, she and Gabe had let go of the past and could move forward in a future guided by God's will.

27

―――――

A month later, Gabe tied every color of birthday balloon to the covered picnic structure at Lost Lake Park in downtown. He'd already strung light and dark blue streamers for Lucy's Bluey-themed fifth party. She loved that character, and Gabe vowed to try to keep things as normal for her as possible.

He'd even bought a professional Bluey costume online and wheedled Jude into wearing it at the party. Gabe would probably owe the guy for the rest of his life, but if it was for Lucy, it was worth anything he had to pay right now.

Satisfied with his work, he stood back and looked at it with a critical eye. His most important question? What would Kenna have thought of it? His most loving, compassionate, and considerate best friend lost to him and Lucy. The day of her funeral flashed into his brain, but whenever that happened, he forced it away to stop his pain from scaring Lucy.

All things considered, she'd handled the loss pretty well. Sure, she was upset a lot of the time and cried often. But she seemed to be able to dig herself out of the sadness by reminding herself that her mother was in heaven.

Gabe couldn't do that. Yes, he knew she was in heaven. A better place, but he sorely missed her. He and El had spent a lot of time together this past month, and that helped fill the emptiness, but his sadness came upon him at moments when he couldn't control it. Like right now. Kenna would want to be sharing in this party. She'd be with them in a way, he supposed, when he played her first video message for Lucy.

Could he hold it together for that or would he fall apart? God was with him, and he would do his very best for Lucy. That was all he could promise.

"You did a fantastic job." El's voice came from behind.

He spun to look at her. "I'm glad you're here."

She shifted a box of Bluey table items to her hip and touched the side of his cheek. "What is it? What's wrong?"

"I wish I could hide my sadness from you as well as I hide it from Lucy." He tried to smile, but couldn't manage it, so he took the box to distract her.

"You're thinking of Kenna. Of course you are. She would be here, right by your side. With Lucy."

"Not here." He stepped into the pavilion and set the box down. "The party would be at Kenna's place just for her, Lucy, me, Mrs. Z., and two of Lucy's friends from preschool." He looked at the pavilion again. "Maybe I should've thought of that. Maybe this is too much for Lucy right now. She already had to change her daycare. Homes. Living in my basic accommodations at the inn, for crying out loud. This might be too much to handle."

"Hey, hey." She took his hands. "You're gonna freak yourself out. She knows about today's plans, and she's super excited."

"You're right." He clung to her hands. "This dad thing is really throwing me for a loop. All I know on most days is that I love my little princess, and I'll do anything not to screw up. Not to screw her up."

"I get it. I have the same feelings, and I'm not an official guardian. Just someone who loves you and is trying to get to know Lucy. She makes it so easy to love her, and all the fear and misgivings are on me."

"She really does like you." He could smile in earnest now as he thought of all the time the three of them had spent together this past month and how happy Lucy had been with El. He let go of her right hand and touched her ring finger. "I don't think it'll be long before I can put a ring on this finger."

"I'm waiting for that day. I really am. More than you know. But being a mother?" She shook her head. "I don't want to screw up either, but we have God on our side. All we need to do is trust that He wants us to raise this young lady. If we remember to talk to Him first, we'll succeed."

"I guess, when my doubts are really bad, I can remember that me being her dad is a far better choice than Sloan, who's rotting in prison for years."

Thankfully, he and the others took plea deals, sparing Lucy from testifying and giving up the missing girls' location so they could be rescued. Tinsley and Ward were also doing lengthy stretches for their part in the terror Lucy suffered, too.

"I'd like to keep discussing this with you," he said. "But my mother and Brad are coming our way."

"I'll get started with the tables," she said, reaching for the box. "You can talk to your family."

He took her hand. "You'll soon be part of the family, and they need to know about you and me."

"Son." His mother stopped next to them. She cast a beaming smile his way. "Thank you for inviting us."

"Ditto," Brad said.

Gabe and Brad had spent some time together while Brad was healing in the hospital, but their contact ended when Brad was discharged. Not because of a disagreement. No, they'd made peace with each other, and Gabe had even accepted that his brother had once planned to marry Kenna and be Lucy's father. Thankfully, Kenna hadn't been ready for Lucy to find out about Brad until he made good on his promise and left the family business. So he'd only met with Kenna when Lucy was sleeping, and she knew nothing about Brad.

His mother looked at El. "I thought you and Gabe were more than business associates when you came to question me."

"We didn't hide it very well, Mrs. Irving, did we?" El asked.

"No, and please call me Denise."

El nodded, and Gabe hoped this meant his mom would someday accept El as her daughter-in-law.

"You should know." Gabe put his arm around her waist. "Once Lucy settles in, we'll be getting married."

His mom clapped her hands. "How wonderful!"

"Congratulations." Brad held out his hand for a fist pump, but sadness lingered in his gaze. "It'll be great for Lucy to have a mom and a dad."

Gabe bumped his brother's fist, still surprised to see him show concern for others.

"How are you feeling?" El asked Brad.

"Good. Been able to work and get on with life."

"I'm so proud of him." His mother gave Brad a fond smile. "He found a great job working for a security firm. They contract with businesses to evaluate their security risks."

"No one better than someone with a sketchy past like

mine to determine risks." Brad laughed. "But seriously. It's a great job."

"Are you still living at home?" Gabe asked.

"I left your father, and we're sharing an apartment." His mother lifted her shoulders as if the weight of living her former life with their father was gone. "Brad has saved enough money to help support me until I'm able to find a job."

Gabe didn't know what to say. A deep ache that had lived in his gut since the day he'd learned of his father's profession evaporated. He might just float up like the balloons in the pavilion.

"We need to run back to the car for the present," his mom said. "We just wanted to make sure we were at the right place before we hauled something so big over here."

"Do you need help?" El asked.

They both shook their heads and turned to leave, but his mom spun back and threw her arms around Gabe's waist. "I hope this changes things between us."

He hugged his mom tightly for the first time in years. "It does, and I want you to be part of my life."

She started crying and pushed back to get a tissue from her purse. "The present. We need to get the present."

Dabbing at her eyes, she rushed away. Brad followed, a loving smile on his face.

El turned her attention to Gabe. "Looks like you'll not only be able to leave your past behind you, but your mom and Brad can now be part of your life."

"Thanks again to God, and we can pray that my dad realizes what he's doing and makes a change, too."

"Everything is working out for us." She let out a contented sigh and rested her head against his chest. "I'm not naive enough to think we won't have problems, but together? Trusting in God? We can get through it."

He circled his arms around the woman he loved and wanted to be his bride. Only one thing that would make this moment even better. To kiss her and let her know how much he loved her.

～

El loved having Gabe's arms around her, but she suddenly remembered they were in public. She leaned back and peered up at this handsome man she couldn't wait to marry.

"Hey," he said. "Don't pull away. We haven't had much time alone this past month, and this is nice."

"We're not actually alone," she said. "Just look at all the kids on the play structure."

"They really aren't paying us any attention. So, before things get crazy here, I want to do this." He lowered his head, and their lips connected.

The same jolt of love she experienced every time he kissed her raced through her. He drew her closer with one arm, eliminating all space between them, and plunged the other hand into her hair. She reveled in how confident he was about his love for her.

She kissed him back, hopefully showing him she felt the same way. She lost track of time. Of place. Of everything.

"Hey now," a male voice in falsetto came from behind them.

She spun out of Gabe's arms. A tall person completely hidden by a giant Bluey costume stood there.

"You're early, Jude," Gabe said. "You'll be burning hot by the time the kids get here."

He lifted off the head. "No kidding, I'm already sweating."

"Jude? Oh my goodness. It is you." El started laughing. "What does Gabe have on you that you agreed to do this?"

"It's that kid." Jude shook his head. "I know you feel it too. You can't help but love the little squirt. But if you tell anyone I admitted it…" He chuckled, carefree as she'd seen of late.

She loved getting to know the off-duty Jude. He was a great guy, and he'd been spending a lot of time with Lucy. The whole team had devoted themselves to her, but him more than others, taking her fishing, to the batting cages, and watching *Bluey* with her, something he seemed to enjoy far too much for a man his age.

"It's not a good idea to walk around here as a headless Bluey," Gabe said. "You'll scare the kids."

Jude turned his back to them. "Then unhook me so I can get out of this and put it back in my truck for later."

El undid the Velcro in the back, and Gabe helped him out of the suit.

"What I do for that little squirt." Shaking his head, he marched across the grass carrying his furry costume.

"Now, where were we?" Gabe asked.

"We were about to set the tables because we don't have much time until people get here."

He grumbled good-naturedly and opened the box. Denise and Brad returned with a giant package that took both of them to carry. They wouldn't tell them what was in the box, and helped them put out tablecloths and set the table with Bluey-themed items.

"Hey, I need you to check this out!" Reece called from the grass. She carried a sheet cake and set it on the food table. "I've never made a Bluey cake before. What do you think?"

El took a look at it. "It's wonderful. Is there anything you can't do?"

"Oh my goodness, yes. Don't get me started on the list or we'll be here all night." She laughed.

Gabe turned to his mom and Brad. "Reece is one of the team. There'll be more coming, but I'll introduce you to everyone once they're all here."

El turned to see Abby and her fiancé, Burke, stroll across the grass. He balanced a large open box in one arm, his other arm around petite Abby's shoulders.

"Goodie bags," Abby said. "Filled, and ready to go. Where do you want them?"

Reece stepped forward. "Give them to me. I want to reorganize this table anyway."

Gabe rolled his eyes. "Mama Reece is here to take over."

She wrinkled her nose at him, but didn't dispute his comment. Neither did anyone else.

"The others are right behind us," Abby said. "And you can barely keep Lucy's feet on the ground."

"It's good she's able to be happy so soon after her loss," El said. "Even if it is just for one day."

Reece looked up from the table. "Is she still having bad dreams about bad guys coming to get her?"

Gabe nodded. "But the counselor she's seeing is helping."

"The heartbreaking thing for me," Abby said, "is that she doesn't ever cry when she's with me. She just holds on too tight, like if she let go, I might disappear on her."

"She does that all the time with me, too." Gabe's tortured expression spoke to the challenges he was facing. "Her counselor says it's normal and could last for a while. That's why she'll cling to your sleeve or shirt and not want to let go. She needs to be reassured that we're there for her, and we're not going anywhere."

His pain got to be too much for El, and she looked away, catching sight of Nolan and Mina coming toward them. Nolan carried cases of juice boxes, and Mina held packaged snacks.

"Over here." Reece waved. "Just set them on the table, and I'll take care of them."

"I won't argue with that." Nolan dumped the big cases of juice boxes on the end of the table.

"You sure you don't want any help?" Mina asked.

The others laughed.

"The last time I saw Reece ask for help was when she locked the food in the car with the keys," Nolan said.

Laughter broke out again as Hayden and Cady joined them with a cooler swinging between them, the ice inside swishing.

"I thought you were bringing Lucy and Mrs. Z.," Abby said.

"We did." Hayden set the cooler down near the juice boxes. "Mrs. Z. insisted we get the ice here as fast as possible. She needs a wheelchair for this distance, and we couldn't bring her and the ice in one trip. So, she opted to wait and asked Lucy to stay with her."

"I think it's Mrs. Z's way of spending time alone with Lucy today," Cady said.

"But it looks like we better get the birthday girl over here before the party starts." Hayden rested his arm over his fiancée's shoulders and led them away.

Gabe slipped closer to El. "You look overwhelmed."

El sighed. "I am, though I hate to admit it. I rarely get flustered, but seeing everyone together and how well they all know each other, I feel like an outsider."

He put his arm on her shoulder. "Talk to Mina, Burke, or Cady. Or all three of them. They were new to the group at one time, too, but they all seem pretty comfortable now."

"I'll do that. Maybe today." She pointed across the lawn. "Here comes the princess."

Lucy clung to Mrs. Z.'s hand as Hayden rolled her up the walkway.

Gabe went to greet her, picked her up, and swung her around in his arms. "I hope you like your decorations and your party."

"Yes!" She wiggled free and twirled in her special party dress, her shiny black shoes tapping on the concrete. "Don't I look pretty?"

"Beautiful." When she stopped spinning, Gabe knelt in front of her and kissed her cheek. "You won't believe who's coming to join your party. He's right behind you."

She spun and shrieked. "Bluey. It's Bluey. He's really here!"

She raced ahead, then threw her full body weight against Bluey. Jude stepped back, but then planted his feet while she hugged him.

She looked up at him. "I love you, Bluey. Thank you for coming to my party."

"Are you kidding?" Jude asked in an imitation of Bluey's squeaky-high voice. "You're my very best friend."

She grabbed his hand and started dragging him toward the pavilion as the first kids arrived behind them. They charged away from their parents, flooding toward Bluey, but Lucy stepped in front of them. "He's my very best friend, and he came to my party."

The others didn't seem to care and pushed past her to hug Bluey. She frowned.

"We need to go to the party to have food and drinks," Jude said in the high-pitched voice. "Take my hand, Lucy, and we'll lead everyone there."

El heard Gabe let out a loud breath, but then the kids and their parents arrived at the pavilion and he was swamped with greetings. Maybe next year, El would be by his side, but for now she hung back and enjoyed watching the children eat snacks and cake and listening to their laughter over just about everything.

Lucy chimed in as if she'd never lost her mother. That was something El had come to understand about her. One moment she could be happy and carefree, and the next moment she would be deep in sadness, all of it unpredictable.

Present time arrived, and she maintained her happy go-lucky behavior as she opened package after package, tearing away the paper and tossing it up, then exclaiming her joy and thankfulness. Kenna had taught this child impeccable manners and must've really been an incredible mother. No pressure for El. No pressure at all.

After all the smaller gifts had been opened, Brad and Denice brought their giant package forward. Lucy hopped up and down, but looked warily at Brad and his mom.

"Remember, sweetie, this is my brother, Brad, and my mom," Gabe reminded her. "They bought this present for you."

"You have a brother?" she asked in wonder.

"I do," Gabe said.

She suddenly frowned. "I wanted a brother, but Mommy said we couldn't have one until we got a daddy."

Brad sucked in a sharp breath, and Gabe shared a sympathetic look with him.

El felt Brad's pain. If Kenna had lived, he would become the father of a boy and dad to Lucy.

With expectant eyes, Lucy peered up at Gabe's mom. "Can you be my grandmother? I've always wanted a grandmother, too."

Denise beamed a glowing smile at Lucy, but then gave Gabe a tentative look. "I'd like that if it's okay with Gabe."

"Sure," Gabe said, without even pausing to think about it.

How far he'd come since El had first met him.

Lucy reached for the wrapping paper. "Help me, Gabe. This one's too big."

"How about if Brad does it, since he bought it with my mom?"

She flashed a look at Brad. "Can you please help me?"

"Of course." Without hesitation, Brad dropped down beside her and started to fling paper away from the box, wincing with pain from his surgery.

"It's a Bluey bike." She flung her arms around Brad's neck. "Thank you. Thank you. Thank you. I never had a bike before, and this one's even more special."

His look of sheer shock, then warmth and acceptance while Gabe smiled down on them, Denise by his side, was priceless to watch. El could now see this little girl bringing Gabe's family closer together.

All of the children flooded in to look at the bike, and Brad stood to get out of the way.

"Hey, thanks, man," Gabe said. "But the person who buys the bike is the one who has to teach the child to ride it."

"No problem. I'd be glad to do it."

Gabe arched his eyebrow. "That'll mean a lot of trips to Lost Lake."

Brad hesitated. "Um, well, not really. We didn't want to mention it until we saw how you felt about our big life change, but we moved here."

Gabe gaped at him. "To Lost Lake?"

"You sound like you don't like the idea."

"No. No, it's fine. Good. I'm just surprised."

El was surprised, too, but couldn't be happier for Gabe.

Brad inched closer to Gabe. "Mom and I figured if we wanted to repair our relationships with you, we had to be nearby."

"So you did this for me?"

"Yeah. You deserve it after how we treated you."

Gabe grabbed his brother in a man hug and clapped his back before releasing him. "I'm glad you're both here."

"Okay, kids," Reece called out from behind one of the main tables. "Time to get your goodie bags before you go."

Pandemonium soon ensued as children grabbed the bags and parents claimed their children, all offering their thanks for the wonderful party. Lucy beamed at them all, but then suddenly sat on the bench, tears sparkling in her eyes.

Gabe was busy with helping families depart, so El sat next to Lucy. "Do you want to tell me what's wrong?"

"I want Mommy." She turned and buried her face in El's stomach.

"It's okay, honey. I understand, and I'm here for you."

El stroked the child's back until she quit sobbing and looked up. El grabbed tissues from her purse and handed one to Lucy. She swiped her eyes and blew her nose, the sound apparently catching Gabe's attention. He picked his way between empty tables to get to them. The team was already packing things away as Gabe settled on the bench next to Lucy.

"You okay, princess?" he asked.

She wiggled her way onto his lap and put her arms around his neck. "I miss Mommy."

"I miss her too, and it's okay to be sad."

She looked up at him. "Are you sad too?"

"Very," he said, the one word carrying a wave of emotion.

El moved to leave them alone, but Gabe took her hand. "I'd like you to stay with us."

"Of course." She swallowed and gave him a smile.

Reece marched across the pavilion and stopped in front of them. "We've got everything packed up and ready to go.

We'll take Mrs. Z. back to the inn unless you want someone to stay."

"No, thanks. Go ahead."

Reece smiled at Lucy. "See you soon."

The team carried everything off, their arms loaded with leftover snacks and drinks and all the birthday presents. Even Mrs. Z.'s lap was stacked with packages.

Gabe looked at Lucy. "I have a special surprise for you. Your mommy left a video for you. She recorded one to play every year on your birthday."

Excitement washed the sadness from her face. "I wanna see it. I wanna see it now."

Gabe reached behind to grab his iPad from the table.

El didn't know if this showing was meant to be for the two of them only. She didn't want to intrude so she started to get up, but he placed a hand on her knee.

Lucy looked at her. "This is a video from my mommy. She made it for my birthday."

"That's really special, sweetheart. Do you want to watch it alone with Gabe?"

"No." She grabbed El's hand and clung tight. "I want you to stay too. I want you to meet my mommy. She's special and you'll like her."

"I know I will." El tried not to cringe when Lucy talked about her mother in the present tense. She'd yet to really come to grips with the fact that her mother hadn't just gone somewhere for a short time and wouldn't come back.

Gabe started the video playing. Kenna came on the screen, and he pressed a hand over his mouth.

El had never seen Kenna alive. She was a beautiful woman with a vibrant personality as she spoke to Lucy, affirming her love for the child. Kenna told her she didn't want to leave her, but she was happy that she was with Gabe. But then, she took a turn and told her that someday he would get married, and Lucy would have a new mommy, and she wanted Lucy to love her new mommy.

Lucy whipped her head around to look at Gabe. "Stop the video, Gabe. Stop it! Stop it!"

He quickly pushed pause and took her hand. "What is it, princess?"

"Are you going to marry El?" She sounded so terrified by the idea that El was certain a steamroller had run over her heart.

Gabe glanced at El for a moment then back at Lucy. "I hope to someday."

Lucy started breathing quickly, her little chest rising and falling under her blue dress. "And she'll be my new mommy like my mommy said?"

"If you let her."

"But I want *my* mommy. Not a new one."

"Remember, sweetie, your mommy is in heaven, and she can't come back."

She flung herself at Gabe and clutched onto his shirt, sobbing.

Gabe flashed a look of confusion at El, then returned his attention to Lucy. "What's the matter, sweetie?"

"I've only ever had a mommy, and she just said that El would be my mommy. So that means you would go away and just come to visit me like you used to do. But I don't want that to happen." She started crying again.

Gabe snuggled her close. "I'll never leave you. Never. Always remember that, sweetie. I'll be with you forever. So will El."

El couldn't stand it any longer, and she placed her hand on Lucy's back.

The child looked up at her and gave her a wobbly smile. "I want to love you as my new mommy," she said, "but you win at Trouble a lot, and I like to win."

El held back a snort at the logic of a child. "What if we spend more time together, and I teach you some things to help you win?"

"Would you?"

"Of course, I would."

She squirmed out of Gabe's arms, and when she was on the ground, she threw her arms around El. "Okay. Now can we go home so I can ride my new bike?"

"Absolutely." Gabe smiled.

Lucy jumped up and down.

Gabe took the child's hand, his broad smile displaying his contentment. He clasped El's hand too. "We can watch the rest of the video when we get home."

"C'mon." Lucy tugged Gabe to his feet, and the three of them started for his truck.

El moved closer to him. "Crisis averted one more time."

He put his arm around her and used the remote to unlock the truck door. Lucy raced ahead to climb into her seat in the extended cab.

"I know her doctor said this was typical behavior," El said now that Lucy was out of earshot. "To be unsure of me. To be happy one moment and withdrawn the next. All while she processes the loss of her mother, but I have to say my heart was crushed there for a while."

"I can imagine, and I hope you're still up for getting married and becoming a mom."

"I wouldn't have it any other way. God's given me a chance to get rid of that awful guilt that's plagued me for so long, so I can be a mother to this child without feeling anything but love."

Gabe swung her around and into his arms. "And what about me? Can you love me after all these years you've avoided a relationship?"

She stroked the side of his cheek. "Not only can but do."

"Good, because I was thinking now that Kenna brought up the subject of marriage to Lucy, we can move up the date when we say *I do* in public."

El twisted her arms around his neck, and her heart fluttered. "Well, kind, sir, I think this is the type of decision that needs to be sealed with a kiss."

She didn't have to ask twice, but his head dropped and his lips pressed against hers. Not a passionate kiss. But the sweet, tender kiss of a promise of working together to keep their pasts in the past where they belonged, so they could enjoy their future together as husband and wife and as Lucy's parents.

He released her and looked her in the eye. "I promise I'll never leave you either."

She held up her little finger and grinned. "Pinky promise?"

He threw back his head and laughed before locking fingers with her. "Pinky promise."

"Hey, no fair," Lucy called out from the truck. "I want to pinky promise someone too."

El and Gabe looked at each other and smiled, then joined her at the truck. This wouldn't be the last time Lucy would want to be included in their newfound family, something El prayed the three of them would experience for a lifetime.

Thank you so much for reading *Lost Lake*. If you've enjoyed the book, I would be grateful if you would post a review on the bookseller's site. Just a few words is all it takes or simply leave a rating.

I'd like to invite you to learn more about these books and

about my other books by signing up for my **NEWSLETTER** at www.susansleeman.com/sign-up-2. When you do, you'll also receive a FREE e-book copy of *Cold Silence*, book one in my Cold Harbor Series. If you're already a subscriber, you can sign up again and get the free book and it won't put your name on the list twice, but you will receive three *Welcome to My List* messages.

You'll be happy to hear that there will be more books in this series. Read on for details.

LOST LAKE LOCATORS SERIES
When people vanish without a trace and those who go looking for them must put their lives on the line to bring them home alive.

Book 1 – Lost Hours
Book 2 – Lost Truth
Book 3 – Lost Cause
Book 4 – Lost Lake

Book 5 – Lost Girls
Book 6 – Lost Light

For More Details Visit -
www.susansleeman.com/lost-lake-locators/

LOST GIRLS - BOOK 5

A chilling secret beneath the surface...
The picturesque small town of Lost Lake suffers when a
series of young women disappear without a trace. The
town's tranquility shatters, prompting the arrival of Lauren
Benson, a determined FBI agent. But before she arrives,
Jude French, a rugged Lost Lake Locator with a haunted
past, is hired to find one of the girls.

Presents them with the ultimate test.

Forced to work together despite their conflicting investigative styles, Lauren and Jude embark on a perilous journey to unravel the mystery behind the disappearances. As they delve deeper into Lost Lake's dark underbelly, they must rely on each other like never before to survive. In a heart-stopping showdown, they confront the true mastermind behind the disappearances, risking everything to bring justice to the victims and closure to the town. And putting their hearts on the line as they do

PREORDER LOST GIRLS NOW!

THE TRUTH SEEKERS

A team of six forensic specialists bound by one mission: to bring the truth to light. But when chilling mysteries land on their doorsteps, the hunters become the hunted—and the truth they're sworn to protect may be the very thing that shatters their world.

Book 1 - Dead Ringer

Book 2 - Dead Silence

Book 3 - Dead End

Book 4 - Dead Heat

Book 5 - Dead Center

Book 6 - Dead Even

For More Details Visit -

www.susansleeman.com/books/truth-seekers/

The COLD HARBOR SERIES

The cost of protection is high, but for these heroes, no price
is too great—not even their own lives.

Book 1 - Cold Silence
Book 2 - Cold Terror
Book 3 - Cold Truth
Book 4 - Cold Fury
Book 5 - Cold Case
Book 6 - Cold Fear
Book 7 - Cold Pursuit
Book 8 - Cold Dawn

For More Details Visit -
www.susansleeman.com/books/cold-harbor/

ABOUT SUSAN

Susan Sleeman writes the kind of romantic suspense that makes you double-check the locks—and maybe fall a little for the hero.

Her clean, high-octane stories are packed with danger, heart, and just enough faith to light the darkest corners.

With 60+ novels, award wins, and over two million books sold, Susan knows a thing or two about keeping readers on the edge of their seats—and her FBI and police citizen academy training doesn't hurt either

She calls Oregon home, where she juggles plotting crimes (fictional ones, promise), spoiling grandkids, and running *TheSuspenseZone.com*.

Ready to lose sleep over your next favorite book? Head to SusanSleeman.com.

www.ingramcontent.com/pod-product-compliance
Lightning Source LLC
Chambersburg PA
CBHW020907060726

47591CB00004B/1128